IBRAHIM

And The Magicians' Rebellion

Kevin Kalu

Copyright © 2020 Kevin Kalu

All rights reserved

The characters and events portrayed in this book are fictitious. Any similarity to real persons, living or dead, is coincidental and not intended by the author.

No part of this book may be reproduced, or stored in a retrieval system, or transmitted in any form or by any means, electronic, mechanical, photocopying, recording, or otherwise, without express written permission of the publisher.

ISBN-13: 9798646414176
ISBN-10: 1477123456

Cover design by: Art Painter
Library of Congress Control Number: 2018675309
Printed in the United States of America

EPISODE 1: THE SLEEPING LION

Wino (pronounced: we-no), like many other citizens, adored his cozy human life. Its tranquil, predictable and equitable nature intoxicated them—almost to the point of blissful submission. As an added bonus, this liberal lifestyle unshackled humans from the brutal dominion of wayward magicians. Their reign had come to a bitter end a few years back. Anti-magician sentiment fueled a bloody overthrow and kick-started the sovereign rule of the Humans. These were to be the golden years of humanity. They believed it'd last forever. But little did they know, the war with the magicians was far from over.

Wino stared at Ibrahim's wand stationed atop his marble kitchen countertop. It symbolized near-infinite power restrained only by the talent of its wielder. He thought it a pity that no life swirled through its amethyst core anymore. It sat coldly for months. Distressed wood swathed the now gray, cold and lifeless orb. It was no larger than a fist, and no livelier than a dead mouse. Wino panned to his best friend slouched over the living room couch.

Ibrahim was a short magician. His foot rocked over the center table. TV rays washed over his Oakwood brown skin draped over by flowing satin dress. This robe swept down to his ankles like an overgrown shirt. Bags hung beneath his sleepy eyes and a single vein bulged above his furrowed brow. He detested this new reality.

Wino didn't want to further irritate Ibrahim. It'd been months since he'd last held his precious wand. Wino hoped Ibrahim might actually let it go if granted enough time. For now, it just sat there. And every day, Wino inched it closer and closer to the trashcan. He hoped that one day, he'd knock it down, and Ibrahim wouldn't notice because he'd moved on or simply wouldn't care enough to do anything about it. He thought, *Then I'll turn the wand into the police for him, give him the reward money and help him to move on. He could try and make something of himself in this new world of ours.* But for now, he'd simply wait it out, measuring time by the inches.

Wino snuck his head around the corner of the door. He peeked out from his room, and analyzed the expression on Ibrahim's face from a distance. Ibrahim, his lifelong best friend, had been kind of down lately and acted rather grouchy. But, Wino considered this part of his transition. *He'll get through this,* Wino thought.

Wino emerged from his room, into a little corridor and stepped into the adjacent living room. He was about one foot taller than Ibrahim, had golden brown skin, and a thin frame. His black hair faded at the sides and coiled along his scalp. His striped socks grazed over the oatmeal-and-raisin carpet. They ruffled as he shuffled past Ibrahim—and the wand—into the stone-walled, polished wood floor of the kitchen. He sparked on the gas stove. Ibrahim reeled one arm over the couch and stared blankly at some sitcom. The warm light stemming from outside the apartment dimmed, as the evening breeze rushed upon the windowpanes. A burnt orange sunset faded just beyond the horizon.

The glittering cityscape twinkled in Wino's periphery like a series of flashlights communicating across the towering concrete buildings. The hazy glints mimicked a Morse code conversation. The lights of this apartment complex switched off and stillness set about the scenery.

The complex was labeled *The U* cognizant of its U-shaped, ultramodern design. The two wings contained multi-unit dwellings while the center mass consisted of a series of lobbies with showrooms topped by a glass-bodied, steel-framed sky bridge. Transactions rang into Wino's earshot. Youths patronized the shops that ran along the inner walls of The U. They enclosed a courtyard creating a mini-shopping complex complete with exotic food stands and flamboyant entertainers.

Suddenly, a loud crackle shattered the serenity of the evening, masking it beneath a surging storm. Ant-sized guests and residents swiveled curiously. Storm clouds swirled about a focal point, forming a whirlpool of frosty moisture. A call echoed from above The U, it heralded from the heavens. Residents inside the opposing apartments glanced towards their windows as others threw them open. They jutted their heads out.

High in the sky, hovering atop a wide cruiser board minus the wheels, sat a Witch. She perched atop this decorated hover board with legs crossed at her knees. She had warm bronze skin that gleamed sleekly in the moonlight.

The Witch laughed, "Come on people! You don't have to give up. Magic isn't dead yet. We can't just give in to this. Let's make some noise. Let's have some fun!"

More people inside The U shuffled to their windows. They pressed up against the glass sky bridge and windows of the walkways. Lights sparked on from within their rooms. Wino *curiously* motioned for his own window while Ibrahim simply glanced over his shoulder. He quickly snapped back to the TV – like he couldn't be bothered.

Eventually, the Witch in the sky raised her arms, conjuring a purple ball of electricity. The flash of light revealed her deep, glittering, and purple blouse with a black skirt. Like a turtleneck, the cut out shoulders and waist revealed her supple skin. She wore boots and fishnet stockings. Her yellow eyes gleamed like a cat's against the night sky.

She shouted, "Don't worry, I'll take the first shot. I'll wake you up myself!"

She hurled the ball skyward where it divided into individual violet missiles. They arced for the crowds beaming towards the ground. They scattered and pummeled the environment: fountains, sections of The U and the distant cityscape. Colorful chairs scraped the clay-colored stone tiles as everyone leapt from their seats. The crowds scattered into the shops.

Screams rang out. Residents cowered in the hallways crouching along the walls while others dashed back into their rooms. They trampled over one another in their scramble for shelter. The shops backed up so much so that fleeing occupants reversed into the hailstorm, forced to search for alternative hiding places.

An elderly man tumbled in the uproar while another guy, likely a resident, curled to shield his fractured arm, wrapped in a caste from further injury. Screams of terror filled the night sky echoing as they rose. Rubble rained down over the pavement from collapsing infrastructure. It sprinkled over the fallen, the weak and the helpless. The chaos stirred confusion.

Some parts of The U, however, were untouched—for now at least. One such space was Wino's room.

Wino calmly scanned the hellish scene beyond his window. "Sounds like someone's using magic. It's been a while."

Ibrahim lurched forward, as he changed the channel. Flickering over it, he read, 'Breaking News.' A suited newscaster came online beside a live-streamed video of the maniacal Witch in the sky.

"I'm not sure what's going on," the anchor started. "But it looks like the popular residential complex commonly known as 'The U' is under fire from yet another magician."

Ibrahim gripped his knees unsettlingly.

The anchor continued, "We're not certain of the details, but we do have live video coming from eye witnesses *inside* the complex as we speak. Authorities have been notified of the destructive use of magic and have been dispatched. Additionally, connections to the *Blue Bandit* have yet to be established. For all we know, she may be acting alone. In the meantime, we're urging all residents to stay inside and lock their doors. All pedestrians need to find shelter."

Ibrahim wore a look of genuine fixation. He'd never displayed this degree of stimulation since he'd moved in.

Wino pivoted back to the window. "Well, The General will get to her and—"

A rumble stirred behind him. He whipped around, as Ibrahim gunned for the door. It flung open.

Instinctively, Wino barked, "Wait! Where are you going? Ibrahim!" A glance to the kitchen countertop revealed the wand disappeared. Wino gasped. "Oh no."

Behind Wino, beyond his windows and beneath the heavens, the Witch projected an inferno of chaos. She volleyed blasts randomly, and with no regard for the lives she wrecked. This attack painfully reminded him of the days when he and Ibrahim used to travel the world. They often encountered these beings—these magicians. A smirk clearly lined her face, her eyes gleamed like moonlight over the ocean, and she energetically launched additional projectiles into the fleeing crowd. She fed on their helplessness and basked in the madness. Her board twirled, exposing hoards of civilians to her sadistic terror. Her own violence enthralled her.

The Witch sang ecstatically, "Come on people, let's go back the way things were. Let's have some fun! Somebody's got to have magic, right? Who's with me?"

Wino sprinted into the hall after Ibrahim. He bolted past frightened people in the hallways, shouting for him to stop. The Witch's voice broke past the plastered walls as they sped past. Paintings, glass panels, and people blurred out of sight. It felt like riding a bullet train through a tunnel. Now, Wino had never been one to fly down the halls at max speed, but this fearless maniac just might do something they both regret. Before Ibrahim could turn the corner and dart into the sky bridge, Wino tackled him. The galaxy-carpeted hallway spun. Ibrahim's robe scrunched in Wino's fist. His back bounced against the floor.

Ibrahim growled, "What are you doing? Get off me!"

"You'll get yourself killed or arrested!" Wino retorted. "We're supposed to stay inside."

Ibrahim tightened his face in response. He squinted, furrowed his brows and grit his teeth. He glanced into the sky bridge and spotted the Witch hovering in front of the glass. There she was, his ticket out of this miserable lifestyle. Floodlights projected her shadow upon the opposite glass panes of the bridge. The light shone from the courtyard. The pair froze.

A voice from the plaza projected, "Well, would you look at this? It's been a while since I've had any takers."

The diminishing echoes of this voice silenced Wino and Ibrahim.

***

Beyond the walls of The U stood a woman in a militaristic police uniform. She wore a confident smile and flashed a row of pearly whites. Her hands folded behind her waist, as she planted her feet shoulder-width apart in a power stance. Her maroon jacket laced with white trim dangled over her broad shoulder. Badges adorned her left breast. Foot soldiers scurried into the plaza from her rear. They wove into position. Many of them stopped to check on the people inside the shops while others took up defensive positions behind shattered concrete walls and toppled objects. The Witch hovered in the sky with a cocky grin upon her face.

She broke the tension with an air of nonchalance, saying, "You must be The General."

This woman, this soldier, 'The General' responded,

"And you must not be from here, otherwise you'd know this town is mine."

The Witch sneered. "Oh? I don't see your name on it. This city belongs to the people who can run it—people with powers."

"People like you?"

"We handled things much better than you lot. Always have."

"Times change."

Wino glared at the Witch with anxiety creeping upon his face. His heart pounded in his chest. He scrunched Ibrahim's shoulder in his grip. Like a child soon to be caught red-handed, his stomach stirred with anticipated guilt.

The General led the human revolution against the magicians. She seized control during Ibrahim's stasis and took advantage of what societal stability Wino and Ibrahim had set in place before his disappearance. Her militarized foundation allowed places like The U to develop. By taming the magicians and restricting the flow of magic, the world metamorphosed. This domestication of wild magicians, however, spawned power-hungry magicians like Ibrahim.

***

Outside, the General commanded, "Bring it in." She twirled around.

Her subordinates rolled in a creaking steel container on a dolly. They plopped it onto the floor with a loud thud bellowing into the atmosphere. One soldier presented himself before the ominous container while others retrieved pieces from the steel crate and clipped them onto him. They clasped smooth, metallic armor plates onto his thighs, his forearm, and neck.

They clamped elbow pads and a biker's helmet on top of his head, veiling his eyes. It lit up with an orange "V." He faced The General. He resembled a humanoid cyborg with very few crevices exposing his uniform beneath. In fact, the soldier had to twist and bend to reveal these openings. The General strut up to him.

A subordinate started, "Chief, you know this is still under development?"

"I'm aware." She hummed flicking particles from the uniform. "Just give it your best shot."

The man inside barked patriotically, "Yes, ma'am!"

He turned into the Witch and clenched his fists. An eerie silence fell over the plaza. Subtle chattering crept into the ambiance. They rippled into the halls.

Wino wedged his palm into Ibrahim's shoulder mumbling, "What is that thing?"

Ibrahim groaned, "Get off me."

The bionic soldier leapt skyward. An emerging sound wave cracked the glass windows of the first story shops. The Witch threw herself back to evade him. He darted by like a spear, snagged his fingers upon the sky bridge, and chipped the glass near Ibrahim. The Witch glared at the cyborg. Turning back, she found The General shrugged with immodest approval.

The super-soldier hunched on the steel frame of the glass sky bridge. He leapt, clutching for the Witch. She dodged the man and threw her palm out to blast him towards the concrete. A glint of violet light shined followed by a thunderous clap. The man plunged like a meteor. He splattered into a cloud of dust, debris and gravel. His subordinates drew their guns at the triumphant Witch. However, from the smoke and rubble, the suited man climbed to his feet. He scrubbed his helmet like he suffered a headache.

The officer that advised the General commented, "It absorbed the impact!"

Astounded, the officers scanned the sheer height of The U.

"What's it made of? Is it magic?" The Witch grumbled in the air.

The super-soldier rose to attempt another grab. He ricocheted against the walls of the U trying to land a single hit. The Witch outwitted his every strike. She swirled like a spinning top and zigzagged to evade suppressive fire. She outmaneuvered the assault while maintaining eye contact with her nemesis.

The General clearly commanded great influence. Those that stood against her risked lifetime imprisonment, or even execution at her hand. However, this was precisely why the Witch challenged her. If The Witch could best The General in front of all these people, the marginalized magicians who observed from the shadows would likely heed her call. Then, she'd successfully overthrow this new world order. This gamble hinged on The Witches desperate performance. But, she may have bitten off more than she can chew. The onslaught prevented her from retaliating. Its pressure was nearly too great for her reflexes.

As, he spun slowed, her hair danced majestically in tune to her dress. The cyborg made for her thigh. She repelled him onto the sky bridge. He skidded to a halt, cracking the glass as he slowed. Determined, he jousted back into the swarm.

***

Ibrahim suddenly broke from Wino's grip. He palmed, Wino's chin and threw him onto his back. Ibrahim dashed for the sky bridge.

Wino screamed, "What are you doing? You'll get yourself killed."

Ibrahim stopped midway. He flailed his arms to signal the Witch. Wino froze at the connection between the bridge and the west wing of The U. He whispered desperately for Ibrahim to stop. Onlookers set their sights upon him with wonder. Wino receded. His mind spun as to how he should quell this sudden inferno within Ibrahim. It's like Ibrahim dismissed the dangers of The General, her team and even the super-soldier bouncing all over the place. Ibrahim saw something in the Witch and desperately sought after it. Wino hoped this battle would end quickly. The sooner the Witch fell, the safer they would be.

***

Outside The U, the Witch dodged the super-soldier until he snagged her board. Drawn nearer, the soldier punched her board in two. He then motioned to pummel the Witch, but she detonated her magic. They exploded apart from each other. The soldier fell while the Witch flew through the shattered glass into the sky bridge. A small section splattered inside, leaving a hole with jagged cracks.

The Witch struggled to her knees, squirming like a snail slathered in salt. She peered up from the shard-stained carpet to make eye contact with Ibrahim. She scanned his face. He held his wand, an artifact clenched within his fingers. Her pupils glittered with crystalline specks—a signature of magic flowing through her arteries. They twinkled like charred wood held over a crackling flame. They danced about as if suspended within fluid.

Suddenly, the Witch's eyes flashed violet. Wino caught a glimpse from a glass chunk as, unbeknownst to him, Ibrahim's eyes reflected the flash. Ibrahim acted as though he felt nothing. He slowly extended his wand. It's not often that Ibrahim is this serious, but he acted like he desired this power more than anything. The Witch smirked agreeably in return and lifted her fingers towards him.

The two drew nearer, almost intimate in their approach, until the super-soldier barked, "Hey! You stay away from him! Don't you touch him!"

The soldier stumbled over the ground. His suit sparked like an exposed power line plopped into a lake. He suffered no damage from the fall, despite bouncing around and being blasted with magic. The suit was foolproof. It shined like a freshly buffed car, but must have absorbed too much internal stress and was collapsing. The "V" screen that covered the super soldier's face, the visor, chipped. Sparks flew from the joints. His rigid motion stiffened, as if he battled with rust.

Another officer called out, "The suit's had it. It's falling apart. Time to take it off."

Soldiers rushed to their subordinate, ripping the pieces off of him and helping him to a resting position. The man wrestled with them. He resisted, eager to resume his fight with the Witch.

The fallen soldier hung his head in failure. "Sorry chief."

The General stood beside him, never having moved. "No, don't worry about it. I think you've proven my point."

A voice buzzed into The General's ear, as a red LED bulb flickered on like a ruby-studded earring.

A voice chimed. "I've got visual on the target chief. Tell me when to take the shot."

"Shoot, whenever you're ready," The General replied with her focus centered on the bridge.

***

Wino inched into the sky bridge. His timidity halted his advance. He thought, *I never knew Ibrahim's passion for magic was this strong. I almost feel sorry for him, like a lost dog searching for its old home in this new world.* The steel frames obscured his vision. The magicians looked like figurines. If only he could hear their conversation, but what would they discuss? Wino chewed nervously on his nails. He nearly muffled his mouth. He wanted to scream for Ibrahim to stop, but Ibrahim was unresponsive like a stubborn cat. Wino wondered how Ibrahim could side with a criminal standing against some of the best in the world. He considered fleeing the scene. Perhaps, he could grab Ibrahim and run away? Scenarios unraveled in his mind's eye at blistering speeds, however none of them end well.

Truth be told, Ibrahim did as he pleased and, right now, that was contacting this Witch who stretched out towards him. Her finger and his wand were an inch apart, when the Witch snapped her head to the dense, dark city surrounding The U. From one apartment building, a glare grew brighter and brighter. The Witch reeled back from Ibrahim and fell away from the hole in the sky bridge. Her gaze fixated on something in the distance. Ibrahim held his wand with desperation – *just charge it* he urged. He inched closer to make contact, when the distant glint of light suddenly flashed into a streaming bolt. It whipped across the night sky, crashed into the sky bridge and snapped across, yanking the wide-eyed Witch out with it. She flew outside and hurled towards the ground.

Ibrahim sprung up. He ran towards the hole shouting, "No! Damn it!"

He leaned in so far that he nearly dived after her. The Witch spiraled out of control and plunged to the ground. Like others that stood against The General, she failed to lay a single scratch before falling to her death.

The General casually turned to her soldiers. "Well, that was fun. Alright, let's round her up."

Her officers bundled up into 5 and 6-man teams. They jogged off to capture the defeated magician.

From the sky bridge, Wino crept up behind Ibrahim. He maintained a safe distance, glancing towards the shard-smothered carpet.

" Is she gone?" Wino asked. He made sure not to insult the solemnity of the moment.

Ibrahim didn't answer at first. His gaze fell within the smoke-filled area. The dust cleared with time and the Witch disappeared. She hit the floor–or *something*– hit the floor, but her remains fled. He grit his teeth and turned back through the other hole at the General. She stood before a couple of soldiers who checked on the vitals of the super-soldier. This woman, this General foiled his once in a lifetime opportunity.

What am I going to do? I didn't even know he still cared about magic like this. What if she saw him? What if she saw me? Is keeping Ibrahim around even worth it?

Questions ping-ponged through Wino's mind while a rail gun-bearing sniper stepped up to the General. Her hair sat in a bun pinned by a silver needle. A black mask shielded her nose and mouth. She bore a long rifle that was slightly taller than herself. A gradient of lights ran along the barrel as it hovered over the ground. Its body pressed into her torso. She stood at Ibrahim's height with a smaller array of badges lining her breast. She dawned a sash and straddled her rifle using both arms.

One of the 5-manned squads returned. Its leader reported, "Target is not at the crash site sir." He drew a disapproving look from the sniper but the cool calculating attention of the General.

The General asked," Did you miss?"

The sniper frowned. She casted a blank stare over the rubble-cluttered ground. "No, the witch moved the shot from her left ventricle to her outer rib. She won't get far though."

The General commanded, "Check again. She's likely in hiding like the rest."

The soldiers never found the Witch that evening. Ibrahim and Wino returned to their apartment, number 5050, left wing of the residential complex. They avoided the gargantuan elephant in the room thanks in part to Wino's timid and conflict-averse nature, but also thanks to Ibrahim's unresponsive attitude. Officers climbed each floor of The U. They checked on the residents and escorted those in need of aid to emergency rooms. Wino retracted into his room. He listened as the city fell quiet. Ibrahim's thoughts and actions were lost to him. His door remained shut throughout the evening.

***

The next day, the sun hadn't fully risen yet, neither had the moon surrendered the nighttime. Wino walked out from his room dawning his business casual work attire—complete with his timeless, diamond-studded silver watch. His romantic partner gifted it to him. He popped over the litter that dotted the carpet. He frolicked into the kitchen, past the living room and all-white dining table. Here, he twirled a golden slab of farm produce over a non-stick pan. It bubbled and sizzled under his simple smile. He made sure to monitor the heat and his noise. He guided the smooth release of his toast from the toaster, poured boiling water into his teacup marked "Cheryl" and had everything set. Finally, he sat down in front of his huge triple windowpanes.

He relaxed. "Such a beautiful day."

Full-sized, electric glass panels opened midway. They mirrored the hotel industry's standard. These panes lined the wall opposite the front door between his room and the kitchen. He reclined and basked in the serenity of this morning's calm. A gentle breeze pressed against them as birds chirped. A tall crane sat in the middle of the courtyard. Its neck hovered near the sky bridge––but no workers were present.

"I could stare at this forever."

Eventually, Wino grabbed his suitcase and made his way downstairs. Outside, he waited street side until a fancy double-decker, ruby red bus rolled by. It swung open for him. He displayed a card stamped with The U's design, scanned it and walked into the bus. He sat in a spacious chair with ample legroom. Few others occupied the bus, exemplifying its exclusivity. The engine hummed as it sped off. It made for the busy city center where Wino secured a high paying job. The city climbed its steady trajectory towards revitalization and earned its title as a Humans paradise.

Back inside his room, the clock swirled from 7:15 all the way up to noon. The construction workers arrived and start hammering, knocking, drilling. Their work generated a cacophony of screeching and rattling. Vibrations danced along the sky bridge.

At first, they drilled but no response stemmed from within the apartment, then they clasped steel beams together, and a bundle of cloth—like a sleeping bag began to squirm over the sofa. They hammered away, it wiggled more and moaning climbed into earshot. The heavy drilling started and then Ibrahim flung off his blanket. He sat up. He squinted tightly and balled the blanket in his fists.

"Someone ought to put your head under that drill," he complained.

He flopped up and over to the window wearing nothing but boxers. His arms spread apart, opening up to The U. He stood groggily, scratching his self with bags hanging beneath his eyes before slumping into the bathroom. A flush and Ibrahim wandered into Wino's room. He reemerged with Wino's now stolen sleeping robes draped over him.

In the kitchen, Ibrahim threw open the fridge. He squatted curiously. Ripe fruit and moist vegetables beading with sweat filled the trays. He searched the shelves, scanning for anything remotely edible for him to eat. In the end, Ibrahim retrieved one small yogurt from the corner and plopped a seat at the dining table. The sunlight stung as he groggily gazed down at the pathetic cup he now had to call a meal. What a dramatic fall he'd endured from magical grace to a bottom feeder.

Within the courtyard, a jubilant crowd of residents and guests attended one of the weekly open house events hosted by The U. Tour guides led streams of starry-eyed attendees throughout the complex.

"Weird."

What was he to make of this sight? Prior to stasis, Ibrahim's magical hibernation, homes were a place of refuge; where one could rest one's head, away from the piercing eyes of the wicked magicians that ruled. In fact, communal homes used to be a common sight.

"It's like they're going to see a parade," he said.

Back in his day, people surrendered personal gain for the benefit of the community––a calculated move towards the preservation of self-interest. Others scavenged, taking whatever the strong left behind and pillaging from the weak and this included living quarters. Now, they're a luxury investment tiered by their degrees of perceived comfort.

Ibrahim basked in this pinnacle of comfort, a spacious apartment quartered all to himself and afforded by a friend who had everything he could ever want. And this friend, Wino, had achieved all this without Ibrahim. In this world, with picturesque horizons and glittering skylines, there's nothing Ibrahim had to offer him anymore. Ibrahim might as well return to sleep.

***

One glass office towered amongst equals within the bustling downtown. The cityscape was rather gray; tall buildings lined the streets, avenues, and boulevards chockfull of lifeless people walking down concrete sidewalks with little eye contact. Puffs of nicotine rose while faces attached to their phones. It's lifestyles like these that uplift The U into the shining apartment on the hill. It explained why it's so gratifying to those occupied it and ideal for those who weren't. The U was green and lively, the people there behaved they resided within the bounds of a foreign country: they smiled and laughed, strolled throughout the complex and smelled the ornamental roses and sunflowers. They lounged outside and basked in the afternoon sun. Most arrived at the conclusion that those who ran The U, aught to run the city.

In comparison to the complex, a bounty of old apartments, dilapidated corner stores, and shops riddled the city blocks. City residents hated these buildings. These factories emanated an oppressive aura. Most slaved away in these buildings trying to make some money and some of them are tried to make it big in this city. Some did, some didn't.

Way up in one particular office space, Wino sat at his desk. His cubicle outsized and outclassed many of his peers. He rose high enough in rank to live happily at The U. He merrily bounced between his three monitors with a stack of documents neatly spread out before him. Wino swiveled back and forth. He checking his emails and fine-tuned document details, when he detected some pictures tucked into the corner. One displayed him with his partner smiling with each other. They attended a ski resort. Together they smiled, hugging each other cheek-to-cheek. The adjacent picture displayed her wearing a sunny yellow dress, denim jacket, and a hat with a feather in it. She posed for the camera. Wino's deep brown eyes dilated. His thumb brushed over the image as he thought, *Man, how'd I get so lucky to have you?* He smiled back into the pictures when his phone buzzed. He flipped it over and read: "1 Message From Cheryl <3"

"Are we still set for dinner tonight?"
He replies, "Time?"
"8?"
"Kk"
"♡"

Wino gazed into his phone with a smile. His attention popped over to her pictures to match a face to the emotions bubbling in his chest.

It'd been almost 2 years since Ibrahim froze his magic to sleep in perfect stasis. Since then, Wino moved into The U and a few months later, met Cheryl. They'd been dating for over a year now and seriously considered moving in together. However, there was just one issue: the vacancy was filled. Wino's watch buzzed. He snatched his suitcase and made for the door. *Time to head home for the day*, he thought.

Wino's door *clicked* before swinging open to his apartment. Ibrahim and a woman calmly sat in the living room. Ibrahim lounged on the main couch, facing the TV while the lady hunched over the dining table in the corner. They glanced over to Wino as he scanned the room.

Cheryl greeted him, "Welcome back." with her chin in her palm.

Cheryl was born in the city, down a lineage of travelers whose roots stemmed all the way from the islands. Her short, dirty blond-brown hair cuffed around her neck cut in a classic bob. Mint-green eyes and a toned musculature running from her shoulders down to her calves.

Ibrahim faced the screen. "Good, you're here. Now take her to your room and keep her busy. I'm watching TV."

Inside Wino's room, Cheryl shut Wino's door behind them as Wino stumbled to his bed. His spacious room was minimalistic with a cool navy blue complemented by wood accent furniture. His closed electric curtains lined the far wall. Crackling wood snapped opposite his bed, simulated by a fireplace on his LCD screen. He plopped his rattling keys on the distressed wood countertop next to his bed and sat down. He reluctantly faced Cheryl standing with her arms crossed in front of him.

"Here we go."

"So, when are you gonna kick him out?" Wino huffed as she continued. "Because this guy is just a jerk. He's a jerk to you, he's a jerk to me, he's just a jerk to everyone he sees. I understand you guys had some beautiful history together; rode ponies, kissed babies, met under the mistletoe, but this is ridiculous. He doesn't work. He doesn't cook. He doesn't even clean. In fact, he makes a mess, insults us and orders you around. I mean–"

Wino turned away from her. The LCD fireplace turned off automatically.

She continued, "We were supposed to move in together but––."

The door slid open.

Ibrahim called, "Wino," prompting Wino to pick his head out of his hands. "Gimme a five, wouldja? I haven't eaten all day."

Wino scrambled onto his bed and through his blazer for his wallet. Cheryl tucked her arms into her chest, swiveling towards the nightstand. The thickening tension between them made Wino scramble faster. He whipped out a five. Ibrahim promptly swiped it and strolled out. Cheryl glared at Ibrahim's back and he glanced back in response just before sliding the door closed.

Cheryl snapped back towards Wino. "And what was that? You just gave it to him?"

Cheryl just didn't understand.

"Back when Ibrahim and I were traveling the world together," Wino plead. "Ibrahim did things that I could never pay back. He gave me food when we were broke, clothes and a place to sleep when we were in strange towns and empty places. Ibrahim took care of things, no questions ever asked. Ibrahim never complained about having to take care of me."

"And that's why you can never muster the strength to tell him no or to take a hike?"

"I've tried to talk to him but–"

"But he never listens."

"Yeah."

"That's why I said to kick him out. Stand up for yourself Wino. We don't live under them anymore, y'know. We don't have to fear magicians. We have The Genera now. Ibrahim is just too stubborn. He doesn't back down and constantly pushes the bounds of your rules."

The living room door shut. Wino sank his head between his shoulders. He wasted another attempt trying to address the intricacies of Cheryl's request. Together, he and Ibrahim saved the world together, twice. In untold stories lost to the ages. They journeyed across inhospitable expanses and battled villainous magicians, witches, and wizards at a time when access to magic distinguished the rulers from the ruled. But now, Wino needed control over Ibrahim, or else he risked losing Cheryl.

The time struck 6 pm. Cheryl left in a foul mood. Wino hoped she'd cheer up for their dinner date that night. He wondered if they'd have a lively discussion or waste more time discussing Ibrahim. The magical rascal took over their relationship. Wino contemplated the time required for Ibrahim to fully assimilate into society. How Ibrahim would adapt as an average individual and no longer a blessed hero. Most importantly, would

Cheryl's dwindling patience diminish before Wino saw this process to its completion?

Outside, Ibrahim strolled across the central plaza or The U.

He mumbled to himself, "Stupid cow. I'd turn her into a goat if I just had magic."

Ibrahim crossed the major street – Ménage Boulevard – into the city side where the gray businesses and rusty apartments shrouded him in a maze of concrete. Another major street – Capone Street – and he'd be at the business center where Wino worked.

Ibrahim had his dinner in a plastic bag. He walked down a dark street. Most of the light stemmed from the second-story windows but people had cheap plugins to lower their rent. There were some wayward individuals dressed in tattered rags and dingy garments occupying the streets. Some hunched on the curbs, and others wondered the tight alleyways between the buildings. Ibrahim tucked his head into his chest and weaved about the occupants like an obstacle course.

"Man, all these people look so sketchy," he thought. "If my wand were charged, I'd walk this street naked and *dare* someone to touch me."

He kept his wand well into his pants, where his back pocket would be. After the incident the other night, it resurfaced more and more upon his person. It pressed upon his skin secured by the waistband to his shorts. At times, the tip poked outside his shirt but he adjusted accordingly and never moved without it.

This clearly drew Wino's attention but thankfully, the guy was too timid to gather his thoughts and even more so to vocalize them. His other half, on the other hand, had ample courage. Fortunately, she wanted to see

Wino do it. The naggy nuisance aught to buzz off with her defiant attitude. The sooner the city girl left the picture, the better it'd be for them—-at least in Ibrahim's eyes. *In fact, all these city dwellers felt like they ran the world all because they had The General to inflate their ego with her protectionist agenda. She prioritized humans above magicians which wasn't a solution, it just reversed the problem. But what else could you expect from a human who seized untold power?*

Ibrahim walked past some five-stair steps before a street-side porch. He glanced at some lady seated on stairs. She wore a royal purple skirt partly masked by a black jacket, grey hoodie underneath, and cowgirl boots. Darkness shrouded her face. Ibrahim glanced towards her and met a violet flash. He immediately turned away, unaware of the gleam his eyes displayed. Ibrahim strolled past her. She panned after him from her seat. A few more steps and suddenly his ear twitched. He planted his foot. A hand reached for him, but more importantly it went for his wand. Pivoting reflexively, Ibrahim took a careful look at the courageous stranger's demeanor. He instantly recalled: The witch on the bridge, the one who fought The General and was shot out of the sky; the one he almost made contact with while Wino protested. A smile slithered across her face. She mimicked his eagerness – just let me take it. Ibrahim froze. His chest fluttered with shallow breaths. His shoulders slacked and he wondered: *what could she want from me?*

***

People crisscrossed the sidewalk adjacent a street-side restaurant. There was an outdoor veranda. Cheryl and Wino sat beneath the redwood pergolas at a petite, pink table. Potted plants dotted the four corners of the foot-high stonewall outlining the wood flooring. Cheryl glanced out the corner of her eye. Bussers scurried by carrying trays bearing gourmet dishes. Sizzling oils popped as they came outside while footsteps squeaked as they head back in empty-handed. Wino followed her lead, eagerly watching the workers. Salivation crept over his lips as his stomach gurgled.

"So," Cheryl asked. "Any plans this weekend?"

"Hmm?" He faced her while she stirred a sunset orange drink.

"I was thinking. We should go somewhere. Get out of the city, y'know?" Cheryl gazed up at Wino.

"That would be great but," he paused. "I can't leave him there."

He did it, and he didn't want to. Usually, it was Cheryl and her complaining that brought Ibrahim into the equation but tonight it was supposedly Wino's turn. Cheryl didn't take the bait, she snapped back at the door and distracted herself with who's ordering what and how entrees crackled and popped above the black serving tray. Wino attempted to reignite the conversation but it's as if she's too intrigued to hear him.

"What're you doing?"

His voice blurred into the ambiance and she failed to respond. Wino's heart fell to the table hovering over the plastic advertisements there. He fiddled with them as they waited for their orders to arrive.

"I'll talk to him."

**

From the alleyway, Ibrahim overheard the choir of voices stemming from around the street corner. He was a block away from the main road, Ménage Boulevard. He turned back as footsteps faded into the distance. The hooded witch, twirled into her steps with a smirk on her shrouded face. She faded into the darkness of the alleyway, with the buzzing streetlights dimming into a violet hue as she passed by. Her voice echoed softly from the alleyway.

"Just don't forget. Now, you owe me."

Ibrahim's excitement fell onto his wand: a charcoal-toned, elongated mushroom formed of distressed wood variegated in its intricate golden lace patterns. The mushroom-capped scepter glowed with a deep purple hue, embroidered with a swirling, but fragmented gold strip. He released the plastic bag in his hand. It plummeted to the floor and splattered all over the concrete. Rats, bugs, and onlookers made their way towards it. With his free hand, Ibrahim clenched the wand. His face brightened, as his lips stretched from ear to ear. His mouth gaped open as an energetic whimper echoed from him. Ibrahim huffed and puffed excitedly with the wand wedged between his two palms. His fingers caressed it.

"Finally," he said in a fit of hysteria. "I have it."

***

The next morning, Wino stared blankly at the ceiling of his bedroom. He listened as the crinkly crane dangled at The U. Last night, construction workers maneuvered supplies into position behind a yellow taped barricade. Residents meandered through the maze of traffic cones and tape to get into the residence. His mind pondered the cold shoulder Cheryl gave him last evening. She'd never been so cold and her words echoed within the chambers of his heart.

I said I'll talk to him. But, I barely got a word in last night. Ibrahim was so distracted and I was reluctant to bring it up anyways. I just mumbled to myself inside here. But now what do I tell Cheryl?

The front door clicked and swung open. Wino twitched towards the sound. His door split from the frame as he peered towards it. His heart trembled at the thought of Cheryl appearing.

No! I didn't tell him anything yet! He's still here, Wino thought.

Beyond the doorframe, Wino spotted Ibrahim making his way out into the passageway.

Wino threw open his own door to call, "Ibrahim? Where are you going?"

Ibrahim continued undisturbed. "Food."

In stepped Cheryl, with eyes set on Wino. Her cotton blouse fluttered past Ibrahim's satin robes. She made for the dining table before coming to halt.

Ibrahim continued, "It's not like I'm getting any breakfast here."

"What about Wino?" Cheryl asked.

"What about him? You're here, make yourself useful. Just try not to make too much noise," Ibrahim lowered his voice. "The neighbors like to sleep in on Saturdays."

The front door closed behind him with Cheryl barking, "Jerk."

Cheryl turned towards Wino. "Did anything happen after we left last night?"

"Not really. He sat in the corner out there where I couldn't see him."

"And?"

"And there was something glowing out there."

"Something was glowing? Like...?"

"I don't know. But he's been very happy lately."

"That was happy?"

"That was *something*."
"Oh brother."

***

Downstairs, The U hosted a continental breakfast in an indoor/outdoor restaurant across from one of their ballrooms. It took place in the center of the U where the makeshift park occupied. Trees, wooden benches, a rocky water fountain decorated the interior while gift shops and other cafes lined the walls.

Despite being the newest building on the block, The U spared no expense when it came to advertising. They hosted guests, events and everything they could to fill those vacancies. Despite overwhelming demand, The U continued to display its major presence on the block. No space outside the business district compared to The U and the management flaunted it. Guests packed the foyer and park; some people stood to eat their meals while others sat on the rim of the water fountain hoping not to fall inside. Inside the cafe, people queued for everything: juice dispensers, omelet line, waffle makers, and more. And Ibrahim, this pseudo-resident strolled past these lines, his hands in his pockets. Filtered sunlight crossed the finely stitched bamboo panes lining the glass walls. Ibrahim continued until his eye caught a lady, seated alongside the sun-kissed wall. She ate by herself. He pulled up a chair and plopped into his seat.

Across from she sat with thin strings of braided hair running down her spine. They're bundled by a golden bangle and rested against her fitted black shirt. Her sunset yellow eyes gazed on her plate of fruit. She poked, prodded, and rolled the grapes around before piercing one forcefully with her fork.

"You made it," the woman said, not looking towards Ibrahim.

Ibrahim's smile from the evening stretched across his lips.

"So how'd you like it?" she inquired.

"Loved it."

The woman's eyes rose just enough to see his smile before getting the message. Smaller plates rested around her with scraps all over them.

"And what about your roommate?"

Ibrahim's smile collapsed as he snapped towards the window. "Who cares what he thinks." He regained his composure and addressed her. "I just want my powers back."

"Does he use magic?"

"No. But screw him. How do you still have your powers?"

To this, the Witch furrowed her brows. She silently stared at Ibrahim while he waited for her answer. "What do you mean?"

"I mean, how come you still have your powers?" The Witch's head pivoted curiously as she processed his question. "No one else has their magic but you."

"Who told you?" she asked.

"I've only seen you use magic."

"Where are you from?"

***

In Wino's room, Cheryl sat by his bedside. His bedroom door hung open granting her a view to the living room. She threw an inspecting glance periodically. Wino lied flat with his arms to his side. He recounted how his conversations with Ibrahim revealed a purple gleam stemming from Ibrahim's eyes – the trademark of a magician. But yesterday evening, it seemed as if Ibrahim himself was unaware that it was happening. If anything was clear from his demeanor, it was that Ibrahim had made contact with something or someone and showed signs of magic aggregation.

"I just don't get why you trust that guy." Cheryl groaned. She stood up, gesturing. "Why don't you let him go? He's nothing but a burden to you now. He's changed."

"It's because of him, I'm still alive. All the things he's done." Cheryl paused quietly. She paced by his bedside. Wino continued, "I just didn't know he'd rebound like this."

"You thought he'd given up on magic."

"He was just waiting."

"Wino, what if The General finds out? What then?"

Wino pretended to ponder it. This exact question, this scenario, was one he'd suppressed for some time now. He knew it couldn't end well.

"That's just the thing. I don't think Ibrahim really considers The General a threat even though he's seen what she can do. And I didn't hear back from him until he showed up at my doorstep a year and a half later," Wino concluded.

Wino fell silent. His gaze rested on Cheryl — flabbergasted. Cheryl huffed forcefully, slacking her shoulders.

"So what now?" she asked.

"I don't know," Wino stared at the ceiling.

"Well. If he takes this too far you'll have to cut him off."

***

Back at the cafe, the Witch leaned forward with a questionable expression on her face.

She asked, "You slept for over a whole year?"

Ibrahim responded, "Yeah, it's a trick I can do. I kinda slip into hibernation."

"You hibernate?"

"Recoil. It's a long story but I went to sleep after our last journey. The magic usage took it all out of me and I enclosed myself within a crystal ball to recharge. This way it doesn't take three lifetimes"

Ibrahim smirked. The light from the window splashed into his eyes. The reflection shined a golden brown like the fur of a golden retriever.

The Witch cheeks rose in reply.

She interlocked her fingers above her plate adding in a soft low tone, "Cus' you know what I want for loaning you my magic."

Her eyes flash from gold to their signature violet.

Suddenly, a deep purple hue polluted Ibrahim's eyes and formed a tight ring just around his irises.

He grumbled, "The General."

The End

EPISODE 2: THE METEOR SHOWER

Birds chirped outside The U. The morning sun climbed over the distant horizon beyond Wino's tall windowpanes. Cheryl cuddled atop Wino's blanket snuggling up towards him while his arm protruded out to cover her. The two rested in the hazy darkness of Wino's bedroom. The curtains blocked the sun with the exception of a slit opening where the curtain met the wall. Here, a bright ray scrubbed the edge, scattering like a light bulb and outlining all the furniture within the dim room. The two rested soundly when struck by a thumping noise. It stemmed from the living room. It sounded like it came from another room or from down the hall. The bass rumbled as if tucked beneath a pillow. Next, their noses twitched in unison. This continued with aggravated frequency. The thumping grew more boisterous. Cheryl jerked to a seat. Wino climbed slowly after her. They glanced at one another. Their eyes flashed open and they made for the door.

  Wino's door rolled open with Cheryl skidding out across the carpet.

She barked, "What're you–?"

A cacophonous whirlwind overwhelmed her ears like removing noise-canceling studio headphones at the height of a live rock concert. Wino clutched the doorframe and jutted his head out too. They scurried back inside his room and slammed the door. Inside, the noise was muffled; however, once they creaked it open, it sounded like being in the center of a professional drum line. The door slid open with Cheryl and Wino stumbling out once more. They smothered their ears with pillows but grit their teeth at the noise. A soccer game played on the TV. The volume read 'max.' A portable radio sat over the countertop with the broadcaster screaming, "*Arriba Arriba!*" and Ibrahim stood behind the kitchen counter dressed in a chef's uniform. He swirled a pan, balancing a Bluefin tuna fish larger than the skillet. He mimicked the announcer proclaiming, "Arriba!" Glancing to the television, he follwed up with, "Goal!" He threw up his free arm like a spear. Cheryl squinted in pain, while Wino panned across the room. The mariachi music blasted onto the walls, but cotton balls lining every vertex of the room absorbed it. The ubiquitous lining worked as no one came to complain about the noise. The music suddenly cut and both Wino and Ibrahim turned in to Cheryl having found the off button.

Ibrahim protested, "Hey" until he spotted Wino lowering the TV's volume. "What're you doing? I was listening to that. How am I going to know if I win if the radio's off?"

Cheryl impatiently snarled, "What is wrong with you?"

Wino added, "Are you trying to bring the whole U down?"

"Not the *whole* U," Ibrahim responded. "And not with you two turning my music off."

He switched on the radio. The announcer said, "Ari-" when Cheryl turned it back off. "Stop that."

Ibrahim glared at her before turning his gaze to Wino. "You better warn her, Wino."

Wino anchored himself over the kitchen counter to see the large fish balancing across the rim of the frying pan. "What're you making, Ibrahim?"

"Breakfast," Ibrahim snapped. "Since you're not making it for me anymore."

Cheryl stepped in front of Ibrahim examining the pan. "But it doesn't even fit–you have to cut it up first."

"Are you cooking it?"

"No, but you–"

"Exactly, so why don't you move out of my way unless you're going to learn how to cook something for once, tomboy?"

Wino's door slammed. The living room emptied and Ibrahim stood beside the counter. Cheryl audibly complained to Wino inside his room. Ibrahim continued to swirl the catfish, watch the football match and proclaim *arriba* after the radio announcer.

Inside Wino's room, Cheryl complained, "Ugh, I hate him so much. I thought we were done with these magicians!"

Wino reclined over the ledge of the bed. He twirled some cotton between his fingers and plugged it inside one of his ears. He angled his head towards the noise, testing if it worked.

When he turned to Cheryl, she sighed and yielded, "Whatever."

"I think Ibrahim just needs to find something to

keep him busy. He gets pretty bored just staying here."

"What a great idea. How about, you tell him to get-a-job? You're gonna have to tell him sometime, Wino, or else, I might just strangle his little–"

The door opened with Ibrahim in the doorway. His chef's cap slanted while he wore a confident smirk. "Breakfast is ready, Wino."

Cheryl asks, "You mean you actually cooked that thing?"

Wino asks, "Your apron's gone. Are you leaving, Ibrahim?"

"Yeah. I have to meet up with someone. I'm leaving the food on the table. I ate mine already." Ibrahim starts towards the front door, adding, "And it's better than anything you could make, tomboy."

The front door closed.

Cheryl clawed her fingers, grunting, "I *hate him*."

"I wonder if he actually cooked it," Wino pondered.

Cheryl snatched her purse, threw on a jacket, and then tugged on her boots. Her keys jingled as she picked them up. "Whatever, I have work anyways."

"What about breakfast?"

"You can eat whatever slop he made you since you won't kick him out."

Cheryl gave Wino a kiss on the cheek and left.

Pacing across the living room, one succulent aroma wafted underneath Cheryl's nose. She noticed a metallic tray on the round, white dining table situated in the corner of the room where the carpet of the living room transitioned into the hardwood flooring of the kitchen. As her eyes washed over it, her taste buds savored a meal not yet eaten - not yet even tasted. She curiously wandered over, sunlight pouring over her golden-brown bangs, to see three assortments of finger food. *Three* columns of tuna sushi rolls with a single red egg, *tobiko*, seated at the center of each one; followed by *three* columns of crustless, triangular sandwiches with alternating tuna-turkey and tuna-ham. There's also creamy pink and red meat seated underneath a green line of lime-green avocado, all perfectly balanced so that one apex pointed towards Cheryl. Finally, *three* columns of tuna salad cut perfectly cylindrical and stacked atop salted crackers with a leaf of basil at the very center. It's not a spice, it's not a spray but it's definitely coming from the food – Cheryl, however, could not determine just what producing that aroma she perceived. Her mouth submitted to the stimulation and generated a pool of saliva that overflowed onto the floor. Cheryl heard the drop plop onto the floor and her focus snapped.

Wino asked from inside the room, "Mmm, what's the smell?" The front door closed when Wino stuck his head out from his room. "Is that Ibrahim's food?" He angled towards the door, confused about why Cheryl disappeared in such a hurry. Wino found *two* columns of assorted finger foods lying on a metallic tray on the table.

"She should have taken some," he mumbled.

***

An elevator dinged open. Ibrahim stepped his sandal onto the office floor. Behind him, entered a handful of employees, all wore black formal attire. They glared at his back. His black satin robe fluttered in the air behind him, shielding his wand seated in the back pocket of his shorts. He stepped onto the office floor. His sandals flopped on the carpet as he passed a pair of plastic rose bouquets, down rows of cubicles, and up to a glass conference room. Some people stretched necks over their computers, while others rolled back their seats to observe the anomaly waltzing down the aisle. Ibrahim remain focused, burning with determination as he grabbed the door handle and threw it open.

Inside, a lady stood with her arms crossed. Her black skirt hugged her waist, swerving around thighs and slanting across her knees. It's decorated with a golden string belt that only looped under one hook while the rest slanted like the skirt. She wore a white blouse with frills at her collar and braided hair, dangling like beads on a string along her back. Violet wire wrapped about her black braided strands, wafting under the soft whirl of the air conditioner.

"Anyone stop you?" she asked.

"No. I mean, people stared but I don't care."

He always came off as shameless or as he put it: *unyieldingly confident.* Ibrahim stood in a category of his own, a human who acted like mountains divided in order to provide him a clear path. This put him at odds with people throughout his travels but forged a unique brand of Ibrahim-ism.

The woman scoffed, turning towards him. It's the first she's seen of his confidence, having bestowed upon him a surge of energy. The Witch's feline eyes were sharp, glaring at Ibrahim behind sunset golden-brown cornea. She wore a calm yet crooked smile. For a split second, her eyes flashed violet. Ibrahim's eyes unwittingly responded with their own violet flash. Ibrahim smirked in response to her expression. She turned away and casted her gaze down at the street, almost thirty floors below.

"So, how're you liking it — feel like your old self?"

"I love it." Ibrahim retrieved his wand. The sunlight washed into the office, projecting their silhouettes for the employees to see from behind their cubicles. "I feel alive again. So, what do *you* want?"

The Witch quietly maintained her gaze beyond the windowpanes.

The downtown area, where skyscrapers punctured the skyline like porcupines, bustled with activity. Its maroon outer core of dilapidated apartments made of red-clay bricks and tight alleyways lied sandwiched by its cozy modern center on one end and high-end residential establishment The U on the other. Here, all-glass buildings towered alongside limestone banks with gold-bordered lettering. At their base, strolled officers of The General's elite police force. One male and one female they dawned *Police* vests with checkered bands running across the back. Bulky all-black pistols rest strapped into their holsters, waist-high above their boots. The female officer wore a gray beret while her partner wore black shades. Unbeknownst to them both, far above, the Witch watched with disgust.

She trailed the two officers for quite some time, eavesdropping on their conversation through magic. As they walked along, she continued her espionage.

"Any plans for tomorrow?" the male asked.

"Why is something happening?" the female responded.

"We're supposed to be having a meteor shower tomorrow night." Her eyes lit up with her mouth aghast. He confirmed, "The whole night sky is supposed to light up with stars. Although depending on where you view it from, they say it's also going to be cloudy."

"Where can you view it from?"

"Some of the rooftops here should be good," he

drew his finger along the skyline, "although most of 'em will be locked or people have already planned to take it." Her expression fell. He continued, " Unless you want to watch it with some strangers. I know some of the good rooftops already have stuff all over them. "

"People marking their territory."

"Sounds about right."

"Well, now I know about it, I'd love to see it." The officer shrugged, gazing at the clear sunny sky. "Just imagine the whole sky with falling stars."

"It'll be a lot of wishes."

Ibrahim pulled his gaze from the sidewalk to the Witch.

"You got a grudge? "

"Yeah," she responded without breaking focus. "I got a bone to pick."

Her nostrils flared and she snarled at the henchmen of her assailant.

"You know, you'll be picking a fight with The General right?"

His comment snatched the Witch's attention. Her curled finger drove her long nails into her own forearms.

"She's the one I want."

***

The sun slowly fell behind one wing of The U as Wino sat at one of the cafe tables along the wing. He balanced a small cup of honey-milk green tea upon a fine-china saucer. From his seat, he took in the sight that was The U's botanical park. Shops lined the two walls, closing the ornamental shrubs and flowering trees. These three-story, open-access restaurants and shops delineated the park with only handrails. Stairwells ran up either end. Tiny pastel-colored chairs and tables bordered just outside the small cafes.

A much larger man, oversized for his seat, joined Wino. This man stood at least six-foot-five inches and wore sky-blue shorts. His small tank top exposed his toned muscles. His tanned-honey skin was smooth and his face was beardless, with only a black buzz cut atop his soft face. He sat with a diagonally sliced sandwich atop a fine-china plate and a clear drink of iced-water sweating from its container.

The man asked is a gentle yet raspy voice, "Alright, so what's the problem?" The man dove his face into half the sandwich, retrieving a large chomp.

"Nedu, it's Ibrahim."

"He still living with you?" Nedu asked with his mouth half full. He swiped a sheet from his stack of napkins. "How's that panning out?"

"That's actually the prob–"

"What does Cheryl think about it?" Wino tucked his head into his hands. The man munched for a few seconds. "Alright, go ahead. Tell me."

"Okay." Wino picked his head back up. "I don't know what to do about Ibrahim. He's always been a guy to do what he feels like, but now–"

"But now, it's messing with your life; your relationship."

"What am I supposed to do? I can't kick him out."

"Why not?"

"I mean it's Ibrahim. When we were traveling, he never asked anything from us. He just did it himself. But now, he can't even take care of himself. I–"

"Ibrahim did all that because he wanted to. You have to do what's best for you, Wino. If Ibrahim's being stubborn, you have to let him know the rules. Either he turns in the wand to the General or he fends for himself."

Wino fell upon the steaming tea beneath his nose. The sunlight flickered through the tight caramel coils of his hair, almost hovering onto the skewed shadow behind him.

"He won't respect you if you don't mean it. So, do you think you can kick him out if you have to? Think about it."

Wino paused. His anxious gaze wandered the darkening courtyard of The U. A miniature stone arched bridge with water running underneath, fed from a fountain surrounded by wooden benches. Colorful floral umbrellas shaded the seats. A wide variety of potted annuals, vines, and ferns decorated the space. LED backlit water shined orange hue. This coordinated effect exacerbated the sunset's calm over the area. The cafes and shops gradually lit the area.

"Anyways," Nedu continued. "You know where you're going to watch the meteor shower from?"

Wino furrowed his brows. "A meteor shower? When?"

"Tomorrow night, The U's rooftop looks like a good place but I heard a lot of people already packed their stuff up there."

Wino faced the central wing of The U, his gaze flew above its rooftop. "But, isn't it going to be cloudy tomorrow?"

"That's what I saw, but people are still hoping to nail a good spot. Just thought I'd ask you."

Nedu downed the entire cup of water, stacking it atop his plate. He gazed at Wino's plate. Wino downed his tea before passing the cup and saucer for Nedu to put up. Wino rose, panning around The U. A constant trickle of passersby strolled about. Shop owners locked up. Wino pondered what he has to do.

"By the way," Nedu called. "D'you see that crazy witch the other day?"

"Oh, yeah." Wino analyzed the hanging metal frame, the moonlight shimmered gleaming across the beams.

"Remember when we used to see that every day?" Nedu smirked nostalgically. "I bet Cheryl was freaking out, huh?"

"Yeah." Wino retrieved his phone. "She was. Cheryl."

***

On a bus riding down the empty roads, Cheryl clung to a pole with her phone in hand. The bus rode along streets striped with streetlamps providing puddles of light. These washed over Cheryl's face like waves rolling past the windows. She swiped through pictures of Wino and herself: on a mountain blanketed in snow, where they posed together with their ski poles waving in the air; on a sandy beach, Wino piggy-backed Cheryl before a boundless sea beneath a bewildering, baby blue sky; the two formally dressed for the wedding of a relative, smiling from their pew; the two kissing on a checkered pink and white picnic blanket beneath a skyscraping ember maple tree. A gentle smile blossomed upon her face. She scrolled past a couple more pictures, her ears plugged with wireless earbuds; Cheryl sat peacefully in a nest of emotions lost in her memories. With one swipe, however, her chain of thought snapped. An image slid into view, of the three of them. Ibrahim had recently moved into the room and Wino was ecstatic to see him. Cheryl initially shared in her partner's sentiment and took a photo. It was timed, Ibrahim lied down on the couch with a magazine in hand, Wino sat at Ibrahim's feet leaning towards the center, and Cheryl leaned over from behind the couch gesturing the "peace" sign. All but Ibrahim smiled; instead, Ibrahim held a neutral and unenthusiastic expression. This image shrank Cheryl's smile. It warranted a cold stern glare, similar to Ibrahim's, at her phone. She swiped to her messages with Wino, scrolled up to an old conversation where she asked him:

"So we're not moving in together?"

"I just don't know if I can fit three people in here comfortably."

"But we've been planning this for months."

"Let's just hold off on it for now. I'm not sure how long Ibrahim's going to be in town."

"So later then?"

"We'll see."

Her thumb hovered over her phone. Her eyes replayed the conversation, making multiple passes over the same statements. Eventually, Cheryl just shut off the screen. Her bangs pulled apart as she rose to view the passing cityscape.

She mumbled, "Ibrahim" underneath her breath.

***

"So?" the Witch asked Ibrahim beneath the starry sky. She faced the windows, arms crossed, braided hair rustling against her hips, and a stern look pointed at the cityscape. She, having discussed at length with Ibrahim the full extent of her plans, wondered, "D'you wanna run this city?"

Back at The U, an elevator dinged as its sliding doors retracted. Out stepped a handful of people alongside Ibrahim. He paced down the hall, his hands in his pockets and his gaze scrubbing the carpet. The crowd dissipated into the rooms leaving him to continue along his path. Alone, the wand in his back pocket emanated a craving. It signaled its unending thirst like that of a scorched desert clawing for a drip of water upon an outstretched tongue: magic. It used to flow so abundantly, now a scarce resource. And here's a witch, one of few beings that generate magic within their bodies, offering Ibrahim just what his wand and, more importantly, what he desired most. The flow of magic pulsing through his veins was his key to exploring his passion without restraint. He'd done it for so long, his humanity could only offer abundant vanity. Ibrahim felt like a dethroned king begging for his crown. He planted his feet before a door, room 5050. The door slid open. The offer she made him rattled his mind. And to be fair, it was a two-in-one deal for him: he gained both his powers back and capsized The General's monopoly over the artifacts. It's perfect for him, except for one unattended caveat: Wino.

The rustling of fabric and foam creaked from the living room couch opposite the sliding door. Seated upon it, Wino's gazed climbed up to Ibrahim's face. Ibrahim's eyes dilated; he stared into this showroom of shadows striving to discern what waited inside. Wino's hands unraveled. The filtered moonlight served as a lamp outlining all the furniture in the hazy apartment.

Ibrahim started off, "What're you doing? Why are you sitting in the dark?"

Wino stammered, "I was – I was waiting for you to come back."

"But why were you waiting in the dark?"

Wino swept the room for a reply. The lights switched on. Ibrahim read his friend's expression, Wino's thumbs twiddled, his knees bobbed, and he blinked rapidly. Ibrahim stepped into the room and towards the kitchen. Before turning onto the ash wood bamboo panels.

"Ibrahim, are you going to turn in your wand?"

"Never," Ibrahim responded, his back towards the living room. He hunched over to open the fridge.

"But it doesn't work," Wino urged. "And you can't recharge it."

"So?" Ibrahim's voice echoed from the fridge.

"And you could go to jail. The General is no joke, Ibrahim."

Ibrahim emerged from the fridge clutching a glass bottle containing a violet fizzling fluid. He walked over, plopped onto the couch, and anchored the bottle cap onto the crown of his molar. Ibrahim, having been to prison and held captive within holding cells, scoffed at the statement.

"I'm not scared of her."

"Everybody else is." Wino lurched his shoulder over his knees.

"Are you?"

"Yes, and I don't want her coming after me. So, if you don't turn in your wand—" Three knocks sounded from the door. It drew Wino's attention, but Ibrahim held his focus.

"Then what?" Ibrahim asked.

Wino's gaze snapped to him. The two paused for a moment. The knocking sounded again.

Cheryl's muffled voice penetrated the wall. "Wino, it's me."

The door swung open, Cheryl stepped inside and found the conversation she interrupted. She had her own contribution but restrains herself in light of the solemn moment she clearly disrupted. Instead, Cheryl snagged her tongue within her jaw and sealed it within. She faced Wino and uttered to him in a hushed voice while Ibrahim sat patiently. Group dynamics made him the villain of the group.

Her voice leaked parts of the conversation, "I wanted us to find a spot."

"For the meteor shower?" Wino replied.

"Yeah, c'mon." Cheryl grasped Wino's hand and tugged him into the bedroom. Without formally acknowledging Ibrahim, she threw out a "Hey."

Ibrahim ignored her, glaring at Wino who simply followed her, avoiding the previous conversation. The door closed as the couple's mumbling burrowed across the frame. Ibrahim took a swish of his drink and belched.

***

The next day, Wino and Cheryl went out for a stroll. In front of The U, kids frolicked about the two fountains. They skipped and climbed over the stone arched bridge bisecting the water displays. Parents and teenagers chatted among the benches. These couples surrounded the central courtyard filled with children.

Wino and Cheryl shared their own umbrella, pink with lotus flower print. Cheryl shouldered it while nestling into Wino's overarm grasp. The two perched on a bench shared with other guests. They split a double-strawed ice-cold drink, beading with bubbles of water. Strawberry sorbet and mascarpone gelato swirled with crumbs of granola and whipped cream on top. Cheryl's yellow sundress fluttered around her shins. A cool breeze whipped past. They sipped at the same time, with noses nearly kissing and cheeks blushing. Cheryl's mint-green eyes glimmered like the ocean floor speckled with pellets of colored stone. She glanced up, unconsciously swaying the umbrella more to her side and exposing Wino's back. Up above The U, a gathering of people waddled like ducks. They packed their sleeping bags and pitched small tents under the sweltering heat. Wino followed Cheryl's lead. Turning back to her, he pinched her umbrella and tugged it over himself.

He said, "D'you want to see if we can get a spot?"

Cheryl shook her head no. "It's probably packed. And with lots of sweaty people." She chuckled.

"Girl, I know, right?" her bench mate, a middle-aged woman with sunglasses, chimed in. "They up there sweatin' and nasty. I don't wanna be up there with them." The woman broke into a crackled laugh. She leaned to nudge Cheryl who joined her.

Wino twirled back. "At least it's not cloudy. That just might be a good spot."

"Oh no," the woman retorted. "It's just not cloudy *yet*."

Another couple chimed in from across the bench, this time a young pair with matching pastel-colored shirts and ripped jeans, "It's supposed to get cloudy tonight. And the meteor shower isn't until like midnight or really late."

"See?" the woman added. "They up there sweatin' for nothing. Leave 'em alone. More room for us down here."

The group meeting diffused as the individual conversations reform.

Cheryl leaned towards Wino. "So what happened with you and Ibrahim?"

She swirled her straw within the gelato, prodding the sunken granola crumbs, waiting for his response.

Wino watched her blankly. His voice climbed, "Well, I was talking to him about it last night."

"About what?"

"How he hasn't used *it* in a while, for a few months actually.

"Go on."

"And I tried to let him know that if he was going to be living with me…That he'd have to give it up."

Cheryl sat unresponsive. The couple down the bench, clad in pastel colored clothing nuzzled and laughed. The sunglassed woman between the two pairs clacked her nails against her phone's screen.

"You tried?" Cheryl's words came out sharp. "What happened?"

"Well, I told him and that's when you came in. I think he was going to say something though."

"No?"

"I'm not sure, but we didn't really finish."

"Well, why didn't you text me? I would have waited outside. Now he's gonna think we're double-teaming him."

"We kinda are."

"Yeah but it's his fault for ruining our moving in together. He should find his own place." Cheryl drained the remaining one-third of the drink. The cup emptied, leaving only their straws and soaked particles of granola. The drink doused her sternness. "So where is he?"

"He said he has some errands to run, but I don't know what he really means."

***

Later in the day, Ibrahim twirled his wand with a grin. The front door opened to him seated upon the couch. He swirled the wand onto the couch parking it next to his extended thigh. His foot rested over the center table. Wino stepped in, alone.

"Hey, Ibrahim."

"Your other half's not with you?"

"No, Cheryl's coming over tonight to see if we can watch the meteor shower."

Ibrahim grunted in response.

Wino continued, "There's a huge crowd up there. I went up to see it and the police actually had to block off access because of the weight limit. Some people are trying to bring coolers while others are smuggling matches to see if they can start a bonfire. The police have a pile of contraband right before the roof access and most of the stuff is lighters and fire starters, some beer kegs, butterfly knives, and someone had a gun but thankfully he had a license so they told him to put it up in his room."

"You won't be able to see it."

"I know, it's supposed to be cloudy. What're you gonna do?"

"Whatever I feel like," Ibrahim said with a smirk he clearly suppressed.

"D'you still have your wand?" Wino hunched over to ask.

"Yeah, so what?"

"I thought I told you," Wino's voice quivered. "You have to get rid of it to stay here."

Ibrahim furrowed his brows. The sunset ducked for cover beneath the horizon, relinquishing the cotton waves against the black-purple sky to bear witness to Wino's challenge. Darkness filled the room, revealing a violet glow emanating from Ibrahim's eyes. They shined like a cat's in darkness, yet Wino, contrary to his timid nature, inched forward.

"You found her. You found that witch, didn't you? I knew it."

Ibrahim pulled away. "So? Is it any of your business? Go watch your stars. And before you say anything else, remember I used to take care of you? D'you care about any witches then?"

Wino, simmering with courage, came closer. "Ibrahim, magic is illegal now. You can't just use it like you used to."

Ibrahim leapt up in defiance. "Says who?" He strutted up to Wino. "Says you?"

"Says The General," Wino implored him, subconsciously retracting his steps. "And her new hyped-up police force. They've taken down a lot of other magic users."

Ibrahim whirled away, "Don't worry about her then."

Wino's arms dangle beside him as Ibrahim retracted onto the couch and twirled onto his back with a magazine in hand. The wand rested on his chest, pulsating violet energy that resonated with Ibrahim's heartbeat and possibly with the witch.

"I didn't know you were this power-hungry, Ibrahim."

Wino fled to his room. The living room went silent. Ibrahim reclined on the couch with his eyes pulsing in sync with his wand.

At 11:30 pm, Wino emerged from his room, phone in hand. It shined onto his face in the dim living room, lit only by moonlight and the ambient 'on' status of all the devices present. He flicked on the overhead bulbs and spotted Ibrahim lying on the couch. Ibrahim wore an all-white nightgown, magazine still in hand but his wand was out of sight. Wino slid open his door to Cheryl in a small denim jacket and turquoise blouse.

After a warm embrace and a kiss, she popped inside. "Could you see it?"

"Not really. I've been checking from my window."

Cheryl peered at the rooftop lining the center wing of The U from the glass panes of the living room. "Ah, I bet that's a great viewing spot. Should we try to see if we can get up there? They might be seeing it better."

"They started making noise a little while ago but I don't kn—"

"Probably just drunk," Ibrahim chimed in.

Cheryl faced Ibrahim but didn't say anything. She glanced at Wino who maintained his gaze outside the window. She read his unwillingness to address Ibrahim.

"So what do you think, should we go up there?"

"Sure, let's try," Wino finally responded.

He rushed into his room and re-emerged throwing on a black sweater lined with a white zipper and collar. The couple strolled past Ibrahim, chatting to each other. The door shut. Silence settled within the room.

A few moments passed of residents strolling along the hallway. Herds of kids and flocks of teenagers trampled past the door. They rolled in and out of earshot. Eventually, Ibrahim peeled down the magazine. The ending of his conversation with Wino echoed in his heart.

Then, a hurricane of voices poured from The U's rooftop. Ibrahim hopped off the couch. His nightgown wafted as he came to the window. With a wave of his hand the light bulbs dimmed. The room faded to black. A speckle of light darted across the foggy evening sky. A sea of clouds blurred the image. A chorus of cheers emanated from what they could see but eventually harmonized into a groaning *Aww* at what they could not see. People leaned over the edge to get a glimpse of a star. Photographers scrambled past limbs, climbing and ducking like ants in a forest.

Rooms across The U parted their curtains while those with window frames jutted their heads out. Lights flickered off. The cityscape fell midnight black as if an electromagnetic surge knocked out the grid. A bus squealed up to the dark courtyard. The LEDs of the rushing fountain lit up. Residents exited the bus immediately pointing up at the hazy meteor shower overhead while others bypassed them. Ibrahim stepped back revealing his reflection in the glass panes. His brown eyes met his reflection. His hand dove into his cloak and retrieved his wand. His eyes synchronized with it and his heart pulsed in tune. *"You've changed,"* he recalled. Had he really? And what of his situation? Had anyone stopped to consider the plight of the magicians, especially those who used their powers philanthropically? *Yes,* he'd changed. The turning tides mandated it; however, some things were worth clinging to rather than allowing them to slip into the rolling waves of time. Ibrahim pulled away to see the strobe lights of an oncoming plane. It flew way out beyond city limits. He swiped one more glance at his wand, his magazine, and the front door.

The door opened to Wino and Cheryl quickly scampering to the window.

"Hurry, hurry, we might see it," Cheryl urged. She dashed across the living room couch and pressed up against the windowpanes. Wino paused to lock the door before joining her. As he came up beside her, she asked, "Where's Ibrahim?"

Wino scanned the place, shrugging. "I don't know."

Cheryl jousted at the window, "Look, there's a plane."

Wino found the oncoming plane. It soared within city limits. Red and white strobe lights flashed along its wings. However, there's one extra light Wino saw: Violet.

***

Along the windows of the plane, falling stars swept across the sky. Passengers experienced a better view than those at The U, however a sea of clouds periodically obscured them. Children clung to their parents. They climbed over their caregivers to get a view from the window seats.

The pilot chimed in over the intercom, his voice screeching over the *ahh* of the entranced passengers, "As we fly into town, there's a meteor shower going on just up above. It is a bit cloudy but I can tell ya, we have a better view than the folks down below. Let's see who can spot a shooting star!"

Flight crew crouched in the center aisle alongside those seated next to them. They swiveled between windows, all in an effort to spot the shower. The cloudiness, however, generated rickety turbulence prompting the seat-belt sign to *ding.* The illuminating tangerine cigarette symbol chimed. The metal bird vibrated and shuttered from the serrated airflow. The pilots fought to keep the plane steady. Especially after calling out the meteor shower, the main pilot hoped the majestic yet hazy scene disappeared so as to clear a path for landing. To his dismay, a rising flare thundered over the cockpit. Its blinding gleam spilled over the glass. The rows of LEDs within the cabin flickered sporadically. The flight crew clutched onto the carts, chairs, and even passengers for stability.

Atop the cabin, Ibrahim's satin milky-white robes

fluttered rapidly in the howling winds. His toes gripped the metal body of the plane. He extended his arms running parallel to the wingtips.

He rode the plane like a surfer screaming, "*Aribaaa~!*"

Ibrahim withdrew his wand from his robe, violet energy pulsing through it. His smile ran from ear to ear. He gripped the wand with both hands, wound back, and swung it across his chest like a baseball player. This move banished the waves of clouds that surrounded the plane. It burrowed a gaping hole in the field of cotton haze.

Beyond this crater, a celestial downpour of liquid crystals fell against a swirling backdrop of stardust and distant galaxies. Ibrahim hovered his wand over the plane, twirling like a spinning top with low rotational momentum.

Suddenly, he whipped his wand out over The U and banished the misty veil for the stargazers. The emerging view entrapped them. As if sitting within a snow globe, lights arced over the world, running across the very boundary of the sky and whatever existed past it. Another swing, another clearance. Ibrahim continued his dance until the entire city could bask in awe at the spectacle above.

Finally, Ibrahim threw open his arms. He closed his eyes and endured the rejuvenating embrace of the world he lost: magic. It's like diving in a pool on a blazing summer day.

"I missed this," he whispered to the array of lights surfing before him.

The pilots of the plane flipped the knobs lining their cabin. They adjusted their dials before rising off their seats. A communal moment of silence settled between them. The magnificence of nature bedazzled them; the glittering lights hurled faster than their modern pinnacle of technology.

"What do you make of it?" the copilot inquired.

"A miracle."

The passengers scrambled back to the windows, gathering with the flight crew to gaze out the small windows lining the cabin. People rushed to the rear, calmed by the gently rocking wings, to find a less crowded experience.

**

Atop The U, flocks of stargazers cheered and roared at the plane while trailing the shooting star. Some shouted in horror while others sat back ready for a show. From their voices, it was like they witnessed a star falling out of orbit, like a firework – a roman torch that plummeted back onto its tower. Drunken cries of exhilaration mixed with those of anxious distress.

Crowds of onlookers hurried back to their viewing positions. Police escorting stargazers off the rooftop saw them scurry back. This congregation of stargazers threw up their hands, following the leads of children, naively trying to grab a star. Others prayed under the starlit sky, some kissed, others hugged, and a few chugged cans of fermented rye to celebrate the rarity. Similar to Ibrahim, they felt the cool evening breeze slither between the fabrics of their clothing. It wiggled between their bodies and washed over their cheeks. Viewers leaned back. They closed their eyes, basking in the solemnity of the moment.

Passengers emerged from the last bus stop of the evening. They hopped into the courtyard while heavenly bodies soared above them. Along the walls of The U, window blinds flipped, curtains tore apart, and windows screeched open. From their apartments, onlookers twirled out over the courtyard of The U. All gathered to bear witness to the spectacle as it unfolded.

The sheer quantity of stars illuminated the courtyard in a deep ocean blue hue like that of a dwindling twilight. The bus driver leaned out to catch a glimpse. He, like all the others within the city, was trapped under the hypnotic brilliance of this display.

***

Wino's apartment fell dark under the *flick* of the light switch. Then, like the sun, a blaze of rays soared past the glass wall. The rays outlined Cheryl. With her back to the glass, the room flashed black and white. It spilled over the space like a rolling tide.

As the waves pulled back, she twirled. "What was that?"

Wino shielded his eyes. "My eyes! Something flashed outside."

Cheryl's hand scrubbed the glass wall. The evening breeze whistled as it passed through the shuffling courtyard trees. Her head nodded and her fell limp.

"Do you – do you think Ibrahim did this?" she inquired.

Wino walked quietly. He didn't answer her but instead approached the glass. Suddenly, down hovered a ghostly Ibrahim. His flowing silky sleeping gown wafted before them. His toe balanced on the one-inch ledge just outside the glass wall. His back faced them. Ibrahim centered his focus upon the cosmic rain while Cheryl and Wino fell speechless in wonder.

The room was silent, The U went quiet and the

city watched as the meteor shower glittered down until there was not a star left in the sky.
    The End.

EPISODE 3: MAKING FRIENDS AND MEMORIES

Wino, like other busy bees of The U, was up and about, in the early morning hours. He paced out of his bedroom with a minty fresh morning smile. Wino made his way into the kitchen in his socks, white shirt, ruby red tie and leather briefcase. On his couch lied a lump on a log swathed in blankets. Ibrahim wouldn't budge or even react to any of the noises he heard. The toaster popped up two slices. Wino caught them between his fingers, shuffled into his moccasins and dashed out the door.

His life was dull, his life was ordinary, but his life was also peaceful. Most importantly, he managed his own life. He thought, *I won't lie and say that I don't at times miss the carefree lifestyle and abundance of misadventures to be had when I traveled. It was like being part of a band: touring cities by foot and rocking out venues by sunset alongside your closest friends. It always felt like charging down a pier, leaping as high as possible and plunging into a chilling lake – skinny dipping as the sun climbed the horizon. Nowadays, my work is my passion, my home is at The U, and my relationship with Cheryl is my adventure. And for nothing would I ever exchange this.*

Around noon, when kids assembled for games within the courtyard, Ibrahim twitched. His delayed reaction to Wino's noise finally arrived. Ibrahim rattled underneath the blanket like a worm. Eventually, his restlessness stopped, the bumps and hills under the covers flattened.

His voice groggily called out, "Wino. Wino? Ugh."

The blanket flopped off his face and poured like pudding onto the living room carpet. Ibrahim slumped to his feet, his shoulders leaned over his torso. He hunched like a swamp monster flopping his feet over to the bathroom. Inside, he gargled and spat; the faucet spilled out rushing water and the toilet flushed. Ibrahim came out, crossed the window rubbing his face and the next moment, he threw open the curtains. He wore only his boxers. Bending over he scratched his upper thigh. He yawned and simply flopped away.

The fridge opened and Ibrahim hovered his face a few inches from the fresh fruit and vegetables. Plump tomatoes rolled onto firm sunset-orange tangerines. Soy and chocolate milk eyeballed Ibrahim from their cartons. He scanned the layers, hunting for something he could throw into the toaster, oven, microwave or straight into his mouth.

Eventually, he whined, "I could use a buffet after last night. Damn recoil. I'm out of shape." The curtains flapped and fluttered behind him.

The early noon breeze rustled his boxers above his

thin legs. A shadow hovered over the living room couch. It stemmed from the windowsill, with interlocked ankles rooted to the frame at the base. Her braids draped over her shoulders like wind chimes dangling against a central plank of wood.

Ibrahim continued his search while saying, "Those windows don't open like that, y'know." He referred to opening permitted by the lower half of each pane. She sat beneath the row of panes, flaring out in an "L" shape.

The Witch responded, "So this is where you live."

The fridge shut. Ibrahim stood erect and turned round. He made his way to the living room and flopped back to the couch.

"For now," he replied. He dove under the sheet and twirled his blanket into a cocoon.

"Oh? You planning on building a castle? Cus, lord knows I could use one."

"It's not mine. It's my friend's place."

"Your friend's, huh? It's nice though, you should take it."

"No thanks. Where do you stay?"

"Don't worry about it. Just build me a castle so I can move in."

"I thought witches built their own castles," he says.

"Does that mean I can't move in?" Her comments fell into the silence. "I know. You just want your power back, but we have to get the magic circulating again or else you'll keep begging for a recharge. Now, don't you want to be a magician again? Free to roam and do as you please? Speaking of, I saw that little performance you put on the other day. Very impressive."

"Glad you liked it," Ibrahim grumbled.

In a low tone, the Witch reflected, "Y'know, I'm

beginning to like you."

"Everyone comes around eventually. And what about you-know-who? We still haven't done anything about her."

A sigh. "I know. I'm working on it." A maniacal look grew on the witch's face. "I wanted to disgrace her and tear her down before ripping her to shreds. But it turns out she's got no file. Or at least, she's hiding it." The witch calmed herself; the violet hue in her eye faded. "Why? You eager to wreck this place? Want to show off more magic? Put on a play for the city?"

"Whatever gets my power's back. I just want my life back."

"Well, a few nights ago, I snuck out of their office tailing a bullion van full of up-there-officers but..." The Witch shrugged.

"What?"

"I got distracted. By the time I came out, there was a meteor shower going on."

Ibrahim poked his head free, guilty as charged. They faced each other, smiling with their cheeks and their eyes, sinister intent coupled with sincere cynicism. Voices of children playing in the courtyard below scaled the walls of The U. The Witch held her gaze on him. In a second, her golden-brown eyes pulse violet, and Ibrahim's reciprocated.

She thought, *Good,* and turned out the window lifting one leg over the glass. "Well, I'm heading out. I'll let you know if–"

"Hold on." Ibrahim leapt from the couch.

The Witch peered over her shoulder. She found him standing before her, stern-faced with his wand outstretched. She smirked and grabbed the other end. Ribbons of royal purple power, swirling like cosmic energy, twirled from her wrist into the wand, emitting radiant heat. Ibrahim grinned, shadows washing over his face in the light of the energy transfer. She held this for a few seconds before relinquishing the wand to him. The Witch carried her other leg over the glass.

"Don't spend it all at once."

"No promises," Ibrahim replied gazing into his wand.

"You'll need it for the party – when this city blows like a firework. I'd stay out of the spotlight if I were you." She plopped off the window and out of sight. In her wake, the windows realigned into linear windowpanes stacked across the wall. The outside breeze whistled against the upper wing of The U.

**

Later in the day, Wino jogged across Ménage Boulevard. He dawned the full getup: headband, wristbands, pulse measuring fitness watch, and wireless earbuds pumping music. He scanned the street, jogging in place before humming his way across to The U on the other side. A family sipping smoothies curiously watched him run by. One of the kids tailed him. He slowed to an energetic pace as The U's glass doors slid open for him.

In the elevator, a dog sniffed and licked the beads of sweat off his ankle. Both the owner and the dog paused for a reaction. Wino's overburdened senses attended to his good stress, soreness, and exhilaration. His toe tapped. His knee bounced with the sway of his arms to the Afrobeats in his head until the elevator door dinged open. He paced to his room, resisting the infectious urge to break out into a dance.

Inside, Ibrahim sat on the couch.

Wino stopped and wondered, *Who are these two?* He iquired. "Um. Ibrahim?"

Two ladies snuggled beneath Ibrahim's arms with smiles gleaming towards Wino. They leaned into Ibrahim whispering, "Is this your roomy?"

Ibrahim mumbled, "Yeah, he lives with me."

Wino searched the room. Ibrahim's folded blanket stacked on the other couch facing the door; nylon bags with Chinese words printed in red sat on the center table; two styrofoam takeouts, one with falafels, the other containing scraps of tilapia; and a Bollywood drama is airing. Wino's uplifted expression plummeted. Finally, he grumpily addressed Ibrahim.

Ibrahim asked, "Were you jogging just now? I thought you went to work." Ibrahim leaned forward, almost looking concerned. "Wino, are you jobless?"

"No idiot, I just jogged back."

A knocking sounded at the door. It slid open to Cheryl on her phone.

She strutted past Wino who held the door open for her saying, "Wino, I found this nice–" Cheryl looked up and intuitively read the situation: Ibrahim grined on the couch alongside two ladies, takeout on the table, Bollywood drama on the TV, and a visibly grouchy Wino at the door. She turned, whining, "Ibrahim! We didn't know you'd be having guests."

Ibrahim snarled back at her, "So? I never know when you're coming yet you're always here."

Wino defensively retorted, "Yes, you do know, cus' I always tell you."

"Well, I-don't-listen. Speak up next time."

The two ladies pulled away from the conversation. An awkward silence wiggled its way into the atmosphere. The tension between the three participants heated up. Cheryl and Wino stared down against Ibrahim until the girls under Ibrahim's arms bounced. Their focus locked onto the television.

One gasped while the other jousted her finger towards the TV. "Oh my gosh, he's doing it. He's really doing it."

The first one bit her nails while the other one hugged her shins onto the couch adding, "What's Romeo gonna do then? What's Romeo gonna do?"

"I don't know!"

"He's going to be devastated. Oh, this is going to be horrible."

Ibrahim used the cinematic tension on screen to pull the ladies in closer to him for comfort. His grin reached across his face while they coddled and clung to him. His attention rested on them while theirs attended to the drama. Wino and Cheryl exchanged glances. They made they're way past the couch sharing in a communal pool of disapproval.

***

Later that evening, Wino's bedroom door slid open. He curiously stuck his head out. Cheryl sat on the bed behind him. He scanned the living room. The mating calls of cicadas among other tree critters provided that orchestral ambiance that heralded the evening calm. Wino moved out into the space. Cheryl audibly plopped off the bed behind him. He flicked on the living room light.

Crumbs and junk littered throughout the space. At least the TV's off but that's probably because of the automatic power-saving feature, not because Ibrahim actually turned it off when he and his accomplices migrated from Wino's room to god-knows-where. He might have left a while ago but nobody heard him. The girls also left but their takeout remained and the place reeked of rapidly rotting remains. Cheryl scanned the area while Wino glared at the mess. His hands rose to his hips and he let out a huff. Cheryl stopped between the couch and the table.

She shows that not-really-smiling smile and sarcastically suggested, "Looks like you guys might need to have another talk."

Wino started out low. "Oh, I'm gonna have more than just a talk with him."

"To be fair, it's not your fault. Remember, I came in the room and–"

"Yeah. And I'm gonna shove my foot where the sun don't shine so that he can hear me."

"I don't think he understands that."

"Well, I'll get him a translator."

Cheryl scoffed to Wino's rant.

"I mean seriously, look at this mess. Does he expect me to clean this up?" Wino retrieved speckles of trash. He grumbled under his breath.

Cheryl protested, "What're you–? Let him pick it up. He and his friends made this mess, you can't pick it up for him you'll just encourage him."

"You don't know him. This'll never get cleaned up."

Wino crumbled the trays between his fingers and threw them into the bag marked with ember Chinese calligraphy. Cheryl reluctantly followed his lead. Together, they tidied the room.

***

The next morning, Cheryl groggily emerged from Wino's bedroom. She wore one of his oversized shirts, one that would be large even on his torso, and petite shorts. Stepping up to the dining table, Cheryl paused.

"Ibrahim didn't come back last night?"

The blanket remained folded on the couch facing the entry door. The mess they cleaned up sat packaged in grocery bags along the front door – a signal to you-know-who-probably-doesn't-care that they had to clean up after him. Finally, Ibrahim's wand was nowhere to be found. The two analyzed the room, meeting at the end.

Cheryl mumbled, "Do y'know where he is?"

Wino simply shook his head *nope*. It was not like Ibrahim to even leave the apartment. One thing about someone who never evacuates their residence is that when they do leave, the options are limitless and the evidence too scant to predict just where they've departed to. With Ibrahim's character, his magic wand, and presence of the Witch, the only conclusion Wino drew was that it couldn't be good for either of them.

***

Inside the downtown skyscrapers, papers were filed, pens clicked, and millions of dollars' worth of services were provided. In the office room, a manila folder flapped open. In it, documents spilled over the dark wood grain of an office meeting table. The documents listed names, ID numbers, photos, and performance records among other things for a number of operatives. Atop each document read Police Records. Just below read: For Internal Use Only.

The Witch inquired, "Well? What do you think?"

She peered down at Ibrahim from over her shoulder. She swirled around to catch Ibrahim's expression. Ibrahim tugged the first document over.

He read, "Car-men San-chez," and tossed it back

onto the table. "What am I supposed to do with this?"

The Witch smirked. She peeled the top file from the stack. Sarcastically she started, "This is called a file. And what you do with it is you're supposed to read it and–"

Ibrahim impatiently smacked his lips and swatted papers across the table. She toyed with his intelligence.

"Don't joke with me. I'm a real magician. If you want something done, just point and shoot. I'll hand the rest."

The Witch huffed, spinning the information side towards her. "Alright, no judgment. Since some of us can't read, I'll read it to you. 'Carmen Sanchez, age 29, born in Cotswell–"

"Don't make me burn that paper."

The Witch giggled mockingly at Ibrahim's aggression. Ibrahim tapped his foot. His thumb grated against his wand and he wore a scowl on his face.

"Why so angry?"

"Cus, I finally have my powers back and you want me to read a book."

"But it's just a few pages. Are all magicians like this?" Gathering some between her fingers, she pinched them up. Her nails extended over her fingers. Her middle fingernail stood out with swirls of green studs on a royal purple back. Ibrahim slapped the papers away to her amusement.

"Put those down," he commanded. Ibrahim sat humorlessly while the file for 'Ms. Carmen Sanchez' slid before him. "Just tell me what you want me to do."

The laughter faded, and the Witch's shoulders relaxed. She lets out a sigh of relief. The Witch peeled herself from the table, and wiped her eye with the side of her palm.

"Okay. Okay. Alright, so here's what I want you to do..." She slipped out another sheet, this time from beneath the manila folders and flopped it atop the others. It was an aerial photograph of the city, more specifically a small subsection – a superblock. "So, I found this guy that lives here, he makes these crystalline orbs that can store magic. And he's been selling them for some time now to — to, well, people like you who can use them. And he's been making big bucks."

"A Whitesmith?"

"Exactly."

"And you want in?"

"I mean, I'd love the money, but that's not what we're going in for." She lifted the map, revealing police records. Within the gap of overlapping files, Ibrahim spotted a unique paper. He hunched forward, cleared away the files to see a folder stamped Confidential. Ibrahim flipped it open, and skimed. "You see our friends are pretty smart and they've been watching this guy for some time now."

"Cus he's sloppy."

"They're just about ready to take him out. And this guy is one of the original Whitesmith's, if you see him he has three gold earrings – right side – just like they used to. You know what the earrings mean, right?"

"It means the police are gonna regret picking a fight with us." Ibrahim's grip crumpled the paper at his fingertips. His eyes glowed violet.

A smirk. "That's why I like you."

"When are they moving in? There's no date."

The Witch leaned in to continue. She and Ibrahim discussed the confidential file, scattered and unveiled files of police officers assigned for the bust. Projected sunlight muddled their silhouettes onto the glazed glass. Once again, the office workers glanced at the room wondering just what department they even worked in? Typing rattled keyboards as phone lines rang. The buzz of the office work faded.

***

Back at The U, Wino and Cheryl spent the whole day together. It seemed like they're getting used to it. The tenderness of their embrace was intoxicating. They shared Wino's room, his couch, and his TV. They felt like they'd gotten away with something even though this was how it used to be before His Majesty showed up. Right now, the pair occupied the couch, ankles overlapping atop the table.

Cheryl tucked under Wino's arm, her own arms sandwiched between her thighs. Ibrahim's blanket disappeared. Twin large plates sprinkled with home-cooked scraps filled the sink. The peaceful couple spent the time with TV. Wino tucked his head into Cheryl's hair, kissing her and rubbing her shoulder. The rustling of shrubs and trees, void of the squeaking cicadas complemented the dying sun in the far distance.

A soft triplet of knocks sounded at the door. The two sat perfectly still, basking in the bliss of feigned ignorance. The knocks repeated, triggering Wino to untangle his ankles from Cheryl's. Wino huffed on his way up. He made for the door, opening it upon the sounding of the third triplet. A large, white board with feet shooting out from the base stood in the hall. Wino paused. He waited confusedly for a moment, before stepping out of the board's way.

It barked, "Move it!" waddling into the room like

an uncoordinated infant.

It resembled an oversized pizza box with Ibrahim marching behind it. He came to a halt before the table. The box angled its flat side of the box towards Cheryl. She got the signal and retrieved her feet. Ibrahim plopped the box onto the table. He leaned back and threw up his arms shouting "Arriba!"

Wino stood over him as Cheryl leaned in.

Cheryl flicked the box, asking, "A board game?"

Wino inquired "Ibrahim, where did you get this?"

Ibrahim grinned. "You're looking at the happy winner of the Arrrrriba sweepstakes all the way from El Salvadoria and sponsored by the Arrrrriba radio show - me."

Wino asked, "A sweepstakes? Wait, you mean that radio show you were listening to?"

"The same," Ibrahim answered.

"So what did you win?" Cheryl chimed in. "Caves-and-Castles. Isn't that one of those wizards and dungeons board games? A role-playing game?"

"Why is a Spanish sweepstake selling a role-playing game?" Wino asked.

"Why's your face look like that?" Ibrahim retorted. Wino rubbed his cheek, stumped for words. "Now then." Ibrahim lifted the box.

Cheryl and Wino exchanged glances. Underneath the box lid clacked a series of two-toned, multi-sided die; stacks of transitioning cards with monster art; a large, collapsible, cardboard pamphlet with a colorful map featuring a fantastic world upon it, character cards and more. They curiously grabbed pieces and analyzed the work.

Wino skimmed over the cards. "What are these

things?"

Ibrahim popped up like a jack-in-the-box. "Those are the monsters." He wiggled his arms like tentacles while rolling his fingers like the legs of a walking crab. "That lurk in dark murky forests and suck your face out." Ibrahim pinched Wino's cheeks, tugging on them.

Wino swatted Ibrahim's hands away protesting, "Get off me, man."

Cheryl juggled the die in her palm while analyzing them piece-by-piece. "The dice are really nice, I like the noise they make when you roll them together." She cupped her hands and shuffled them around listening to the clacking like marbles rolling over one another. Wino and Ibrahim picked out more things until Cheryl eventually drops the die to withdraw the world map. "Whoa, check out this art."

Ibrahim and Wino leaned over prompting her to lay it flat against the table. The art appeared freshly painted. The fantastic world transitioned dramatically from tropical wetlands to scorching desserts to mansions of an estate located in the clouds. These all had rails that linked them together except for rare and excluded locations. The pop-up art added an extra flair to the scenery. Cheryl and Wino could not help but run their hands across.

"Wait, what are we going to do with this, Ibrahim?" Wino asked.

"We're going to learn how to play it and right now," Ibrahim responded.

"But I have work in the morning."

"Screw your work! Come on, it'll be fun."

Wino and Cheryl shared a glance. Ibrahim organized the game pieces on the table encouraging Wino to sit down. Cheryl smirked at Wino as if to say that this is a good time to try and either connect with him or make your decision to be firm with him. Wino read this from her expression and resigned to sit down.

A few moments later and the table was set. The room lights dimmed and everyone sat around the center table. Wino and Ibrahim sat on the floor while Cheryl scooted the sofa closer. The couple continued with uncertainty now that they were seeing a different side of Ibrahim.

"Alright," Ibrahim started. "This is just a trial run but let's see how this game works." He grabbed some die and character cards. Wino passed them around. The pair scrambled through the cards and mumbled whatever they could read to the group.

"So are we going somewhere or – what're we supposed to do here?" Wino inquired.

Ibrahim mumbled through a paragraph on a scroll. It unravels as he speed-read his way through it. Over twenty seconds passed until he finally came to a stop.

Cheryl doubtingly asked, "Did you read all that?"

"So what're we doing?" Wino questioned.

Ibrahim released the scroll onto the floor. "I don't know. I got bored after the first sentence. Let's just start a battle! Everyone pick a character."

"What?" Wino protested. "That's not how you play the game, you're supposed to-"

"I'll be a warrior knight!" Cheryl interjected.

"Alright cool," Ibrahim answered. "Let's start…" He circled his finger over the map. "Here. Cave Marx."

Wino followed along with this train wreck until he detected a glint from behind Ibrahim's back.

"And just to make this a little more exciting…"

Ibrahim added as his eyes gleamed violet.

From his back, a spark of light flashed over the room. It engulfed the space and washed over the trio.

As it dimmed, Cheryl removed her arm shielding her face. The heavy weight of body armor tugged at her forearm. Withdrawing her hand, she spotted her black glove and glistening white armor. The eyepiece to her helmet fell, obstructing her view with vertical slits that mimic a grill. She threw it open and found smooth limestone pillars lining the walls. Their apex towered like skyscrapers over her. She occupied an inner sanctuary located deep within a cave. On either end of this space, were caverns running into voids of darkness. Totems with flames atop them lit the area and a cage dangled from the rooftop.

Cheryl spotted a massive blur as it descended from on high. Its weight shuttered throughout the cave. The vibrations rattled the cage and flung loose pebbles from the rooftop. Before her now crept a pepper-red dragon whose scales each outsized her. The beast jousted forward, screeching into her face.

She nearly fell hysteric, screaming, "Wh-what the hell is that!?" but the monster's face immediately morphed into that of Ibrahim's.

His voice echoed, "Ugh, here we go."

Another flash and they reappeared within the living room. Ibrahim sat with his arms crossed and a scowl on his face.

Wino inched in front of her, nudging, "It's okay, you're fine now."

Cheryl clutched Wino's collar. "D-Did you see that? D-d-did you just see any of that? I saw a huge room with a giant dragon and ... and I-bra-him."

Wino answered, "Don't worry, it was just his–"

"Nice job, Cheryl," Ibrahim complained. "The least you could do is play along."

Ibrahim wore a cardboard box over his head. It had a cutaway for his face and squiggly scales doodled on its sides.

"Wait," Cheryl inquired. "What are you doing? Why do you have a box on your head?"

"It's called role-playing. Look it up."

"But I swear! I saw all this stuff. But you weren't there, Wino. And I–"

"Nice girlfriend you got there Wino. She can't even play along to a simple game."

Cheryl leapt to her feet, balling her fists. "You know what, Ibrahim? I've had it with you and your snide remarks–"

A flash shined before her and she's spoke to the dragon. It faced away from her but spun to screech in her face again. She dashes into the corner shaking and whimpering. Her arms covered her head. Rattling bellowed into the cavernous space.

Shaking in terror, Cheryl heard the voices of Wino and Ibrahim, albeit muffled, behind her.

"Ibrahim, that isn't funny," Wino complained.

"So what, it's not my fault she can't role play."

Cheryl considered the absurd possibility that if she could not only hear the boys they may also be a part of this alternate world. She peered up and found a straight sword plunged into the ground. Its handle glittered with golden embroidery wound about with a midnight blue band for grip. The tail of the handle sparkled with a sapphire gem in it. Behind her, the dragon scoffed with disinterested. Cheryl wasn't worth the trouble.

Suddenly, a blade jousted towards its rear.

In Wino's room, a paper towel roll aimed for Ibrahim's jaw. Ibrahim glanced towards Cheryl, at first surprised, and then a grin slowly crept across his face. Her eyes shared in his violet glow while that of the knight's glittered hazel. Her eyepiece fell. She snatched the shield of a fallen soldier from the floor. Now, she clearly challenged the dragon. Cheryl had never been one to stand down to a challenge.

Ibrahim's voice echoed in the cave, "Here we go. Now we're role-playing." The dragon lunged onto four feet as it inched closer to her. A sinister glare beamed down at her.

Cheryl refused to back down. Instead, she gathered her courage to bark, "You're going down, Ibrahim-dragon!"

With this, she bravely charged, leapt skyward and arced towards the beast. With her blade she drew the first blood, nicking the beast on its nose. Still suspended within the air, the beast twirled and swatted her back to the wall above the cavern. She slammed with a thud and crashed before the cavern opening. She rose to the beast engorging its mouth with magic. Streaks of ember flame leaked from the slits in its pursed lips. The knight wobbled to her feet, distracted by the imbuing power before her. Ibrahim threw open his mouth, and releases a blast of hot breath.

Cheryl scampered along the couch. She took shelter behind its armrest. Within the sanctuary, the knight planted her shield and took refuge behind it. A torrent of fire engulfed the warrior blazing its way down the tunnel leading away from the sanctuary. It illuminates the hole and after the attack receded, it left scorching residue all along the walls of the path.

Small fires burned like candles as Cheryl climbed from behind her anchored shield. Steam streaked from the openings in her armor, including her eye slits. She stumbled into the sanctuary, leaning her head back to capture the majesty of this enemy. Her arms slouched, her sword and shield dangled from her hands. The monster reeled back.

Ibrahim's voice echoed, "What's wrong? Tired after just one move? I thought you were going to slay me?"

Cheryl gazed up. She had absolutely no idea how to handle this challenge. She considered surrendering. She never asked for all this craziness in the first place. As usual, it's Ibrahim and his shenanigans that led to this.

Wino's voice cried out, "Ibrahim!"

The dragon angled towards the cage. Inside the dangling prison a fair maiden, with ivory skin clung to the bars. She wore white gloves that veiled her elbows, a multicolored floral dress, and a glittering diamond tiara. Her black hair ran alongside her arm, down to her elbow. This maiden gripped the bars of the cell and threw her head out.

"How come I have to be the princess?" She complained in Wino's voice.

The dragon's head morphed back into that of Ibrahim's as he responded, "I like you better that way. It suits you."

The knight proclaiming, "Wino, is that you?"

Wino glared at Ibrahim as the dragon's head reformed.

"Don't worry," Wino responded. "I'm fine. It's just a ga—"

"Don't worry, hun, I'll save you!"

Wino watched with speechless amusement. His mouth hung open as Cheryl took charge of her role. Her grip bent the paper roll she pointed at Ibrahim. Ibrahim now stood upon the living room couch. A threatening foe, his claws hung by his face as he marched towards her. She held firm.

Nothing ignited Cheryl's spirit like protecting the defenseless. She's a nurturer at heart and could not stand unsightly wickedness. It rang unsavory memories of magician's rule into her mind. Although a game, the less privileged Wino made her heart skip a beat and provoked her to action. Wino sat at the table. He watched curiously as the two plunged deeper within the confines of their conjoined imagination.

Ibrahim rattled Princess Wino's cage. Cheryl inched forward, vigilant for signs of distress. Out swung one of Princess Wino's gloves – it danced in the sanctuary breeze like a falling leaf in the wind. It twisted and twirled until landing upon Cheryl's blade. The power from the rare material used to forge Wino's gloves reacted with Cheryl's character.

A gleam of light poured out from the crevices of the knight. The abrupt dispersal of sunrays blinded the dragon and princess. It subsequently faded to reveal the exquisite brilliance of Cheryl's transformation: a surge of blazing heat that erupted from the steel of the knight's sword, a dazzling cross of gold carved across the face of her shield and a majestic cape. For but a moment, Wino and Ibrahim shared a astounded glance. They wondered, *Is she really getting into this though?*

"Hang tight honey!" The knight lunged at the scaly beast.

Once again, she leapt, although this time she torpedoed directly for the eye of the monster. It swerved to avoid her but failed to anticipate her rebounding off the wall. She took aim and inflicted a critical strike. With her momentum, the knight continued her assault. She rebounded off the walls like The General's super soldier.

Cheryl leapt off the couch towards Ibrahim. Ibrahim hopped around the room, Cheryl closely tailing him. The two engaged in life-or-death combat as Wino quietly took in the site. He avoided them, wide-eyed from his central reference point.

The beast palmed Cheryl's knight to the sanctuary floor. Restrained beneath its nails, Ibrahim engorged his mouth with another potential outpour of sizzling gas and fire. This time, however, he restrained himself. Flames leaked from his cheeks. Their colors shifted along a gradient from burnt-orange to sky-blue, from sky-blue to royal purple. Cheryl managed to slice his dragon's finger with her paper-towel roll so that she could roll back. Ibrahim sprayed fire like the pressurized hose of a firefighter.

The inferno diverted into two halves, bisected by the rooted shield of Cheryl's knight. The swordswoman withdraws her blade; the beast screeched and the two once again engaged each other.

Ibrahim and Cheryl clashed countless times throughout the evening. Their enthusiasm filled the room, motivating him to participate but from a safe distance. He didn't want to ruin their evening. They're battle spiraled into the night fueled by the machinations of their childlike imaginations.

***

A few hours later, Wino emerged from his bedroom. The

living room had been turned upside down. Chairs scattered all over the place, paper towels draped over the carpet, cards scattered across the floor and die tumbled off the table. Cheryl curled on the floor unconscious. Her fingers still clutched the paper towel roll. Ibrahim resumed his normal sleeping position; his fingers barely touched the unfolded flap of his cardboard box. Drool seeped from his cheek onto the carpet.

Wino crossed over Cheryl to unfold Ibrahim's blanket atop his sleeping body. He also draped Cheryl with a thin sheet that she immediately snuggled into. Wino brought a pillow with him and slid it beneath Cheryl's head. She adjusted herself while he lied down beside her.

In the quiet of the evening, Wino wondered, *Caves and Castles huh? I'd never think of it, but look at how things turned out. If I can get these two to play with each other like this ever again – maybe they can even learn to be friends. This was nice.*

The trio fell asleep, and the room went quiet.

EPISODE 4: ENEMIES CLOSER

C heryl's hair rustled against her supple cheek. She spent the night on the living room floor, having slept there after playing Caves and Castles with Ibrahim. Bands of matted hair wrapped her groggy head. She scrubbed it against the oatmeal and raisin carpet floor. Cheryl sat up. She squinted into the dim living room with a blank stare.. Glints sparkled about the space.

"Where in the world am I?"

Ibrahim slept on the couch, his blanket dangled off his body, wrapped about thigh-high on the seat. One arm and leg hung off the edge while his mouth opened. Snoring stemmed forth. Cheryl's arm anchored onto her neck while.

She groaned, "My neck."

Trading cards and paper towels littered the kitchen countertop. The rolls tumbled onto the white dining table. The living room table shifted towards the wall with the adjacent couch making room for them on the floor.

"You awake?" rasped Wino.

Cheryl faced him lying, snuggled under a blanket with his head balancing at the edge of a pillow.

"What happened?" she inquired.

"You and Ibrahim fell asleep out here. I tried to put blankets on both of you but he rolled it off and you hogged it all."

But what of the creature she wondered – or was it a dream? She could have sworn a dragon bucked and charged her. Glistening armor shielded her. She fought fearlessly with sword and shield in hand. She leapt skyward, higher than ever thought possible and lashed out at the beast, locked in life or death combat. But more notably, she basked in the adrenaline-fueled thrill of it. She had fun. Now, she couldn't recall how it ended. But, putting this timeline together, she assumed it must have all been a dream after she fell asleep from exhaustion.

"Looks like you two had fun together."

She cringed at the embarrassment like a bad memory. Having fun with Ibrahim was almost unheard of – at least when it came to the two of them. Don't get her wrong, Cheryl had done more than extend an olive branch his way, but it often comes back without the olives.

Ibrahim was magician at heart, a practitioner of magic whose interests were often piqued by his own actions. Cheryl preferred to invest her interest in more productive things like volunteer work and charities. So, excuse her if it was difficult to imagine the pair having fun. Cheryl scanned the cluttered living room full of die, figurines, and whatever else came in the cardboard game. She peered to Wino's room. His alarm clock sat on his bedside table.

"What time is it?" she asked, to which Wino sprung up in shock.

He scrambled in his striped socks, sky-blue boxers, and white T into his room. The door slid further open to reveal his bed, naked except for the cover sheet and one pillow on it. Wino clutched his clock. Cheryl crawled on all fours, following his lead. Wino turned, snatched the last pillow and hopped onto the bed, hugging it like it's his partner. Cheryl stepped into his room.

"You work at 8 right?"

Wino shushed her from his back. "Fifteen more minutes," he whispered.

Cheryl inspected the clock; he usually woke up 6:15. He straddled his pillow between his arms and ankles. She threw the door to a sliding close, but it stayed a hair open.

Wino's blanket flew over him similar to how he tossed it atop her. She climbed into bed with him and lied with her arms at her side atop the duvet. She stared at the ceiling, uncertain of how the evening played out. Cheryl flicked a glance at Wino. His shoulder rose and fell. His diaphragm expanded in tune to his breathing.

Turning back at the roof, his voice softly broke the silence, "Did you have fun?"

"I don't remember too much of it," she answered. "But I had this dream." Cheryl cusped her shoulders adding, "It was so vivid. I could feel everything. And-and there was this monster–"

"You looked like you were having fun."

"You mean that was real? You saw the dragon?" she barked, rocking the bed on her way to a seat.

Wino shushed her again. "I still have eleven minutes."

Cheryl climbed over Wino. She rocked his shoulder. "Wait, but how did you know?"

"It was Ibrahim. He used his wand on you – on all of us."

Cheryl rolled away from Wino. Ibrahim gargled saliva bubbles from the living room. His noise paused, a gulp and then the boisterous snoring of a drunken sailor resumed. Her mind raced.

Wino added, "I never would have thought you'd like it, but you got pretty into it. Let me know if you want to do it again and I'll tell Ibrahim."

Cheryl spotted a game card on the floor of the living room. It featured a red dragon with thick scales running from head to toe, twin thick black wings and radiant gold eyes like the sun – just like the one in her dream. Who would have thought that the unbearable magician would share a moment of companionship with anyone besides Wino – more so with Cheryl? If only she could recall the specifics, Cheryl could decipher what made him more amicable that evening. Of even greater interest, she'd construct a method of approach that would be effective at bridging the gap between the two. After all, she harbored no ill will for magicians with consciences. It's the injustice spurred on by the wicked ones that made her blood boil.

Soon after their discussion, Wino's alarm chimed. It beeps in triplets.

Ibrahim's voice growled from the living room, "Turn it off!"

The door slid open with a grouchy Ibrahim bearing his wand in hand. He marched inside prompting Wino to leap in a startled panic. Cheryl gasped as Ibrahim swung his wand overhead, glaring at the beeping clock with murderous intent.

"Ibrahim, wait," Wino protested. "I'm awake!"

Wino dove over Cheryl for his clock. Scattering furniture and grunting from the collision. There went the bedside lamp.

"Turn that damn thing off!" Ibrahim commanded. Next went the bedside drawer.

"Ibrahim, you jerk, get out!" Cheryl retorted.

Wino's hand popped up reflexively. He begged, "It's off! It's off! I got it."

Ibrahim froze with ears poised to detect anymore incessant beeping. His fingers unbuckled and his hands unclasped as his arms retracted. The trio shared in the silence until Ibrahim retreated into the living room. He slid the door shut behind him. In wafted the gaming card, sliding just before the toppled woodwork and into Cheryl's sight. Wino huffed a heavy sigh in relief. That's just like him – a wild card.

***

A botanical footpath meandered behind The U. The park featured manicured lawns spotted with tall trees and ornamental shrubs. Residents dozed off in the cool shaded areas. Ruby-red rubberized lanes wove in and out of one another meeting at large pedestrian intersections. Small children broke from their parents to pounce on gatherings of leaves.

As the leaves danced in the air and tangoed with the breeze, Ibrahim walked past. He strolled along the outgoing lane, forcing joggers to swerve around him onto the oncoming lane. Dimpled light broke through the veil of branches and fluttering leaves. Bikers whizzed past him on the sidewalk at the edge of the park. As they enveloped him, Ibrahim emerged with his partner in crime at his side. The two blocked traffic. Distasteful glares and glances landed on them from passersby.

The Witch asked, "Why this place?"

"I'm sick of that office."

"Then why not your place? Don't want to show me to your friends?"

"No, I just needed to get out of the house. Besides, this trail weaves throughout Uptown so you can show me whatever building you're talking about."

The Witch smirked at Ibrahim's straight face. He scowled at the oncoming runners and even scared some of them onto the grass around him. "Alright then. So, you remember the guy we talked about, right?"

"The Whitesmith," Ibrahim mumbled, peering over his shoulder.

"I found out when they're going to bust him."

He nodded and they head to their new destination.

In the Rusty Belt – a ring of dilapidated apartments and office buildings sandwiched between the newly developed Uptown and wealthy downtown regions of the city – there's one building. Thin, red clay, bricks formed its facade with a black steel staircase climbing its side. Rows of black window frames decorated the structure. Nails held some of them shut; charcoal stains crept along every vertex like remnants of a fire. Wooden steps riddled the front porch. Puddles of cigarette butts hid amongst blades of grass that grew between them. There building bled into the field of run-down building schemes running along both streets that intersect with its location.

"It's not what it used to be," the Witch started. She stood on the rooftop of one building opposite the street.

"It's a dump," Ibrahim commented.

"It is. Now if some benevolent witch was in charge," she sings. "It just might be a little bit better. Who knows, it might even become paradise."

"Why does he live here?"

"Hiding in plain sight, cheap, maybe he's got a lovely lady. Could be anything really, but that's not what matters."

"Does he know we're gonna help him?"

"Actually, I managed to get a word in with him a few days ago. And, it turns out, he knows he's being watched."

"So what's his plan?"

"Doesn't have one."

"A last stand?"

"A grand stand. Turns out, he's just like us. Sick of living under The General. So, he wants to go out with a bang."

Ibrahim sternly angled at the Witch.

"Hey," she defended, "if you want to talk him out of it, be my guest."

"Idiot whitesmith's and their pride. So what are we going to do? If he goes down…"

"I know. Unless you can find someone to grant you some of their power, say a beautiful witch…" The Witch threw back her hair while Ibrahim rolled his eyes. She folded her arms and continued with a smile, "This's your next best option. And this guy is all our community's got left."

"Even if he beats the first round of officers…"

"They'll just send another batch. That's why I found a place on the outskirts of town. It's a run-down shack, but we can throw him in there for the time being."

"Why not do it now?"

"Being one of us, he probably won't listen, not unless the police are trampling on his throat."

The pair gaze scanned the building and its surroundings. They analyzed the tight avenues and winding back streets of the area. Ibrahim and the Witch highlighted little nooks and crannies available for an easy exit as well as points of entry for the police to camp at. Major roads sliced through the Rusty Belt, linking the Uptown and downtown districts together.

Ibrahim met the Witch amongst one of these streets. It flashed in his mind as she slid closer to him. Her outstretched arm crossed his blank face. He recalled her seated on the curbside and most importantly that gush of succulent energy. Like butterflies in his stomach, it made him nauseous yet electrified; he could feel it zing and tingle throughout his body like a high voltage cable slapped right onto his spine. Next thing, Ibrahim smelt the Witch's perfume.

"We could use that one. You see it?"

"Say again."

"That room right there, I think that's his room. We could use this storm drain."

***

The apple-red sun set over The U. The rooftop normally attracted flocks of stargazers by days end. This night, however, only one viewer appeared, but they certainly had a bounty to feast upon. The U's dedicated blue bus pulled up in front of the courtyard. Offloading passengers merged with flocks of residents coming in from across Ménage Boulevard.

Wino's door opened to his living room, neatly arranged and reorganized from the night before. The couches were realigned – one faced the door from across the table, while the other faced the TV to the left. The vacuumed oatmeal and raisin carpet stood fluffed and soft. Standing on it barefoot, he scrunched his feet, hugging them into the floor.

Cheryl stepped in, planted herself before the table, and curiously panned the room. She held her little black bag with rose imprints on it before her lap. She wore denim and a navy blue round neck. Atop the center table sat the pizza box container for the Caves and Castles game. Cheryl hovered over the artwork. It wasn't closed properly. The 10 and 20-sided die lined the ridge of the box. Its artwork was a collaboration of the game pieces. Knights stood in pristine sparkling armor beside purple mages with their peculiar pyramidal hats. The mages flamboyantly casted spells that swirled bundles of mystical, ghostly energy about them. Together with other creatures, they faced off against giants with blackened bodies and hollowed out red gleaming eyes. These beasts towered in the background amongst the mountains. Hawking green dragons with black wings huffed red, blue, and hot white pillars of fire encircling them.

Subconsciously, she smiled at the box and wondered if it would be feasible to have that much fun again. Who knew? She may even find a friend in Ibrahim, a farfetched goal she trialed while still getting to know him. Cheryl knew how much Ibrahim meant to Wino. She knew what lengths Wino would go to defend Ibrahim, even Ibrahim wouldn't do the same.

She kicked off her sneakers in the corner.

"I didn't hear you come in." Wino crossed into the living room.

"You left the door open."

Cheryl plopped onto the couch. He matched her in

denim, but wore a striped shirt. He made for the fridge. Cheryl stared blankly into the Caves and Castles box as he opened the door.

"You cleaned it up?" she inquired.

"Yeah, this place was a mess when I left, and I knew Ibrahim wasn't gonna clean it." He closed the fridge and made his way towards her. "I just finished a few minutes ago." He offered her a soda and snuggled right next to her. The two crossed their ankles over the glass and mahogany table; however, they rested only on the corner as to not disturb the box. Cheryl continued to scan the box and its contents from the slit openings in the corners.

"So? How was your day?"

"Fine," she answered, preoccupied.

"You wanna play it?"

Cheryl snapped to him. Catching herself, she slowly lowered her head back onto his shoulder, mumbling, "Why'd you leave it here?"

"Because I thought you might want to play it again."

"Have you asked Ibrahim?"

"Not yet, but everything's set just in case. Would you play if he said yes?"

Cheryl answered incoherently while tucking in one knee onto the couch. Wino leaned in very close to her.

"Hmm?"

Cheryl smothered her face into his chest answering more audibly, "I said yes."

Wino chuckled. Her cold soda chilled his thigh as they sat in the quiet of the evening. Wino lost his focus in the game box just as Cheryl did. Cheryl joined him from the corner of her eye, peering out from under his chin.

"I wonder where Ibrahim is?" Wino pondered.

***

The moon made its appearance over The U, casting a spotlight along the rooftop. One onlooker from the evening stood beside the oval ray emerging from beyond the hazy clouds of the night sky. A second silhouette joined, heralded by the sound of the iron hatch slamming shut. Within this second character's hand glowed a dim flashlight. It swayed to and fro until jousted up to the taller of the two.

Next thing, a gleam of white-hot light flashed akin to that of metal rods being soldered together. Then a violet bulb gleamed over the building for over thirty seconds before dying down. Upon closer inspection, Ibrahim stared into his wand.

The Witch folded her arms beside him. The shifting clouds unveiled them. Random bands of energy strafed the two as clouds move in and out of view. The light of the wand calmed and then dimmed to a solid, steady orb. The Witch's braids fluttered in the breeze.

"Is that enough?"

Ibrahim tucked it within his robes. "No. But I'll make do and I want more after."

"We'll make the new guy do it for you, so you can take some home."

"Sounds good to me."

The Witch gestured him a small black ball. Ibrahim squinted into her hand, trying to make out what it was.

"Put it in your ear."

The Witch informed Ibrahim. "I tagged the area already since I can't get too close. I'll let you know if anything goes wrong or I'll tell you where to go if everything goes right." The tandem rattling of multiple engines climbed into earshot. "Looks like it's show time."

Along Ménage Boulevard, a herd of vans, crossovers, and trucks quietly grumbled towards the downtown area. They traveled with their headlights off, bumper-to-bumper and disciplined. This single-file line of black, large-bodied vehicles maneuvered around corners and into the alleyways of adjacent streets.

"Here they come," the Witch sang.

Ibrahim grinned, leaning over the edge. He glanced back with a violet shimmer. "Wish me luck."

"Have fun."

Ibrahim leapt up into a swarm of dancing, jet-black crow's feathers. They twisted and twirled in the air as a crow soared into the cloudscape.

***

As the crow flew outside his window, Wino asked, "Is he coming back?"

This prompted Cheryl, who now sat upright, to turn back to him. "Hmm? Did you say something?"

"No, nothing."

She immediately returned to her objective, fondling the box with her foot until it opened. Her piqued interest stemmed deeper than mindless fun supplied by a simple game. Instead, the Caves and Castles game board retained a world of limitless possibilities; it housed a universe where the most ludicrous realities were entertained; and most importantly, it represented the untapped connection and forbidden friendship between herself and Ibrahim. This is why, although interested, she refused to take direct hold of it, as if to convince Wino – and herself – that she's moderately curious and not enthralled by its enticing allure.

***

In the Rusty Belt, bordering Ménage Boulevard and The U, a train of cars parked along a narrow alleyway. They're tucked behind three large apartment buildings. Two more parked alongside the road leading downtown. Lastly, one parked before The U's courtyard. From these vehicles emerged squads of armed soldiers sliding into position.

They leapt from their vehicles. Boots clomped across the road under the veil of twilight. They linked up on the sides of the wooden walkway of the apartment building. Squad leaders wore bulky jackets, jet-black baseball caps, and boots, while their soldiers dawned knee and elbow pads, helmets and assault rifles. Besides these people and a few stragglers wandering the dark streets, the roads and walkways of the surrounding district were empty. In fact, those within The U making their way to the front door found their exit halted.

A small group of friends hugged each other goodbye in the main lobby. A resident girl dawned her pajamas while her friends dressed in casual clothing. They'd outlasted their guest passes and must leave or face fines. They turned and waved to her one last time while stepping up to the front doors. They approached to no avail, however. The automatic door didn't open. One male leaned back and then stomped in front of the door – still no reaction. They gazed up at the sensor. A dim red light glowed but the door simply ignored them.

They swiveled back asking, "Hey, are we locked in?"

"I guess we get another night since we can't leave."
"What's going on though?"
As other residents continued past them, intending

to exit The U, they're stopped. Soon the lobby piled up with residents, guests, and workers all looking to exit the front doors. All halted before the automatic gates.

A little blond girl in a pink blouse relinquished her mother's grasp. She scurried over and pressed her face against the glass protesting, "Open up. I wanna go home!"

The black van parked across from her along the courtyard. The potted plants of the courtyard obscured her vision. The soldiers rearranged them. Her mother clasped her arm and tugged her out of view while others returned to their rooms.

From their elevated perspective, the parked van came into view. Over time, the news spread that The U was locked down. This then provided the perfect breeding ground for rumors to circulate. The prevailing theory turned out, however, to be correct as some residents witnessed operations of this nature before. This untimely lockdown was a result of a raid: when The General's police were dispatched to eliminate or apprehend those who would break her laws. The question at this point was: *who was being raided?*

***

The Caves and Castles box opened. Its contents explored although the pieces remained intact. A game board featuring the map of the fantasy world sat below two decks of cards, small gatherings of two-toned, multi-sided die – some 10 sided, others 20, and so on – miniature figurines, and sheets of character artwork.

In the hallway, the voices of passersby returning to their rooms echoed past the walls. Word of what's happened circulated. Management and security were nowhere to be found and the hatch to the rooftop had been sealed shut. A sign marked the area, 'No Rooftop Access.'

The fluttering sounds of heavy-footed herds pounded in and out of earshot while an insistent chattering hovered in the atmosphere outside of Wino's room.

Wino glanced towards the door.

Cheryl's raspy voice asked, "Is he back yet?"

"No." Wino hushed her.

The two returned to their restful quiet as The U stirred. A buzz chimed from the corner. The vibration rattled a few times, prompting Cheryl to investigate. Cheryl grunted as she peeled herself up from Wino. She dove into her bag, pulling out her phone. A teddy bear charm dangled atop her sunlight-yellow phone case. She groggily gazed into the glaring screen, adjusting her distance to read its message.

Wino ruffled the couch behind her. He came to a stand, asking, "Is it your roommate?"

"Yeah, Melanie just texted me." Cheryl turned worriedly. "She says we might be locked in. That our own apartment is blocked off."

***

A crow hovered atop the building, targeted by the police force. Its silhouette casted no shadow upon the cityscape below. It circled, climbing and falling out of the clouds' cover. It discerned the police's location dissecting their intricate formation.

The Witch sat along the edge of the rooftop. Her forearms crossed upon her thigh with two fingers from one arm holding her chin atop long nails. Her vision projected beyond her closed eyelids.

She mumbled to herself, "Now that's a lot of officers. I count a little more than a dozen." Her eyes narrowly split, revealing a violet gleam. "Need me to hold your hand?"

The crow, at this point, vanished from the sky. And atop the targeted building, a ring of clouds permitted the moonlight to shine down highlighting the apartment. A black pillar rose from the rooftop. Two violet gems punctured its head as its undulating body contours into the morphology of a human.

His voice cracked through to the Witch. "Y'kidding me? This is all mine."

***

The moon shined a spotlight upon the police. One or two officers gazed up in response. They crouched over one another, waiting for commands from higher up the totem pole. In the meantime, the light reflected the smooth surfaces of their armor and the barrels of their rifles. The white light, lined with a sky-blue rim, washes their shadows upon one another and fills the alleyways, granting visibility for over fifty meters.

One squad leader radiod from the alleyway behind the building, "That's a lot of light. Are we still a go?"

Another one responded, "What're you scared of? Werewolves or something?"

"Quiet," a command chimed in. It emanated from inside the apartment building.

The lobby, albeit much less crowded, rested blissfully unaware of the operation manifesting around them. It was a shanty space, a dainty living room with stain-riddled rugs atop wood flooring.

In a small section centered between the double-door entryway and the single screen-door back exit rested a wooden check-in counter. Between this counter and the rear exit was a small table in the corner. Seated upon it were two casually dressed officers. The attendant nervously inspected these two every few moments.

Any slight movement, any cough, any sip of their coffee, and she offered some interest towards them. One officer played on his tablet while the other scrolled through her novel. This reader, stationed in the very corner of the room with her seat against two walls, focused her attention on the central elevator. On every floor, security officers prevented residents from taking the stairs or the elevator. Their efforts slowed the resident's reaction time. However, the city slowly grew cognizant of the lock down.

"You ready?" the Witch asked.

"Move in," the reading officer commanded from her seat.

***

"She says she saw police rolling down the boulevard," Cheryl announced from the living room.

Wino flicked off the light. Noises seeped in from the hallway. He paced towards the window and pulled apart the curtain. Cheryl slid in beside him. Together, they spotted the parked van.

"It's another raid," Wino mumbled. Cheryl snapped to him. He responded with a smirk. "What're you scared? You haven't seen a raid before?"

Cheryl read into his expression for a moment. She gently reached for his wrist.

"What if it's Ibrahim?"

Wino paused in the moonlight. His lips twitched, but he suppressed the thoughts. On the other hand, Cheryl's considered a heartfelt proposal. No crisis should go to waste. Moreover, he'd be better for it. But was it the right time?

"Do y—? Is it Ibrahim?" she inquired.

His lips peeled apart reluctantly, revealing his

inner apprehension. "I hope not."

"You hope? You're the only one who knows this guy – or at least you say you know him. Is Ibrahim behind this or not?"

Wino shook his head in surrender. "I don't know."

His uncertainty preyed on his mind. Perhaps this Lock Down could have had something to do with Ibrahim. The howls of the corridor faded and grew outside the living room.

From across town, a fire burned in his heart as Ibrahim grinned. "Showtime."

The End

EPISODE 5: LOCKED DOWN

Before The U, parked along Ménage Boulevard sat a jet-black van. It'd been there for some hours now. The U, like all other buildings in the area, complied with a Lock Down Order, where no residents were permitted on or off the premise. This situation ensured clear streets, pathways, and parks

A five-man team of The General's police force made their way across the four lanes of the wide road. They crouched with guns drawn and green tactical lasers attached to their scopes. The team approached the building. Single file, they squeezed into a narrow corridor between two towering apartment complexes. Their main objective lied deeper within the Rusty Belt. They're still a few meters away. However, they're only a support squad.

The main team had already established their position at both the main entrance and exit of the apartment. These two units had about seven soldiers each, including their squad leaders. Their target: A Whitesmith, a craftsman skilled enough to forge orbs capable of storing pure, mystical, magical energy. With such an item, a black market could flourish between suppliers – witches and wizards – and consumers – artifact users such as Ibrahim and other undesirables, enemies of The General.

One of the officers at the rear exit of the target apartment aligned two fingers with her ear canal.

"Cap'n," she called out. "We're sitting ducks in this spotlight, is this thing a go?"

From within the building, past the door this officer called from, sat the unit leader. She and her subordinate adjusted the table to clear the doorway.

The leader replicated the finger placement and commanded, "Blue Falcon, White Tiger, the mission is green-lit. You are clear to breach."

***

Simultaneously, Wino and Cheryl's phones buzzed. Assuming it's her own, Cheryl twirled to retrieve her phone. She discovered the messages and alerts piling up.

"Is that Melanie?" Wino asked as he lifted his own phone from the living room table. It shined at the ceiling.

"Yeah," Cheryl responded. "Who's texting you?"

Wino stood unresponsive. She crossed the room to him and leaned over his elbow to see his screen.

'Is Ibrahim with you?' she read.

Wino panned towards the window. This time, however, his focus cut across The U's courtyard to a room on the eastern wing of the complex. It's mirrored Wino's, albeit one or two floors below.

Wino whispered to himself, "You think it's him, too?"

His ominous statement referenced Nedu, his long-time friend alongside Ibrahim and confidant. It's times like this that conjured vocal recollections of stern warn-ings whose predictions came to fruition. Nedu once warned Wino of the threat Ibrahim posed and offered a suggestion that coincided with Cheryl's – kick him out. Now, those words of wisdom echoed with momentous gravity as the reality of Ibrahim's treachery was dangerously in reach.

***

The doors to the target apartment burst open. Simultaneous floods of soldiers poured in from both entryways. They met in the middle, just before the wooden check-in counter, and proceeded up the stairwell in perfectly aligned pairs. Their synchronized march climbed the steps, splitting on each level, circling back around and rejoining up the next flight. The two leaders of the packs ran parallel to one another.

The woman of the two asked as they proceeded up the third flight, "Shouldn't one of us have taken the elevator?"

The two split apart.

Regrouping, the man responded, "Looks like someone didn't do her homework." They split. Regrouping, he addsed, "Elevators are down for this operation. Security risk."

As they split, the female slipped a glance down one hall from underneath her solid black baseball cap. Elevator remained shut. A security officer stood at attention with arms behind his or her back. Regrouping, the male further added, "And as for the stairwell outside. Well, there's no ground access and Delta Squad has that one covered anyways."

True to his word, the soldiers that emerged from the jet-black van arrived on scene. They position themselves along the corridor previously connecting the two units before commencing the operation. Delta squad had guns drawn at the black stairwell that zigzagged its way up the side of the building.

***

Along the opposite side of the building, leaned Ibrahim over the edge of the roof.

His earpiece chimed in with the Witch's voice, saying, "They're moving, they're moving."

Ibrahim's grin crawled from cheek to cheek. He drew a line from his ankle to the ledge of the building's rooftop. Like a thick piece of gum, a pink band accumulated and glued itself onto the ledge. Ibrahim faced The U. He spotted a violet flicker from the distance. He threw one arm overhead waving at her.

The Witch mumbled to herself, "What is he?" before she realized he waved at her. She barked, "Would you just jump already?"

Ibrahim leapt off the ledge. Twirling in midair, he grappled the silky wire and rappelled down the wall. His irises shined violet. A gleaming ring encircled the gaping black hole at the center. His pupils dilated. Ibrahim's vision distorted slightly, blurring at the periphery. The image bled; however, he could now detect violet energy emanating throughout the building. The speckles tagged dirty laundry, jewelry, jagged stones, and ancient relics.

He mumbled to himself, "Sure are a lot of users in here. Trace magic everywhere. Now, where are you? Come on, show me where you are."

He slithered down the brick wall while the soldiers climbed onto the seventh floor.

***

The soldiers crouch-walked hurriedly along the walls of an adjacent corridor. Every other light of the hallways turned off and those that remain only managed to flicker hazily. The bulk of the squad fell in line behind the male as the female hugged the opposing wall.

The man asked, "Pop quiz: what room we going to?"

The woman responded, "Looks like someone didn't do their homework," withdrawing a folded sheet of paper from her shirt pocket. Unfolding it, she paused.

"7761."

The two team leads read the door they paused at. It read 7221. Slowly, they all come to a similar conclusion as the soldiers turned and faced the woman.

"Wrong side." The man said.

"Ah, crap." the woman responded.

***

A moonlit silhouette sat in the darkness of room 7761. An influx of air filled the creature's leathery chest showered by a plantation of frilly hairs. Subsequently, it huffed a heavy sigh, dropping its shoulders. Silver eyes pierced the darkness and sparkled like the soaked hair of a swimmer that dove in and gently rose out of the water.

He growled in a raspy voice, "You've come."

Outside, Ibrahim continued his scan. He squinted at the brick wall, searching through a haze of dust and mist. After scanning one end, he swiveled over to the other side to investigate.

The Witch chimed in, "D'you see him yet? They're past my illusion."

"Nothing," Ibrahim responded. "You sure this is even the – oh."

Ibrahim peered harder. He leaned closer till his nose scrubbed against the charcoal stains of the red wall. He vaguely detected the globular aggregation of trace magic. Once he spotted it, Ibrahim retracted. His smirk grew. Ibrahim braced his feet. Crouching, he swung inches off the wall.

The figure inside the building sensed the disturbance within its surroundings and its silver eyes darted to the corner in anticipation.

Suddenly, a white circle formed along the wall behind the silhouette. The white circle morphed and wobbled with a violet outline. Through this interface, Ibrahim phased through the wall onto a springy mattress. He rolled onto it, coming to a halt, crouched like the officers outside.

He balanced atop the bed and aligned his fingers with his ear canal announcing, "Never fear, the cavalry is..."

"Do you see him?" the Witch inquired.

Ibrahim caught the glint of silver hovering above him. The hairs along his neck stood on end as he struggled to discern what figure stood before him. In a rush, he rolled away, protesting, "Whoa whoa whoa!"

A burly man bellowed in the air as the bed caved under the impact dumped on it. The mattress collapsed the bed frame. Large chunks of splintered wood clambered atop one another in a heaping pile of furniture and fabric. Ibrahim cowered in the corner of the room beside the moonlit window. The creature's outline bled in and out of the hazy atmosphere. This bearded, shirtless man, it seems, towered before the crumpled bed. He heaved menacingly with silver-stained eyes beading towards Ibrahim.

In a deep and gurgling voice, the man asked, "Come to claim my head have you?"

"Whoa. Slow your roll their, jumbo. I'm here to get

you out of–"

"Well, you'll just have to best me for it," the man exclaimed. The Whitesmith threw out his arms exposing his bare chest. Coils of golden frills blanketed his torso as his hands clasped an iron hammer. Glints and flickers of electricity flung about. He conjures a whirl of sparking hydroelectric energy about the head.

"Hey!" Ibrahim pleaded. "Listen, Lumberjack, you and your hammer don't want what I can g–."

Down came the hammer. The noise blasted throughout the apartment. In the hallway, the officers exchanged glanced before scurrying over towards the appropriate doorway. The two squad leads, at the front, geared up. They strapped on bulletproof vests.

They positioned themselves along the wall of the correct apartment room; two on one side, while the others queued along the other side. One soldier crouch-walked up to the door. They attached a reel of explosives tucked within a black mat upon the door's face. It hung on the wall as she retracted to his position.

Inside, Ibrahim leapt and bounced within the confined bedroom. He dodged the boisterous strikes of his target.

The man yelled at him, "Come at me! Is that all you can do? Run like a coward?"

Ibrahim tired of running and backed a short divide that segmented the bedroom from the living room. The wall's opening flanked him on either end.

Ibrahim planted his foot before it, "Alright." He turned towards the man, gripped his wand like a baseball bat and swung it back against the Whitesmith.

"Oh my lord," the Witch grumbled into her palm. "These two are fighting."

Their weapons clashed. Beams projected into the room. These photons briefly illuminated the environment, revealing the neon in their eyes as the light faded.

The Witches voice chimed in, "Any reason why you're fighting him?"

Two more clashes and the warriors' faces glowed visibly. The electrifying collisions jettisoned photons. The two pressed up against one another, Ibrahim sliding back as his feet scraped against the carpet.

The burly man clearly outsized him. The beast mirrored that of a Viking, frilly golden hair, hide and leather boots, and bulging muscles for days. Ibrahim barely reached Cheryl's height and here's this man, dwarfing him with both height and weight. The burly man hurled Ibrahim over to the wall with an overarm clang. The impact projected a boom, cracking the wall along the hallway. The Whitesmith pressed up against him. The handle of his hammer held Ibrahim in place. Ibrahim's wand dimpled against his own cheek. Ibrahim kicked and squirmed. He searched for the ground. Ibrahim desperately gasped for air.

The Whitesmith growled, "Come on then! Show me what else you can do!" He pinned Ibrahim up, huffing humid air between his gritted teeth. The Whitesmith released him. Ibrahim fell while The Whitesmith prepared to smash the hammer against his skull. Before lowering his weapon, however, a lamp flicked on. Its violet and brightness reflected Ibrahim's wand.

Ibrahim wheezed, "Hold on!" his wand jousted out towards the lamp. The man froze. His attention snagged by the corner. Ibrahim crouched wide-eyed at the man. His free hand massaged his throat. Ibrahim hushed, "Just, just calm your nipples. God. And 'ave you ever heard of deodorant, mouthwash, or even a shirt?"

Silver irises scanned the violet image before them. The man paused like a museum display; a mummified monster; a caveman trapped in ice.

Ibrahim added, "I'm-on-your-side, okay?"

The man lowered his weapon, dropping the hammerhead within his palm. His voice grumbled steadily, "You wield that artifact. A true magician?"

"In the flesh."

"Then, why do you come here? This is not the time for requests!"

"Well, I was trying to–"

An explosive detonated. Its blast projected into the room. The door erupted into a cloud of smoke and particulate matter. Its shockwave ran along the walls. Ibrahim and The Whitesmith jerked in response to the bellowing crash and splatter of building materials. Soldiers poured into the room.

From beyond the fog, barely visible within the dimly moonlit space, emerged a silver canister. The pin had been withdrawn. It rolled to a stop along the divide.

Quickly, the man shielded his eyes with his hammer. The device detonated into a solar flare. The light faded as fast as it splashed over the walls. The gassy electromagnetic pulse knocked out the lamp. The man lowered his hammer. Green lasers scanned the area from beyond the fog. Their lines of sight overlapped, almost creating a spider web of laser trails.

Ibrahim groaned. His wand ebbed and flowed in the air as he crawled about the corner, complaining, "My eyes! What kind of toys are y'all playing with?" A loud thud echoed from the corner. Ibrahim hobbled. "Oh for the love of—!"

The web of lasers divided into two, a few pointed at Ibrahim while the majority aligned with the Whitesmith's chest. Slowly, they climbed up to his face and gathered along his forehead.

A voice barked from the shadows, "Police! Get on the ground!"

The Whitesmith cupped his hammerhead into one palm. "I see," he grumbled. "You're the ones that seek my head."

"Get down now!"

The lasers wobbled, some diverting from Ibrahim towards the beastly warrior.

Soldiers barked, "There's two of 'em!"

"Which one's the target?"

"Oh damn, my foot," Ibrahim mumbled from the corner.

The Whitesmith made for the officers. He inched across the divide. His burly torso towered over them. His hammer rose up to his forehead. A whirlwind of aquamarine energy swirled about his weapon's head. It grew to encompass his body within its sway. Rows of silver spikes dimpled along the iron face.

"Well, I'm right here," The Whitesmith howled. "Come and have it!"

He delivered an earthshattering pulse to the ground. The shockwave rolled like an emerging hurricane. It scrambled the soldiers, scattering many of them back into the hallway. The living room couch splintered into hunks of fabric, iron nails, and heavy chunks of oak.

The wall behind the soldiers quaked under the assault of hurled officers. It shattered into the living room of the adjacent unit. The light poured in from the gaping hole and filled onto the Whitesmith's area. This, along with the cleared fog from the front door breach, permitted the hallway's flickering light to also infiltrate the space.

Beyond the hole in the wall, a middle-aged woman sat in her rose-pink nightgown, jaw agape at the hole burrowed into her space. She hunched over her knees. Her arms dangled as she quietly gazed into the silhouettes of the next room. Officers, including the male squad leader, moaned and groaned. They rolled on the slushy, electrostatic floor.

From the hallway, a remaining few officers, opened fire on the Whitesmith. The unit captain blasted her pistol; the female squad leader followed suit and a few other officers fired their assault rifles in bursts alongside these commanders. Together, this resistance force hugged the edges of the doorframe. The Whitesmith rolled out of their line of fire, but they tracked him. He twirled his hammer to deflect the onslaught of ammunition, ricocheting the bullets back towards the muzzle flashes. Violet bolts discharged from the corner. Ibrahim supportively disabled what shots he could.

The middle-aged woman screamed from the other side of the wall and scrambled over her couch. A glass cup shattered over her center table. Holes burst from her sofa. Purple steam emanated from the singed fabric.

She cried, "Oh! Wait! Uh-uh, don't shoot me!"

Eventually, the Whitesmith, crawling along the living room rubble, whirled his hammer like a windmill. He plopped it onto the carpet. An aquamarine shockwave scrambled along the stitches of the carpet, propelling the soldiers further away and torpedoing them like ragdolls. They flew into the hallway and into the other room. Those in the doorway blew away. Only the two female commanders and one subordinate remained.

This trio hid behind the doorframe as the vested unit leader commanded the jacketed squad leader, "Let him have it!"

The squad leader assembled a canister, injecting it with an ember-red fluid. The squad leader loads the foil canister into an all-black launcher.

The squad leader yelled, "Fire in the hole!"

The canister bounced into the room. It rolled just underneath the Whitesmith and detonated. Like a torch, the outpour of blaze scorched his stomach. The flames climbed his torso, uppercut his jaw, and wiggled between his legs. The Whitesmith howled in agony. The blades of fire tattered his clothing. Like cinders of burnt logs, streaks of fireworks burst forth. The white streams of heat shredded his skin. The Whitesmith's arms collapsed. He fell flat upon the scalding canister.

In the hallway, the squad leader nodded to her subordinate. "He's down! Move in!"

The pair charged inside with guns drawn.

"Wait! The other one!" the unit leader barked after them.

The two fired upon the Whitesmith, unloading a clip of their fully automatic weapons. Their bullets, however, slowed to a halt just after emerging from their barrels. The accumulation of propelled lead hovered in the air, trapped within a membrane of violet plasma. Like firing into an extremely dense sponge or fluid, the plasma congealed around the projectiles.

Ibrahim waited in the corner of the room. His retinas shined as his wand hung outstretched.

"Sorry, I'd like to have him alive so I can, y'know, piss you off."

With a fling of his wand, the columns of lead bullets flew back into the guts of the officers. The two tumbled onto the lead-showered carpet. Ibrahim walked over to the Whitesmith. He hurdled over the debris within the tattered room – pictures hanging by strings of fabric; scattered splinters of oak from the doorframe, living room furniture, and other sources lie about; and groaning officers with glints of electricity sparking over their soaked uniforms. Ibrahim waddled over all of this. His wand lit the path. He steered his way past the debris over to the Whitesmith.

Ibrahim paused over the man. This pitiful burly whitesmith sloshed in his own energy. Static sparked. The soaked wood creaked. Whimpers emanated from the opposite room. *Why am I even saving this man?* Ibrahim wondered. Of course, Ibrahim knew the man's value as a Whitesmith. His raised his wand over the man.

A thick glob of syrup strung from his wand. Like galaxy artwork, a drop of dense, deep purple liquid drooped slowly over the Whitesmith. It glittered as if shattered speckles of diamond and minerals saturated the substance. It fell like honey-poured syrup onto the Whitesmith's back, forming a gelatinous pyramid atop his spine. From here, the substance spread, flowing into the channels, creases, and valleys formed by his muscles. It poured over him. Ibrahim aimed with cold stoicism plastered upon his face. The substance flowed along the ribcage of the Whitesmith until encircling his wounds. From there, the liquid disconnected from Ibrahim's wand. It dove underneath the man's body like an animal hiding from its predator. The liquid quickly disappeared.

Ibrahim's hand gently lowered to his side. He commanded, "Get up."

The man's eyes flicked open and he gasped for air. He scrambled to his feet, snatching his hammer from beside his carpet imprint.

Beyond the gaping hole in the wall, the middle-aged woman peered around her couch into the dark room. Despite the lighting difference, this lady discerned the bearded, burly warrior's outline.

She squirmed behind the cover of the couch, overlapping her fingers in prayer. "Lord, get these crazy people out of my home. I thought we were done with these magicians!"

The Whitesmith scanned the room, wide-eyed. He skimmed over the outline of fallen soldiers, soaked carpet sloshing around his toes, before he finally came to Ibrahim. Ibrahim smirked confidently.

"Ready to go?" Ibrahim asked.

"It would seem you're worth your weight in gold," the man huffed, following Ibrahim back into the bedroom.

"Don't say that. I'm worth more than my weight." Ibrahim glanced back at the man. The moonlight splashed over his face.

The victorious pair stood on either side of the widow. Flashing red and blue lights painted the buildings opposite the street. Tomato red clouds of a signal flare bubble into the street.

"I think that's for you," Ibrahim suggested.

"Y'all done having fun?" the Witch chimed in.

Ibrahim plugged his fingers into his ear, "Just about." He spun away from the window fluttering his robes. "You got a plan for our fans here? Looks like they want an encore."

"Maybe if you two weren't trying to kill each other,

we could've skipped the paparazzi."

The Whitesmith curiously drew the curtain using his hand. He peered into view as Ibrahim paced around the room.

"Hey, it's your friend over here that swung his hammer at me. He's lucky I didn't barbecue him. So what's next? You got a plan for us to get out of here or—"

Glass shattered behind him. He twirled to see the curtains drawn outside the window. A booming thud roared from the street.

Ibrahim gasped, "No."

"Ibrahim," The Witch inquired. "What was that noise?"

"Your friend just jumped out the window. I mean, do we really even need this guy, I mean seriously. Why do we–" A blast of white light shined into the street, closely followed by flashing white and blue. "Here we go,"

"I was trying to tell you guys. They called in backup once things got loud."

"Well, the cavalry has arrived."

Below, the Whitesmith rose from a squat. Beneath the man's bare feet, the cement cracked and crumbled. It shattered the road and drew the attention of other officers who swarmed the street. The Delta Squad smothered the Whitesmith's body with lasers.

"Don't move!"

Unit members lined up in a V formation. They knelt and took aim. The Whitesmith grunted. He stomped towards them, huffing like a bull. His silver eyes scanned the officers. His hammer swirled with a turquoise whirlwind of hydroelectric energy. It sparked, firing electric bolts along the street like a plasma ball. The strings of white-hot voltage disintegrated street poles, burrowed holes into the concrete, and ignited street signs.

The Whitesmith barked, "You came looking for me? You wish to tame me? Well, here I am! Do your worst!"

Weapons drawn, officers scooted nervously away from him. His muscles rippled as his hammer climbed overhead.

The Delta Squad officer commanded, "Fire!"

The Whitesmith howled, hurling his hammer into the concrete. Up heaved a wave of stone and rebar. It rippled towards them, deflecting their oncoming bullets skyward.

The officers flailed and ran away as the wave descended upon them. Their cars flipped over. The soldiers scattered like surfers wiped out by the sea. They scattered amongst piles of rubble. Gravel rained down as more squad cars swerved up behind the Whitesmith. He retrieved his hammer from the destruction and faced them.

"I'm not afraid of you!" the man called.

He marched down the street, leathery shorts hanging tattered around his thighs. His fuzzy chest shined, and frizzled strands dangled from his beard.

The cold glare of a beast on a rampage met the calm, cool, and collected gaze of an experienced warrior. The General emerged from the fleet of soldiers. She strolled before them into a clearing. Her hands interlocked at her back.

"You," the man grunted. The woman smirked at him, squinting slightly. The man radiated a burning passion. "So you want my head?"

"Here we go," Ibrahim grumbled from the windowsill.

This woman stopped before the haze of lightbulbs. A glossy charcoal insignia punctuated her honey-yellow beret; it signaled her command over the other officers. Besides this, the woman dawned polished, black boots, slim dress pants climbing up her thighs, and tucked into a white corset, a military vest suspended by black straps that ran up her torso. Golden accents adorned her left side. Buttons and badges complemented her golden shoulder chain. At her neck, she strapped two midnight-black chokers, adorned with golden embroidery. The tall collars of her overcoat veiled these trinkets and draped down with empty sleeves.

"It was just a matter of time really," she responded. "Listen. Whitesmith – you have two options: you can either give in, or we can take you down just like all the others."

The woman motioned forward, her arms swallowed by the sway of her jacket. The Whitesmith's glare traced her across the gleaming field of snow-white radiance.

"You sound confident." The Whitesmith grinned.

"It's your move."

The General came a halt. She stood erect, her chest out and feet shoulder-width apart. The Whitesmith hunched over, his shoulders rose and fell. He peered up at The General as his fingers rolled over his hammer.

***

Inside the room, Ibrahim carefully leaned out the window. He made sure not to expose himself, tucking his shoulders within the frame. He gauged the situation below. A beep sounded.

He muttered, "Hey, your friend might–"

A fist hurled into his cheek. Ibrahim tumbled into the corner. Ibrahim glared back into the bedroom as a moonlit silhouette closed the distance between them. Ibrahim rolled from the second strike. Its force drilled a crater into the plastered wall behind him. The figure pursued him carefully; it tracked his muddled steps as he waddled past cluttered material, jumbled furniture, and scrambled officers. A flurry of fast, twitchy jabs showered his face. Ibrahim reflexed his way past these. He struggled to find an opening. He surrendered control to his nervous system, dancing atop soaked hardwood floors. The moment he jousted his wand, the silhouette restrained it. A fist torpedoed into his ribs.

***

Down below, sparks flickered from the Whitesmith's hammer. The General poised for a showdown. Officers advanced behind her. And unlike the other two swarms, these ones adapted to specialized equipment. Crossbows bubbling noxious, vomit-green gas from their arrow tips lined up alongside marksman rifles, fitted with variable scopes and adjustable barrel lengths taller than the shooter. These and many other weapons' experts waited in the light of their vehicles to pounce upon the eager Whitesmith.

The General grinned.

"Sorry to burst your bubble," a voice echoed from the atmosphere. "But the big lug is coming with me."

The hammerhead glanced over his shoulder.

"Witch," the Whitesmith muttered.

"You're getting a collar after this stunt," the Witch said from his side. "I'm taking him back now."

"Y'know, I had a hunch you'd still be in town," The

General said. "And something just told me that I'd see you again, especially since my men couldn't find you. No one has spotted you roaming the expressways, nor the country roads. Either that makes you smarter than the rest or just suicidal."

The Witch grit her teeth. The insult singed the wounds she sustained that night, reawakening them with an unyielding sting. They'd never truly recovered. The design of the bullet cursed her and prevented healing magic from penetrating. The wounds would take much longer than trauma to a regular person at this point.

"You'll get yours," the Witch responded. Her fingers grated one another. Her brows furrowed but she smiled maliciously.

"I'm ready whenever you are."

"Read to go, big boy?" the Witch sang. She spun away.

"Leave," he answered. "I'm going to end this, here."

"Fine by me," The General interjected. "Two-in-one catch."

"I said, let's go," the Witch repeated with rising sternness in her timbre.

The Whitesmith angled into her commanding, "Leave m-!"

He paused. His lips hung parted. The Witch's stare pierced into his skull. Clearly, a raging fury possessed her, simmering deep into her bones. Despite the tone of her voice, a passionate rage swelled within.

The Whitesmith scanned the crackled concrete. Like a speechless he grumbled to his self.

The General chimed back in, "Don't take it personally, I'm sure that look's for me."

The Whitesmith's bounced between the two

women on either side of him. Their caught fiery tension baked the air between them. The women share an identical smirk – more similar than they'd care to ever admit.

***

Above them, in the Whitesmith's room, Ibrahim danced with a soldier – the remaining leader. He torpedoed into the bedroom space. Rolling his legs over his head, he skidded to a halt. Out from the shadows, a shadowy soldier emerged wearing a red beret. She charged into the rubble of the shattered bedding and wood frame. In a diagonal stroke, like that of a samurai, Ibrahim painted the air with the light of his wand. It sliced across the torso of the figure, blasting shards of tattered rubble and hardwood beams towards the ceiling. The soldier swerved back to avoid this torpedo.

In a similar fashion, Ibrahim painted another stroke, completing the air-drawn X. The soldier dodged the second barrage and lunged to close the distance between them. Up close, their noses nearly kissed. The figure clutched at Ibrahim's wand again, but he rolled away and into the moonlight. His back scrubbed the window, darkening the room. Ibrahim mimicked the Whitesmith, throw his wand up and driving it into the carpet with both hands. Up roared a wave like an unraveling rug. Violet static surged within the cracks and water spilled out over the space.

The officer acted quickly, leaping over the wave like an Olympic jumper. She twirled her body over the waves as they roared below. Armor-padded thighs wrapped in black boots unwound as the officer spun in midair. Ibrahim rose as the soldier descended upon him. The boot bashed Ibrahim's cheek, propelling him through the shattered window.

Ibrahim plummeted outside. He fell towards the concrete. From around the wall, the gummy-like pink cable Ibrahim used to descend the walls whipped after him. It swerved around the edge and strung itself around his ankle. By the time the knot completed, Ibrahim dangled about one foot from the street. He swung like a pendulum. He cried out in a low groan as the officers adjusted their guns. As they fixed their sights onto Ibrahim, the Witch snapped her fingers.

A dustbowl of violet sands engulfed the trio. It blanketed them like a tornado and obscured the shine of the alternating police lights. It swallowed them like a black hole. By the time the grains of the centripetal winds settled, the trio had disappeared.

The General grinned at the empty street. She seemed satisfied, almost pleased with the unfolded of events.

Behind her, officers chimed in, "They're getting away! After them! They're trying to make a run for it!"

She threw up her palm to calm the officers.

"But Chief, they're going to get away."

"So?" she glanced back. "Let them run. They'll be back and we'll be waiting for them."

"But Chief."

"Our subordinates are inside that building and others lie helpless on the street. We should attend to them first."

"Yes, ma'am!" the soldiers responded. They dispersed around the area.

The bulk of the officers stormed the building, flooding the stairs on their way to the Whitesmith's room.

The fearful called woman from across the hole in

the wall, "Are y'all gonna fix the hole in my wall?"

Others hurried about: carrying stretchers to and fro, and loading their comrades into their vans.

The General scanned the target building. At the open window, she met the face of her subordinate. Like an athlete frustrated at their performance, this crestfallen soldier's disappointment fell upon The General. The two shared a moment of silence as the sirens of ambulances filled the air.

***

Back at The U, Cheryl arranged the pieces of the Caves and Castles game. Her fingers scrubbed against the ridges and jagged edges of the creatures. She reviewed the fine details of each figurine, including the cards and the board's artwork. Wino sat on the cotton-white dining chair, read the news feed on his phone. He flicked a look at the window every once in a while. Cheryl asked if the van was still there. Wino, for the millionth time, inspected and confirmed.

He swiveled to his phone. His chair shuffled over the carpet. Wino sprung up from his seat. He scurried over the chair to show Cheryl his phone. Images poured in of streets flushed with high-powered lights, rows of officers in a standoff, and the violet swirl of grains before the escape of the magicians. In none of the images, however, did Ibrahim show up.

Wino silently wished to himself, "Thank goodness."

Cheryl pointed out that, "Ibrahim isn't in any of the pictures."

"Yeah."

"Then he may just be holed up somewhere, due to the lockdown."

"I hope so." Next thing a text came in from a 'Nedu.' Cheryl openned it and it read, "Yo, people are streaming on Utalk. Most of it is from their windows but none of em have him in it. I'll keep looking." Cheryl mumbled, "Your friend's worried too?"

"Yeah"

"Are you?"

"No."

***

In a shack somewhere on the outskirts of town, the trio of magicians rested amongst crumbles of amethyst jewels. It's like that of a run-down eatery - considering the its condition, it could've been an abandoned old restaurant. Booths ran along the wall lined with windowpanes. A bar lined the opposite wall where customers could chat on their stools.

The Witch sat on a booth table as Ibrahim leaned on the frame between two others. The Whitesmith passed behind the counter. He checked the old cash register and swept his palm across the garnet, granite countertop. His fingertips clogged up with dust particles making a Q-tip about his nails.

The Witch angled at Ibrahim. She asked, "You look angry. Something happen?"

"No," Ibrahim pouted.

This drew the attention of the Whitesmith who uttered, "You might as well turn it in. There's no way you'll learn to *use 'at* now. Not with The General on your tail."

Ibrahim folded his arms with his wand crossing his upper arm. "Who're you talking to?"

"I'm talking to you, little one. You and that wand ya got. How long you been holdin' that for?"

"Long enough."

"You're thinking it'll grant you some great big wish, yes? What are ya lookin' for eh? Money, gold, women?" He pointed towards the Witch as an example. She giggled as he continued, "What we're protecting is our livelihood, you understand? Our passion. Not some fantasy. Listen, if I were you, I'd turn that thing in." He turned away fanning the air with his hand, "Let'em give you a couple hundred bucks or even a couple thousand. They'll take pictures uh'ya and show what a good citizen looks like. If not, you'll be hunted by The General forced to live in the shadows just like her and me. *Is 'at* what you want?"

"Yeah," Ibrahim responded defiantly.

The Whitesmith faced the Witch, who watched the two with a smile. "And what're you doing bringing a novice into this? He can barely hold his own."

"Novice?" Ibrahim snapped.

"Ibrahim can take care of himself," the Witch gleefully replied. The Whitesmith scoffed at the statement. Ibrahim pushed off from the booth and stood erect. His arms unfolded. The Witch caught his energetic response and made her way towards one of the double-door entryways. She said, "Anyways, I think we've done enough for tonight. Let's lay low for a while so the police drop their guard."

"The General never drops her guard," the Whitesmith argued.

"I know. I just want things to cool down for a bit. You can work on this place. And we'll check on you. Try not to give yourself away, would you? Come on, Ibrahim."

Ibrahim pulled away from his stance. He followed

the Witch out the double doors.

***

The double doors to The U opened and people trickled in and out. Residents trapped outside, found their way back to The U. Cheryl, having decided to return home, came out the double doors and into the courtyard. She peered about. The General's troops disappeared and their black van had relocated. Her head on a swivel, she briefly spotted Ibrahim.

Ibrahim's hands stuffed his short pockets. A scowl plastered his dirtied face. Cheryl diligently tracked him despite the obscuring flock of people. *I wonder where he was*, she thought. Bags hung beneath his unwavering eyes. He limped stubbornly past Cheryl, only a few feet away. She pulled away from him and started for her home. She thought, *I hope he knows Wino's been worried sick over him.*

In Wino's room, the door slid open. Ibrahim's eyes flickered like empty batteries. He slumped inside, then squeezed himself between the table and the couch. He gripped the cushions and gently lowered himself upon it. Ibrahim grit his teeth on the descent. Finally, a sigh of relief, one leg rose over the sofa while the other dangled over the edge. He sat in silence. Darkness swirled overhead leaving him unable to discern the image before him. He's unaware of how far the ceiling was from him. *Man,* he thought, *I'm out of shape.*

The magical recoil imposed upon a human wielding limitless power took its toll as they progressed along their timeline. It's like a debt they owed to reality for making the impossible come to fruition. It's usually paid off with years withdrawn from their lives. Ibrahim's interrupted hibernation, meant to account for these drawbacks, left him weaker than ever.

Nonetheless, he sighed and blanketed his dimly-lit violet eyes behind their lids. His wand sat beside him. It glowed strong than ever. The Witch had charged it prior to their departure.

Wino spotted the ambient glow from within his bedroom. The door edged a hair open. Wino's fingers cusped the doorframe. Gently, he slid it closed and went to bed. The rumpling from the bed awakened Ibrahim, who turned into the noise. The figurines of the Caves and Castles game board stood out on the table. Ibrahim curiously scanned the various objects. Eventually, he reclined over the sofa and passed out.

The End.

EPISODE 6: TOMBOY

From within the recesses of her mind, Cheryl recalled the insightful words of an elderly gentleman. "Cheryl," he called. "You like to win and you fight with the spirit of a warrior. You are very competitive."

Cheryl planted her feet atop straw mats. She trained within an empty studio. The environment resembled a dojo: spears lined the walls with red cloth wrapped just beneath the spear tips; samurai swords rested neatly stacked on small stands at the short end of the room alongside, nunchucks, punching bags, armor, and other weapons. A hefty thud pounded into the air. Cheryl jammed her fist into a standing bag, weighed down by an encased tub of water at its base. White strips of tape wrapped her fingers. She popped back, a fire in her belly and a black belt strung about her waist.

"But Cheryl, you wrestle with frustration. With injustice."

She threw her foot skyward, swathed in tape just above her ankle. It climbed over her hips, splicing through the air. The strike pulsed into the atmosphere followed by a flurry of explosions. The ripples rattled the keychain dangling from the zipper on her pink backpack. She neatly tucked it into the corner, near the front door and beneath the images of two men.

Of the two images along the back wall of the dojo, one clearly read, "Corbin Tucker - Dojo Owner" in gold lettering atop a bronze placard, while the other read, "Kisame Yamamoto - Founder." The images of the two men shuttered in the quake of Cheryl's assault.

"You must find balance or power will not help you."

Her knee drove into the sturdy red foam of the punching bag, driving a crater into it.

"What do you want power for?"

***

Ibrahim spun his wand, scrubbing his fingers along the groves of its spiral handle. His grip left imprints and the wand's warmth comforted him. His opposite hand flopped the remote over, flipping it along the aquamarine couch fabric.

"Is it the park behind us?" Ibrahim inquired.

"No," Wino projected from his bedroom. "It's another one." He slid into view, "The African one."

"An African park?"

"It's not a theme. It's just the name of it. It's–" He searched the ceiling, "Olu park."

"Where?"

"Midway downtown," Wino pointed at the wall behind the TV as if the park lied in eyeshot or maybe on the screen, "It's pretty close to Cheryl's apartment so we're meeting there."

"Why's the park African?"

"The donor it's named after is from the Tropicana region, but no one can say the real name so we just call it Olu park."

"What's the real name?" Ibrahim asked.

Wino presented his phone to Ibrahim. Ibrahim swiped it, slowly lifting it onto his thigh. His eyes shuffled between the edges of the screen. Wino eagerly awaited Ibrahim's response with a growing grin. The television punctuated the silence with cheering crowds celebrating a goal. Wino huffed forcefully through his nose in anticipation. His teeth shined over Ibrahim whose only action had been to tap the screen as the backlight dwindled.

Eventually, Ibrahim took the phone and lifted it up to him. Ibrahim's eyes center on the TV as his hand hovered over his legs. Wino chuckled to himself, his arms unresponsive to Ibrahim's gesture.

"Take it." Ibrahim softly commanded.

"Did you see it?"

"Yeah, I saw it."

"Can you say it?"

Ibrahim froze; his eyes fixated on the TV while his arm descended to the tabletop. He leaned forward and dropped the phone near his foot. Wino retrieved it, chuckling.

Wino made a cautious attempt, "O-lu-wa-sin-dar-aa-yo-fun-mi Park."

"Oluwa-sin," Ibrahim attempted. "Ol-olu-olu-wasin. Wait, let me see it again." Ibrahim swiped the phone back and mumbled the name. He then annunciated, "Oluwasin-dar-ra. Oluwasinda-ra-yo." Smiling, he concluded, "-funmi park."

He handed it back to Wino stubbornly suppressing

his rising cheeks.

Wino giggled, "You give up, cus' that's not how you say it?"

"Olu park. Leave me alone. I can say it. I just need more practice."

Wino's phone buzzed, dancing in his hand. They turned into the sound.

Wino pulled away into his room narrating, "Oh, I need to start heading over."

"How're you getting there?" Ibrahim asked.

"I'm walking. It's not too far. You wanna come?"

Wino glanced back from my doorway. Ibrahim paused. The TV crowd cheered as if to support him.

"Sure," Ibrahim retracted his feet from the table. Wino smiled brightly as he pulled into his room. The TV switched off. A few moments passed and the two made their way for the front door. Ibrahim hung the basket from his fingers hooked over his shoulder. Wino trailed him, smiling and clicking on his phone's screen.

"I'll text Cheryl and let her know we're coming."

***

Olu Park was an extensive grassy strip bisecting the local commercial district into four quadrants surrounding it. It resembled the small city park situated behind The U, yet expanded to accommodate a variety of activities. Similarly, red brick trails weaved throughout the mile-long green block. One side featured a terraced slope allowing for metallic rails and concrete stair steps that linked the skate park, caged basketball and tennis courts to the park proper.

Overall, its green ratio marginalized the stone dwellers but appeald to the picnickers, joggers, Frisbee players, singers, and sunbathers. Lush vegetation including fur-textured, foxtail shrubs, skyscraping canopy trees, and floral accented water bridges decorated the atmosphere. Benches dotted the deep, forest-green landscape. Occupants preferred however, to either doze off on the lime green lawn or stretch out over their checkered blankets.

A red Frisbee, twirled like a spinning top through the park. It brushed between branches, swerved over heads and arced past joggers. The disc twirled past a tree with a thick, reddish-brown bark. The specimen was medium-sized with fuzzy leaves angled upwards like a pinecone. It projected an oval shade over a couple resting atop a red and white blanket. They shared food out of a woven picnic basket.

"Funny thing is, you can't buy that in the city anymore," Cheryl stated, sliding her fingers into a bag of chips.

She dawned a floral, summer yellow blouse with white sneakers.

"Yes, you can," Wino argued, grinning over a bowl of grapes. Wino wore a fitted black, graphic T-shirt, silver necklace, jeans, and brown shoes. "I've got plenty."

"Oh yeah? From where?" she asked nonchalantly, ready with her response. Wino paused to ponder as she concluded, "Because, they're illegal in the city. Soon as The General made this place her stronghold, she shut down that whole trade. No more Dragon Fruit."

"Why not? Is it toxic or something?"

"No, it's too dangerous to get." Cheryl smirked. "Where d'you think they come from? Hunters have to kill real dragons to get it." She veiled her chewing while her eyes squinted at him.

"Wow. I didn't know that."

Ibrahim strutted by in a white shirt and swim short. He hid wand –it inconspicuously bulging along his hip like a holstered weapon. He walked over with a scoop of violet ice cream with dark chunks atop a waffle cone in his hand.

"Hey, Ibrahim," Wino greeted. "Ooh nice ice cream – did you know that Dragon Fruit was illegal because they hunted the dragons too much? How come we never knew that."

Ibrahim silently processed Wino's question. His gaze bounced over to Cheryl, shading her face before he snapped back to Wino. "Don't be stupid Wino."

His knees collapsed and folded underneath him. Ibrahim sat away from the picnic blanket, leaning onto the shady tree. Cheryl giggled as Wino bounced his bewildered face between the two of them.

"Did you just make that up?" *Yes,* she rocked like a rocking chair nodding her head. "Oh my gosh, I hate you." Wino blushed to the floor, brushing his knuckles against the carpet of grass.

Cheryl sighed a breath of relief turning to Ibrahim. She pointed her salty, chip-smothered finger at the swirling tip of his wavy ice cream. "Hey, where d'you get that?"

"Sure, just point all over my food." Ibrahim replies.

Cherly palmed the blanket, "I so want that."

"Where'd you buy that from Ibrahim?" Wino inquired.

"I found it."

"You found it?" Cheryl asked adoring the sumptuous swirl.

Wino scoffed, "It means he's not going to tell us."

"But I want one," she grumbled in a pouty voice.

Ibrahim sprung back up. He started away from the couple. "You two are ruining my food," he said licking the ice cream. He cut around the tree and hid.

Cheryl trailed him, nonchalantly mumbling, "Ass."

Wino plopped a 1-gallon tub onto the blanket. He peeled off the lid and withdrew two waffle cones from within. "Ibrahim's just being Ibrahim."

Cheryl scanned the small container inquiring, "What's that?"

"He left it for us. He was just acting like a jerk."

"Could've fooled me. What's in it?"

"Whatever you want. What flavor would you want to try?"

Cheryl pinched the rim and tilted the tub over. She peered into the nebulous galaxy within the tub. Like looking into the night sky, it contained glints of sparkling light amidst a swirl of ominous clouds and shadows. The void appeared deeper than a well. A scrolling image like that witnessed by a pirate beyond the lens of their monocular in the dead of night. No way could she discern just how far this image reached beyond her eyes. Her mind churned. Cheryl leaned closer and further in until Wino reached before her.

She reclined as the void curled over itself and solidified. It's like he scraped against a glittering night sky. Cracks rippled across the ball as a frosty mist slithered out from underneath the metal scooper. This cool breeze wisped past Cherly's nose and gently pecked the tip of her lips. The heat of the sun broke past the leaves of the tree baking her back. Yet, the chilling kiss of the ice cream tingled her face. Wino made a pass through the tub.

Closing his eyes he called, "I'll have a mango passion fruit," and drew the scoop skyward.

At the utterance of this wish, the nebulous colors transitioned like the skin of a chameleon. The scoop brightened to a zesty yellow and then deepened with a sunset-orange hue around the top half. The ice cream appeared like a gradient of the two colors, like the gold of a lemon's skin was stripped out and mixed with red a hot chill pepper. Wino calmly opened his eyes. He met his treat with a soft smile. He shuffled the two cones between his fingers, "What flavor do you want?"

Cheryl sat with her lips hovering apart from one another. "You–can you eat magic?"

"Of course you can," Ibrahim answered from behind the tree. He leaned on it with one palm bracing a surface root. "*Can you eat magic?*" he grumbled. "I swear."

Cheryl's innocent gaze, like that of a child, fell from the tree back to Wino, eagerly waiting to make another pass.

"Just tell it what you want," he gently advised.

She rested her fingers on her chest, "I can tell it anything?"

"Yup."

"Okay. Give me," Cheryl projected like she spoke into a microphone, "a blue Coconut, Pineapple, Cherry-lime-margarita-swirl. Oh, and with Dragon Fruit."

She inched forward as he made another pass over the nebulous cream. It curled into another ball, riddled with breaks in its soft skin. He swept it up to witness the transition.

Like mixing creamy milk, golden honey and the baby blue of the clear afternoon sky upon a palette, the colors fuse. Together, they produced a sky blue ball with varying hues of violet and green transitioning throughout the scoop. Small chunks of pineapple stuck out from the ball while the top bore a large raspberry-like fruit. He plopped this scoop onto the waffle cone and gestured it to Cheryl.

Carefully, she retrieved it, analyzed it and licked it. She reeled back in shock. Cheryl glanced across the tub. Ibrahim and Wino enjoyed their own scoops. Returning to her own, she swiped another lick. She squealed *Mmm* to the soft served treat. Taken aback, she inspected at it after every few licks as if it might disappear.

Together, the trio shared in the quiet moment of their treats. Chirps filled the ambiance along with the soft flapping of floppy slippers along the brick road and chatter about the park. The gentle hum of car tires gliding over the concrete climbed into earshot. The ambience echoed like the tides of ocean waves upon the seashore. The canopy above them shivered in the afternoon winds. Its leaves rattled. Like a giant mattress, guests sprawled out all over the lawn. Across the brick road, guests reached for the vast empty sky, people rolled over into the sunlight and an aura of lethargy entranced them.

Since the arrival of The General, humans had known a relatively peaceful world. This new world provided stability, void of the wars and chaos stirred by erratic magicians.

Subtle clangs and clattering chimed from the skate park just beneath the concrete staircase. All of the dunking, hanging on the metal rim, scuffed soles over the court and intimidating barks converged. The players produced the percussion to this organic orchestra. Even the banging against the metal fence contributed to the urban concerto.

***

Wino's fingers combed over Cheryl's golden brown scalp. Her head wrested against his lap. He leaned over her with a smirk. She smiled with her eyes closed and waddled her unsheathed feet. He puckered his lips and huffed to flutter a fallen leaf on her chin. She clipped it between her fingers and planted it on the grass. Wino hastily replaced it. He persisted in trying to blow it off to her amusement.

Shortly after blowing at it, Cheryl noticed the tingles upon her face fade away. She waited patiently, doubtlessly interpreting his every twitch to understand what he was doing. Eventually, one eye peered open to see his chin. She followed his gaze to see a tricolored beagle painted with black, white and brown.

It wagged its tail for them. The owner kissed at the dog from the brick road, over one meter away. It twirled into its owner, again to the couple and strutted away.

"I wanted it to come and lick you," Wino grinned.

"I totally would have freaked out," Cheryl chuckled. "I would have thought you did it!" She whispered, "You know, who I want it to lick?"

"I can guess," he responded, glancing out the corner of his eye towards the tree behind them.

Against the root flare of the tree, Ibrahim slumped like a log. One shin crossed over the opposite knee as his arms folded over his chest. His belly inflated like the ebb of a boat. Next, his diaphragm deflated with a huff, shrinking his stature and withdrawing his shoulders. Besides this wave, Ibrahim slept with stillness. A squirrel scurried a few feet from his arm. It banked and swayed its head. Cheryl climbed over Wino's leg. She squealed with her eyes fixated on the furry critter. Unfortunately for her, it turned and frolicked away from Ibrahim.

"Aww," she moaned as Wino guided her back towards his lap. She rolled onto him complaining, "I really wanted it to jump all over him and just wake him up."

"It knows better than to try that," he responded in a hushed tone. "Ibrahim would have cooked it."

"He can't do that. He'd get in trouble."

"You still don't know Ibrahim. Even after all this time we've spent together?"

The couple mumbled under the ambiance of the park. Unbeknownst to them, Ibrahim slithered his eyelids apart and slides a glance back at the tree just as Wino did; instead of bloodshot eyes, his projected a shimmer of his signature violet.

"Sorry, not sorry. He's not my priority. He might be to you, but he's the reason why we can't move in together. At least, he fed me ice cream."

"I told you he's not a bad guy."

"If you say so," she sang.

A thunderous clang ruptured through the atmosphere. It rang through the park; a fading jingle as it flew overhead. A choir of *whoas* howled after it and the guests of the park were drawn towards the courts beneath the staircase. A congregation of onlookers swarmed the basketball court. Chattering buzzed amongst the crowd surrounding the court and infests the people of the park.

Cheryl rolled onto her side. She inquired, "What happened?"

Wino followed her responding, "Sounds like they're fighting."

Ibrahim sat on the other side against the tree, silently investigating. It's as if they'd disrupted his sleep. Patiently, he waited until, as he expected, a secondary yelp sounded. This time, the outer rim of the crowd scattered. Their departure thinned the remaining group that distanced them from the court. The court became a cage, trapping those inside that clung to its edges too scared to approach the opening.

At the gate of the basketball court, a shirtless, dreadlocked player knelt before a much scrawnier and shorter boy. The boy appeared in his teens, trimmed, short wavy hair rolled to one side, sun-kissed tan and a jersey draped over his thin frame. He clenched the kneeling man's wrist; a black and rose tattoo swirled down the boy's arm. Like a simmering stew, the man's skin sizzled along his forearm; bubbles blew up and popped under the agony of the player.

"Go ahead, call your boys," the boy said. He tugged at the guilty fear in his teammates' eyes. "Since you wanna jump me," He palmed the dreaded man's face to the ground. "I'll take on all of you." He threw open his arms and exposed his chest.

From his fingertips crawling down to his elbows, the air rippled, crackled, and snapped. He strutted into the center of the court, intimidating the crowd surrounding him. The helpless players avoided eye contact, staring at the ground or towards those beyond the clanging walls for help. With a clap of his hands, a heatwave rippled out and into the court. It simmered the skin of the onlookers, too close to the boy and scattered the outer ring of watchdogs.

The fleeing mob sparked panic across the park. People spun around their strollers, retrieved their dogs in their arms, and pulled one another away from the court. Uproars enveloped as a premature stampede scampered across the lawn.

Out from under the tree, Cheryl extended her neck to peer over the hill. "I think we need to go."

The pair sprung to their feet. Cheryl wrapped the woven basket within a ball of the underlying blanket. She strung together the four corners and tied a knot.

Wino hooked the tree and swings around it calling, "Ibrahim we've got to…" Wino discovered Ibrahim whom he had thought to be asleep to be awake and aware. Although he could not detect the violet in his eyes, Wino could discern a familiar expression on Ibrahim's profile. "Ibrahim?"

To this, Ibrahim dragged himself up, bracing the tree. "Yeah, I know," Ibrahim responded nonchalantly.

He started away from Wino going around the other side of the tree towards Cheryl. The couple exchanged glances as Ibrahim walked and passed them. It's as if they asked each other, *what does he make of this?*

Wino made a move to retrieve the blanket and sack. He promptly escorted Cheryl away. The couple curiously peered towards the courts to discover the young man had disappeared. Basketball players and other enthusiasts littered the floor. They rolled and groaned like soldiers from the raid a few days earlier. The young boy rose up the stairs.

He tauned, "Where're you running to? Don't you guys want a piece of me? If I was powerless you would. No magic, no power."

***

In the stampede away from the man, people jogged across the zebra crossings into the city proper. In their excitement, some lunged into the street while others hesitated to stop for the traffic lights. This generated a trickle of pedestrians, clogging traffic compounding the commotion. Onlookers bit their nails and others shielded their children. From the streets, curious citizens reached for their phones to record while few called for The General's police.

***

Within the park, Cheryl, Wino, and Ibrahim made their way down the brick path. They maintained a light jog, pacing with one another while periodically gauging their distance from the magician. The magician strolled down the road barking incoherently. He was either a madman or had gone too far to stop now. In either case, his actions were sure to attract The General's police force.

As the trio made their way past the trees, Cheryl noticed what the occupants left. The scantily occupied park bore clear plastic sacks, checkered blankets, soccer balls, rainbow Frisbees, and other picnic essentials blanketing the grass. Despite the rush to exit the park, some goers remained. They hid behind benches, stabilized their footing or waited for The General to inevitably arrive.

The flurry of information whooshed past Cheryl as she scurried through the park. Cheryl glanced back to witness a small, curly-haired child emerge from behind a tree. The child stood at least five years old, a ruby red fidget spinner twirling between his hands. He strolled out from behind a tree onto the brick path in a tiny striped red and white shirt and short denim jeans. Up towards him marched the crazed young basketball player.

The angry teen shouted, "What, you guys don't want to fight anymore? You sure did when you thought I just a regular guy."

He energetically leapt and sprung up the path, gawking at those fleeing from him, and hurling heat waves at objects, melting them over time. He came upon the child, the two drawing each other's attention.

Ibrahim swirled back, following Cheryl's gaze. Using one arm, he pushed her out of the way of an oncoming tree. As she realigned her footing, Ibrahim found what intrigued her. Ibrahim regrouped with the couple, his focus returning towards the path.

He announced, "Welp, sucks for the kid," to the dismay of Cheryl who stopped dead in her tracks.

Wino snappily followed suit and slowed to a stop. Ibrahim continued his escape. "Cheryl?" Wino called. She grit her teeth and clenched her fists, eyes centered on Ibrahim's back. She instinctively spun and rushed into the park. "Wait! Cheryl don't."

The basketball player growled, "How's about I bring the fight to you?" glaring into the eyes of the child who timidly backed away.

The basketball player's fingers stiffened into a claw. The heat waves rippled about them. The child scooted away from the heat. The teen inched his claw closer to the boy's curly hair. Hypnotized by the danger, the boy subconsciously reeled away but failed to lift his sneaker over the brick path.

He tripped over the ledge as the teen came over him.

"Let's start a riot," the teen said.

His palm rose over the boy's neck, the rose tattoo undulated beneath streams of glistening sweat. The teen's claw dove to scald the boy's bronze skin under the sizzling heat of his power.

Before making contact, a fist hurled into the teen's cheek. It threw his head back and flung him past one tree. He barely caught himself, scraping against the edge of the curvy brick path and skidding atop the lime-green grass.

In shock, the boy peered up to find Cheryl.

Her fist wound up tightly as she heaved in her yellow dress. She glared at him with an indignant passion before the reality of her actions overtook her. Her brows relaxed and her fingers unwound. She thought, *what have I–?*

The magician slowly reconciled what just happened. He scrubbed his rosy pink, freckled cheek and climbing to his feet. Cheryl froze as he rose. Her foot slid back and her arm searched for the little boy.

"L-leave him. Alone," she frightfully commanded.

Witnessing the waver in her confidence, the teen turned the tide. His brows furrowed and he came to a stand. The air baked and wobbled around him. Cheryl clutched the boy's arm and scooted away. *Oh my god,* she thought faced with a deadly magician before her.

"Not bad," the teen complimented her. His deep, scarlet eyes met her own, a predator before his prey; a challenger for him to finally unleash his pent up frustrations onto. He wiped his chin. "Now it's my turn," a malevolent smile grew on his face.

The teen threw out the hand he wiped his chin with. Then, he sprung forward and blew Cheryl back. The heatwave scalded the grass and sparked against the brick. Cheryl flew like a flying arrow, past trees and smashed into a stone bench. She crashed into the bench, the arched seating area collapsing over her. A plume of smoke encircled the space as rocks skipped out onto the grass. The explosive impact bellowed into the atmosphere.

Within the park, those in hiding covered their gasps. Yellow like a Frisbee, Cheryl flew past many of them and was a victim due to her kindness – a traumatizing throwback to the days of magician rule.

Wino's voice screeched, "Oh my god!" as his arms dangled by his side. His eyes shrank, while his lips hung parted.

The danger posed by the magician repressed his protective instinct to run towards his partner. Fear rendered him a coward and anxiety swirled in his belly. Had it been during their travels, Wino would damn the consequences and act. How could he ask Ibrahim to continue blessing others if he didn't participate? Ibrahim's presence provided him security permitting Wino to disregard other magicians. Now, Ibrahim's a shadow of his former self and the presence of The General had reduced battle-front heroes to back-seat onlookers.

Before them, the rubble cleared. Cheryl emerged from the limestone clutter. She shoveled herself out so that she could stand. She braced one large chunk and anchored herself up. On her feet, she scanned her arms, analyzing them as if they're not her own. Her palms slid along her arms and worked their way up to her face. Inspecting her cheeks, she detected a few grooves. Scratches outlined the point of impact but no major injury appeared. On the ground, she retrieved a black phone and gazed into the screen.

Looking at her reflection, she pondered, "I'm not dead?" in breathy suspense.

"Damn," Ibrahim sang, slightly impressed.

Ibrahim knelt on the grass, his wand in hand and the orb planted into the ground. From there, Wino traced a violet string, running between the blades of grass and winding around the trees. The cord disappeared within the lawn but ran towards Cheryl.

"That was close," Ibrahim commented.

Wino swirled back. Cheryl stood flabbergasted at the outcome. She glanced over the rubble. Pebbles fell off her dress as she twisted and twirled around.

"That all you got?" the teen called from across the lawn. His arms opened wide as he marched past the child. "I'm ready for more if you are."

Cheryl's gaze climbed up to him. The child scampered to a run. The boy made his way from down the brick path, making very little gains despite his effort. The teen outstretched his arm aimed at the boy's back.

"Let's get rid of you first," with scathing eyes centered as if aiming upon a bull's-eye.

His wrist is crumpled before unleashing the heatwave. He traced the arm to see Cheryl standing before him, her yellow dress fluttered from the wind of her translocation. This time, the confidence within her grew firm and faintly shimmered in the sunlight. *Don't you dare lay a finger on his head,* she thought. Her fingers curled, grinding his wrist bones. He fidgeted, motioning away from her. His wrist folded and his skin wrinkled under her grip. Cheryl's skin sizzled and popped from the close contact. His ember eyes shined upon her in shock as she squinted at him. He wondered if she felt the scorching pain from his heat. Cheryl drew him nearer. Winding back her arm, she threw a jab at the teen's nose. She released him but followed up with a flurry of punches aimed at his ribs, nose, and cheek.

Wino squealed "*What*?" in shock at her comeback.

Ibrahim protested from behind him in distress, "Whoa now! What's she doing?"

He retracted his wand from the ground. The slender thread-like violet line thickened like an unclogged stream engorged with water. Particles gathered around the orb and solidified, forming another two strings. These lines dipped into the ground and made their way towards Cheryl.

Cheryl regressed the teen further into the park. She hurled a punch into his gut, knocking him meters back; she swerved around a peripheral tree to kick him across the brick path and let out a yelp as she drop-kicked him through the body of a thick oak tree. The tree snapped with the crackle of wood, mud-brown fibers of chipped bark flung about like shrapnel. It tumbled over the severed stump and rustled along the ground. Cheryl stuck her landing, skidding along the grass as the teen tumbled down the rail, flopping onto the concrete below.

Cheryl stood on the grass with her feet apart, one arm extended over her thigh while the other tucked in beside her chin. If she were in her martial arts uniform, strapped in her black belt, the image would be complete. *I feel amazing,* she thought. *It's like I can do anything.* The fire in her eyes burned violet. She waited, poised for a counter-attack. Her fingers popped as she rolled them. The exhilarating rush spurred on by the surge of Ibrahim's magical deposit fueled her with a seemingly unending bounty of courage and strength.

As the light broke past the nearby canopy of the very same tree that shaded the trio earlier, violet strings shimmered behind her. They danced in the passing breeze, attached to Cheryl's elbows, the nape of her neck and the occipital lobe of her skull. She's unaware of these chords as well as the oyster pearl gleam in her eyes. It mirrored that of Ibrahim's albeit less bright.

Wino cheered with exhilaration, "Holy cow! Ibrahim, did you see that? How's she doing that?" He spun around, a bright smile on his face.

Ibrahim scowled at his wand, "That tomboy of yours is stealing all my magic that's how."

"You mean she's controlling it? I didn't even know Cheryl could wield magic."

"Neither did I. If I did, I'd have just told her to get her own."

"Just let her have it, Ibrahim. She's kicking his butt!"

"You don't get it, do you? That tomboy of yours is taking too much. Why d'you think I had to hibernate after our travels? Too much magic, especially for a novice, deals massive recoil damage to the body. You think she can take crashing into a concrete bench? She can't, so unless you want her to feel it all at once, you'd better get her to stop taking so much."

Wino pleaded, "But-but she's doing great! She's taking him down! She saved the kid and the whole park!"

Ibrahim tugged on his wand like a fisherman fighting against a large bass snagged by his line.

The wobbly wires dragged him over the grass. "You're not listening!" he shouted. "She's taking too much! If you want to have a girlfriend after this, make-her-stop!"

Wino hurried into the park. Cheryl climbed into view. Her toasted honey short hair wafted in the breeze. Up slumped the teen, a thin field of wavering air around him. He'd endured more punishment than Cheryl during their scuffle. He glared at her but with the eyes of prey. A curious expression dawned over his face. As if to say, *Who is she? Shouldn't she be sympathetic to another magician's dilemma?* He rocked and swayed to his feet, a speckle of blood rolling from his shoulder and along the rose petals of his tattoo.

Wino sprinted towards Cheryl, flailing his arms and barking her name. He approached from along the ridge, dividing the park proper from the concrete playground below.

As he drew near, Cheryl lurched forward. *Now's my chance,* she thought. *I'm going to beat him.* She clenched her fists, charged towards the teen, and tackled him into the adjacent road. The pair hurled into the street, smashing into a parked car and tumbling onto three others down the road.

Upon the last car, Cheryl straddled the teen. One arm restrained him onto the roof of the sedan as she reeled back her fist. Her fingers crunched and curled upon one another. The teen yielded. He didn't even resist or put up a fight. Cheryl read the wrinkles beneath his eyes. Her gaze scrolled up towards the shop before her. Inside of this beauty salon, employees and guests retracted towards the far wall. Their fear likened Cheryl to a monster.

In her heart, Cheryl felt that she fought for them but realized in her reflection that her eyes shared Ibrahim's glint; the very magician that wreaked havoc upon her relationship. Worse still, this gleam mirrored that of the basketball player beneath her arm. Magic – the source of all evil in her world had infected her at last. In her desire to make the world a better place, she'd fallen into the very vice that corrupted it in the first place. What of the countless sorrows magic had caused? What of the gut-wrenching tragedies she'd witnessed throughout her lifetime at the hands of evil magicians? What of the oppressed people of her hometown and the liberation The General brought by standing for those who could not? What would those matter had she become that which she hated most?

Her arm gently lowered. Cheryl tugged upon her lower eyelid as she peered at her reflection. She'd never known her eyes to shine so brilliantly. She relaxed her grip upon the teen and retracted from him. A voice called her from across the street.

Wino scurried towards her, brows furrowed, panting, and waddling like a frightened child towards their caretaker. She read it as further evidence and rose from the teen. He groaned as she carefully plopped down the hood of the yellow cab and onto the street. Wino ran up to her, his form failing as he closed the gap between them. Winded, he approached her and she hugged him. He panted heavily, almost wheezing as Cheryl stroked his back.

He asked, "Are, are you. Are you ok–"

"I never want to use magic again," she mumbled.

He huffed over her shoulder. His arms rose to mimic her own.

The teen rolled along the roof of the car.

In the park, Ibrahim braced a tree with one arm. His other arm extended towards the embracing couple. A band of strings tugged at his wand. He grit his teeth and wrinkled his lips in an effort to tug against the pull of Cheryl's body. He stretched beyond his limit. Ibrahim relinquished his grip. He stepped away from the tree and planted his feet. He leaned back at a 145° angle against the drag of the chords.

Sirens sounded as a train of three black, unmarked, armored cars pulled up along the intersection that Wino crossed. Out poured a squad of armed soldiers, clad in military gear and each wielding unique weapons. They followed the trail of destruction and aimed their weapons towards Wino and Cheryl. Cheryl buried her face in Wino's chest, the strands of magic dwindling and falling to the ground. They faded and dispersed through the air like cobwebs lost in the breeze.

Glancing back, Wino peered past the soldiers, past their cars, and over the hill. The strings relaxed on Ibrahim's end. Ibrahim tumbled backward into the tree and crashed headfirst into it. He slid down the bark until peeling himself from it. Ibrahim inspected his wand, softly glowing in his hand.

He sighed and mumbled, "Don't worry, tomboy'll make it." Looking back, Ibrahim peered through the slight opening back at Wino.

**

The squad leader of these soldiers marched up to the couple. She dawned a black beret and thick bulletproof vest. Before she spoke, she heard he teen groaning over the car.

"Are you two okay? Looks like he wore himself out," she concluded turning towards her team. "Alright! Let's bag him up and take him to the station. And get these two looked at."

The soldiers stomped over to the teen. Others retrieved stretchers and first aid kits from their cars. They dispersed into the park. They jogged past the canopy tree and along the brick road, attending to the injured and displaced. One soldier waited patiently beside the embracing couple with a kit in her arms. She'd seen it before, the remaining threads of a world plagued by magicians. It wasn't perfect, but at least this world had a system in place to weed them out until one day, they'd be all gone. Along the opposite end of the park, Ibrahim strolled across the zebra crossing, his hands in his pockets.

He grumbled to himself, "Who'da thunk the tomboy could use magic?"

The End.

EPISODE 7: NEDU

An alarm chimed at 6 a.m. ringing over a wooden countertop. Out from her bed, a middle-aged woman groggily leapt out. She dove her index finger into the back of her bed-head fro as she stomped into her living room within the darkness of her apartment. Her pink satin sleeping gown draped over her body. Past the doorframe, flickered a lamp. The middle-aged woman connected an HDMI cable from her television into her laptop. She opened an app with a beeping black line ready at her search bar. She twirled around and retracted into her room.

Later, a fluffy white sweatband lined her forehead. Hot pink wristbands covered her wrists, and she marched like a soldier in her black sneakers. A cream sports top covered her torso and black tights ran down to her shins, hugging her thighs on the way down.

***

A preteen within another part of the city combed over his lochs with his fingers. He retrieved his phone, projecting its light onto his face. His scrawny, bare chest glowed in the ambience and bags hang under his eyes. Nonetheless, the teen swiped away his *buns of steel (Workout at*

6 am) alert, clicked on a streaming app, and rolled his blanket away. His golden brown, luscious locks bundled into a man-bun while the teen sat cross-legged upon his floor. Before him streamed a video with a caption. It reads: *1 minute till broadcast.*

***

Wino emerged from his door into the black living room of his apartment. Panels of moonlight extended beyond the pearl-white dining table. He strolled in charcoal dress socks, sky-blue boxers with clouds, and a marble-white dress shirt. Wino twirled a knot with his tie as he entered the kitchen. As he assembled his meal, a voice broke the serenity.

"Y'know Nedu's got his thing this morning?" Ibrahim rolled open his arm, dangling it over his head and onto the armrest of the sofa.

Footsteps shuffled over the carpet. Wino and Ibrahim angled to the sound. A groggy Cheryl moved into the moonlight. She reclined into a seat at the dining table and folded her arms.

"We wake you up?" Wino inquired from the shadows.

"No," her raspy voice responded. She curled over the table, wrapping her feet together.

The toaster ticked as Wino set it.

Not before long, Ibrahim persisted, "Wino."

"What *thing*, Ibrahim?"

"His morning challenge."

"I have *work*, Ibrahim."

"So? Does that mean you're not going to do it?"

Wino walked past the living room towards his doorway. Ibrahim rolled off his blanket and sat upright. Outstepped Wino as the television shined over Ibrahim.

A menu of selections, including streaming, rose. Ibrahim scrolled through the apps, drawing Wino's attention and stopping him in his tracks. Cheryl's panned her chin over the table. Her gaze crept towards the screen. It read *30 seconds till broadcast.* Wino dropped his hands, his tie unwinding around his neck.

"Are you going to do it too?" Wino asked.

"Sure." Ibrahim stood up. He scooted the table into the corner, freeing up space for the two of them.

"Are you doing it?"

"Nope," Cheryl grumbled.

Wino and Ibrahim met in the center. The two aligned themselves with the TV. The broadcast counted down: *5…4…3…2…1.*

A tanned, muscular man, oversized for the camera, posed before a crowd of jocks. They imitated him, albeit human-sized and less chiseled. This man stood at least six-foot-five inches, and he wore magenta red shorts and a tight black tank top exposing his toned and plump muscles. His tanned-honey skin was smooth. It wrapped his beardless chin, with only a black buzz cut atop his soft face.

"Hey, guys, Nedu here and you're tuning in-to…"

The ensemble behind him roared, "The mor-ning chall-enge!"

They're an ecstatic bunch and enthusiastically leapt across the room, rolled along the galaxy, jigsaw puzzle floor and danced like maniacs. The stream took place within a gym, cast iron weight plates stacked like towers; benches were tucked into the corners and glass mirrors lined the wall behind Nedu. He maintained a professional demeanor exemplified by his palms, folded together. With one swing of his hand, the crew realigned themselves before the wall. Nedu stepped back from the camera narrating,

"I'd like to give thanks to each and every one of you who's tuning into this broadcast right now. It means a lot to us that you'd get up while everyone else is sleeping. And if you know someone who doesn't want to get up early, they can always join us for our citywide jog happening this morning. I don't want to get into the whole shebang about health 'cause you already made the commitment. I mean, you're awake right now. So what do you say we get right into our warm-up, huh?"

The gang of gym rats behind him jeered at his prompt.

"That sounds like a deal to me. First thing we're going to do is, we're going to get into some lunges. You're going to want to make sure you get a good stretch going, especially if you're going running with us."

Within her room, the middle-aged woman lunged three elongated steps. She then pivoted on her foot and returned the opposite direction down her room.

Cheryl watched with expressionless focus. Her gaze ping-ponged between Ibrahim and Wino as they lunged past one another in a square. Wino could not contain his grin as they stretched past one another. His half-knotted tie slinked over his shoulder. His shirt draped over his boxers.

The preteen arched his body over his phone, anchored by his palms and the balled of his feet. He jogged in place, driving his knees up towards his chest. Nedu demonstrated this motion from his studio.

His eyes centered on the camera, and he commanded, "Now, make sure you really drive those knees up and flex those abs. You want to feel the burn." Turning to his energetic crew, he barked, "Do you feel it?"

They shouted in response, "It's sizzling!"

Turning back, Nedu whispered to the camera, "I think they feel it."

Next thing, Wino knelt, sitting his hips on the heels of his feet.

He panted lightly, whining to Ibrahim, "Let me take this off. I'm gonna be sweaty at work."

"Quit whining!" Ibrahim snaps. "Just do this last set. Come on, hurry up."

Wino reluctantly plopped his palms onto the ground. Upon the TV screen, Nedu planked perpendicular to his crew. His form was meticulous, his body sculpted, and his confidence unwavering.

With eyes on the camera, he demonstrated. "Alright, one minute, nonstop push-ups. Go for as many as you can do com-for-ta-bly."

Head to head the pair mirror Nedu. They assumed the position, Wino's tie dangled into a pile on the floor between his arms. The two lowered themselves, retaining an inch from the oatmeal and raisin carpet. Together they rose and repeated. Over time, their synchronization decoupled and Ibrahim paused to recapture it as if he tried to encourage Wino through partnership.

In the last few seconds, Nedu leapt up from his stance. The cameraman pursued him as Nedu hopped over to his crew. "Keep that form, come on, we're on our last 10 seconds." He dropped to the floor, eyeballing some of the men as they roared into the room. Others, he tickled and more still, he instigated.

Within her room, the woman's arms rattled. She grit her teeth. Pulling away from the ground, a bead of glittering water splatted on the teen's phone.

"Come on, Wino," Ibrahim growled as he too struggled to rise.

The pair levitated their torsos slowly from the ground. Rising to the top, they heard the words of Nedu calling the workout to a stop.

"Alright and that's the morning routine."

He clapped his palms prompting his crew to scramble to their feet. Sweat glistened along their foreheads while moist patches lined their torsos. Some panted, others howled, and some rolled off their shirts to twirl them in the air. Nedu stood perfectly dry, not a sweat broken across his body.

"Now we're going outside to see *you guys* for the city-wide jog this morning. Thank you again for tuning in and we'll see you in a little bit."

The crowd jeered behind him. Wino and Ibrahim flopped onto the ground. Ibrahim threw open his arms and heaved a sigh of relief. Wino curled over his knees like a man in prayer.

"Time for work," Cheryl said almost cynically, the toaster popped up behind her.

Wino powered through his exhaustion to his feet. He stumbled over into the kitchen to retrieve his slices of bread and back to the living room to snatch his tie. He waddled into his bedroom as Ibrahim calmed his chest. His belly rose and fell over the carpet while his fingers grazed over it.

Wino emerged from his room five minutes later, fully suited in fresh clothes with a briefcase in hand. He hurried out with a slice of bread in his mouth and headed for the door. Cheryl leaned onto his chest.

Tiptoeing to his face, she nibbled at his bread.

Wino mumbled, "Want me to make you some?"

with half still in his mouth.

"No, I just wanted some of yours. I'm going home."

"I'll see you tonight?"

"Yeah."

The couple strolled out of the room. Cheryl draping her nightgown over the couch, walked out in her shorts and a t-shirt. Her hair stood in a frizzle, and it was a long walk to her apartment. Wino accompanied her to the bus stop, where the two stood quietly in wait for Wino's bus line; they watched as a procession of people filed out of The U. This stream of fashionably dressed sports enthusiasts conjoined with pairs of participants trickling in from across the boulevard. They merged into a congregation behind The U. Chattering replaced the ambient fog, filling the air and livening the serene atmosphere of the morning dawn.

Wino boarded the first line headed towards the city center while Cheryl waited for another to take her to the nearest stop within the Rusty Belt. As Wino departed, he detected Nedu, towering over the crowd around him. It lasted for a split second but Wino's eyes spotted Nedu just before the burly man takes off into the park. The crowd tailed him. Wino lost track.

The bus made its first turn, and Wino pulled away from The U. His gaze fell on the passing buildings as the bus sped down the road. He couldn't help but reminisce about the time he met Nedu. Back then, Nedu's stature was the complete opposite of what it was now. As a matter of fact, Wino's memories replayed themselves a few nights every month. He's experienced this phenomenon for some time now but refrained from sharing it with Cheryl and even Ibrahim. He expressed his fascination with the events that unfolded during his journey to her, but never revealed the unwarranted simulations stirred by REM sleep.

This rolling screen of towers resembled figurine sculptures carved throughout Kala Mountain. An earthy red, like the tangerine-ember of the rising sun, baked into the mud beneath the grass. The narrow corridors were riddled with life-sized still art of hunters, poets, and native dancers adorned with a peacock feather and leather hides. It was a secluded area, located at the intersecting outskirts of nearby kingdoms and villages. Back then, magicians ran everything from empires to shantytowns. The luck of the draw was where you were born and what you got yourself into. It was a mess, but they had the most fun. And Nedu, that's where he finally got Ibrahim to experiment on him.

Wino recalled: *A scrawny little guy, Nedu was even shorter than Ibrahim. Even Cheryl was probably taller than both of them by that time, wherever she was.* He shook his head at the image, remembering how Nedu kept bugging Ibrahim and Ibrahim adamantly refusing to help him. Nedu was born into a tiny kingdom. The kingdom only housed a couple hundred people, so when some thugs came in and overthrew the king, it went pretty unnoticed.

Wino nodded to himself.

I think Nedu tried to recruit some other magicians to counter coupe those guys but no one would take the bait. His hometown was off most people's radar's and the thugs were of no value bounty-wise. They were low-level magicians, the likes of whom witches glossed over.

Wino had always felt sorry for Nedu then. Having challenged them himself, Nedu was tortured, scalded with oil, starved, and banished from his homeland with no chance of returning. Next thing, he found Ibrahim and Wino strolling by.

Gosh, he bugged Ibrahim to no end, thought Wino. Nedu had been desperate to get his mother's pendant back and had no other choice but to seek the help of another wretched magician. Wino scowled. Ibrahim was still just a novice at the time, and he couldn't risk the consequence. *Ibrahim warned him time and again that the repercussions could be disastrous for both of them.*

Wino leaned back in his seat on the bus, watching the city slide by, but trapped in his memories. Despite magicians running things however they saw fit in the past, they still agreed on some common pact of performance. It was like they had a rulebook, an honor code, among thieves. One of their most sacred rules banned the metamorphosis of humans that could result in the generation of an untamable beast. It was outright forbidden, especially by a novice. Apparently, magicians could kill countless innocent people for amusement but god forbid one of them absorbed that energy and surged into a phenomenal creature.

Regardless, Ibrahim didn't want the magic community's attention and so he turned down Nedu at every twist and turn possible. Wino smiled.

He said very little about it, but I'm fairly certain that Ibrahim doubted himself as he was still deciphering the technicalities of his wand-artifact.

Anyways, Nedu one day bugged Ibrahim up to the last straw. He wrapped his arms about Ibrahim's ankle and whined for over an hour as they all made their way through the mountainous labyrinth. Near the flat apex of the Kala Mountains, Ibrahim tugged Nedu away and made the risks explicitly clear to him. If something went wrong, Nedu could lose his humanity and become an unspeakably hideous creature that Ibrahim himself would have to put down – assuming that he could. And even his ability to defeat Nedu, should the project fail, was slim as Ibrahim would be exhausted from the process. In essence, it was a death sentence should Ibrahim fail to correctly transform Nedu into the mystical being he sought to become. Nedu wanted the power to not only overthrow the thugs that threatened to sell his precious mother's pendant but also the strength to dissuade potential raiders from assaulting his homelands – the power to help others. The very utterance brought tears to Nedu's eyes as he spoke from his heart. Ibrahim saw this as good-and-all however he doubted the success of the operation. Nedu persisted nonetheless and was stationed between two pillars.

Wino drums his fingers on his thigh as the bus takes yet another turn and rumbles down the streets. So much has passed between the three of them, and yet the memories remain so fresh. He can still remember the dirt-red soldiers, carved out of the walls, stood with scimitars drawn. Their weapons crossed just below Nedu's chin. Their gazes pierced into one another's eyes just as Ibrahim and Nedu did on that fateful day. Dusk hovered over the horizon as Ibrahim stood a few meters across from Nedu. The stone pillar behind Ibrahim divided the sunset into fluttering blankets of light, flanking him like radiant feathers of a holy peacock. His eyes glowed with razor-sharp opal-rainbow energy. It transitioned like a strobe light flashing behind a haze of clouds.

    Wino shivered at the thought of what came next.

    Next, Ibrahim raised his wand; its brilliant magnificence projected beaded strings wafting from the orbital core. They exaggerated the shadows along the crevices and feet of the sculptures. He swerved his wand about his wrist, drawing a translucent, fading ribbon like the hazy exposure following a camera snapshot.

His brows furrowed, Nedu's followed suit with his teeth and eyes gritting. Ibrahim centered his focus upon Nedu's torso and swung his wand out at him. Out spurted gushes of lightning, searing sparks splattering off the wall and deflecting back onto Ibrahim. This blinding connection spurred on for at least thirty seconds, Nedu howling from within the engulfing haze of white-hot light flaring out from the impact. Ibrahim fought desperately against his better instinct to turn away and glared into the heart of this electric combustion reaction. He adjusted the stream of energy, at first reducing it to Nedu's cry but eventually turning up the heat when he decided that it was taking too long.

The bus lurched to a stop and a rolling sensation filled Winos stomach as he recalled, *At some point, it became too blinding and the heat could scald a human's retina. When the deed was done, however, it was certain that Ibrahim had killed this scrawny kid. Nedu must have been roasted to bits and pieces. It was clear that the boy was no longer there and that his mother's pendant would definitely be lost to time. Pitiful solemnity filled the air at the realization of electric scorch marks, splattered all along the walls.*

It's charcoal aftermath wriggled out from the center like the branches of a tree. The statues fell and melted under the blistering flare streaming above them. Ibrahim sat on the ground further back from where he ejected his energy, his arms draped over his lap and his wand rested upon the ground. The boulder he braced himself against had collapsed. He sliced through it and slammed into the cusp of the wall. His face was burnt with soot and his clothes slit at the hems. Despite his poor condition, his eyes peered up into the static aftermath. Suddenly, a smirk cracked upon his face.

Next, a shiver from the charcoal-smothered wall. Up stood a man from the scalded remains. He rose six feet tall and stood towering over the labyrinth walls like a giant. His clothes barely hung onto him. Nedu normally wore a tank top, hanging over his scrawny frame. But now, this man's chest tugged his shirt into strings, expanded to capacity around his honey-tanned, swollen pectorals. His shorts rolled up his bulging quadriceps. He gazed coldly into the palm of his hand, clenching it and relaxing it as if to say, *Is this mine?* After some time had passed, Nedu turned to Ibrahim and mirrored his smirk.

He said, "You did it."

"Of course I did," Ibrahim replied with rising excitement.

Ibrahim had thrown up his hands, roaring with hysteric laughter and consumed by ecstatic exhilaration. *Words could not explain the miracle.* That magical novice had set his mind to do something and actually achieved it despite the overwhelming odds and his personal lack of confidence.

Little did Wino know, this was only the first of a serious of spectacular displays that Ibrahim would perform. His enthusiasm reeked of charm and infectious charisma. He jeered and cheered until he nearly passed out.

Nedu returned to his home. Wino and Ibrahim followed suit to watch from the front row. Nedu stormed the three-story palace alone and emerged with not only his pendant but also three stooges eager to make it for the hills. Wino remembered being in awe at the entire scene, mouth agape and wide-eyed. Ibrahim howled in laughter the whole thing over, and in the end, recruited Nedu to their party.

Nedu raised a flag over his kingdom and left to make a name for himself. This name would serve to protect his homeland for as long as others knew that harming a single blade of hair on the heads of those he protected, would result in their extinction. Nedu had always been a carefree guy from that day forward. The neurotic brat that pestered Ibrahim and talked big was exchanged for a docile hunk-of-a-man that exuded a charisma that Ibrahim happily took credit for.

The bus lurched into motion again, and Wino chuckled to himself. *It wasn't too long after the second adventure that Nedu disappeared. Fortunately, he moved into The U and they reconnected every once in a while.*

***

Packs of runners trickled into The U's courtyard. Many that started off eager to sprint the whole thing, now jogged to keep ahead of those that are walking. The entourage of fitness enthusiasts dwindled into a train of pony-tailed stragglers and hairy-chested fashionistas. Kids handed out tiny plastic cups to returnees along the waterpark. Nedu's crew of hyperactive jocks joined the kids, zipping across Menage Boulevard to escort fatigued runners. Others high-fived the runners as they crossed the finish line.

One dawning a pink headband called into the courtyard, "If you're finishing the run, we've got drinks for you. We've got merchandise, wristbands, t-shirts and more! Once again, we just want to say *thank you* to all our helpers—!"

***

Inside the gym studio, where Nedu initiated the morning broadcast, he crouched to retrieve his neon-orange duffel bag.

Standing up, a voice chimed in, "Did I miss it?" Nedu found a man strolling into the room.

The door swung shut, clamping behind him. The man wore a checkered shirt, charcoal leather belt, black slacks, and brown dress shoes. His head wasn't bald but scantily carpeted by bundles of tiny gray curls. He spoke with a tinge of an accent, adding emphasis and colorful depth to every syllable.

"I'd come out to help but you know I just don't do mornings."

Nedu suppressed his smirk. He gestured his hand at the man replying, "Well, that's a shame. We could've used the help. I mean, a big celebrity like Mr. Fayode out there and we'd have the streets full of people."

Mr. Fayode laughed, "Oh no. I don't think you want to see me out dy'ere sweating with d'ose, pink bands you all tie around your heads. I t'ink we'd have people running the opposite direction. They'd be running away from me! No, I'm sure you guys can handle it." Mr. Fayode scanned the room. He leaned towards the door, peering past the distorted glass of the window carved within the door. He pretended to see into the street. Leaning back he asked, "I think you all started with more people no? Or did you lose some?"

"Oh, no" Nedu threw out his hand gesturing towards the door, "Some people went home, work and you know. Mo's keeping count." The door creaked open. One jock with a thick black beard strapped to his ears and dangling from his chin poked his head inside. Glancing between the two, he threw up his thumb at Nedu.

" All good?" Nedu asked gesturing his thumb up. The man nodded and twirled back out. "Yeah, Mo's keeping count."

Mr. Fayode smiled at Nedu. His eyes rolled over the ceiling. Falling down, he scuffed his shoes along the jigsaw puzzle mat.

"You've really got this under control." His eyes perused the lineup of gym bags against the mirror panels of the back wall. "Let me ask you a question: You t'ink you can run d'is place. One day?"

Nedu frowned at the man, his lips parting, "You're not leaving are you?"

"Maybe. But you t'ink you can handle it? Running t'ings, if I were to leave?" Nedu dropped his eyes onto Mr. Fayode's feet. "I'm just asking. It's not'ing set in stone yet. Just a thought."

"I'd rather you stick around for a little longer Mr. Fayode." The man smiled, turned towards the door; his eyes still roaming along the jigsaw cracks and crevices of the space. He tugged open the door and whispered, "Alright," as he stepped out.

Next thing, Nedu strolled down one street within the commercial district of the Rusty Belt. He marched across a zebra crossing onto the sidewalk. Cheerful pedestrians capture snapshots of him as he proceeded in a whirlwind of his thoughts. His eyes scrubbed the concrete grains of the floor while his mind spured on. Held up by the expulsion of cars from a T-intersection, Nedu paused. He peered over to the yellow *caution* tape enwrapping the adjacent Olu Park.

It was not too long ago that a magician went lose here and endangered the lives of many park-goers. The

General's Police had since dealt with the assailant, locking him behind bars underground. It's a place he definitely didn't want to go. The streetlight signaled for him to pass and Nedu strolled alongside the park; parallel from across the street. He walked on for a bit carrying his chin up only to bear witness to Ibrahim standing before him. Upon his forehead, Ibrahim bore a striking pink, fuzzy sports headband. Shamelessly, he dawned a slack 32 silver basketball jersey with ocean blue trim dangling over his shoulders. He smiled brightly at Nedu, his palms resting on his hips.

"Am I late?" Ibrahim grinned. Nedu scanned him up and down, silent for the duration of their interaction.

***

Three knocks sounded at the door. It swung open to Wino, standing comfortably in a long cream woven shirt, cotton grey joggers and white socks. Wide-eyed, he strolled back into the edge of the couch.

"Nedu?"

At his door, Nedu braced the doorframe, dragging his foot into few. Upon his leg, Ibrahim happily clutched Nedu, wrapping his arms around Nedu's shins.

"I believe this is yours," Nedu grunted.

"Wino!" Ibrahim barked. "He's just like we left him." Hugging tighter, he squealed, "He's beautiful. It's just like old times."

Onlookers poked their heads out from their doors along the hallway. Passersby inconspicuously snapped shots of the two within the doorway. Giggling chimed into the room as residents strolled past the opening.

Inside, Cheryl could not relocate her eyes from this chiseled creature seated perpendicular to her. Nedu hunched over his knees, Ibrahim smiling happily next to him. Wino entered from the kitchen, handing Nedu a cup.

"So you've been mooching off Wino then?" he turned into Ibrahim.

Nonchalantly, Ibrahim waved his hand, "No."

"Yes," Cheryl countered.

Finally, her eyes slid down to Ibrahim. He glared back at her as Wino moaned in displeasure.

Wino said, "Ibrahim helps out here and there." Cheryl rolled her eyes towards the door in response.

Nedu chuckled and Ibrahim countered, "I do and I shouldn't even have to 'cause I already saved this world two times! Put it on my resume!"

"Ibrahim, are you ever going to get over that?" Nedu asked.

"Nope. Get used to it. More importantly, *this* lazy goat was going to sleep in," Ibrahim jousted his finger at Wino startling him to rise to his feet. Bringing his finger back to himself, "But I got him up to exercise. I even worked him through the pushups." Ibrahim hopped up from the chair and scooted the table out from the center.

Nedu watched with a half-smile on his face. His face brightened like Ibrahim's and he commented, "He seems in a good mood."

"So Mr. Nedu," Cheryl chimed in. "You live at The U?"

"Oh yeah, I'm just on the opposite wing."

Nedu gestured towards the glass panels across The U's courtyard. Turning back, he spotted Ibrahim hunched over the table, his mouth hanging agape, cheeks puffing and twinkles in his eyes. The two were frozen glaring at one another.

"You stay by yourself?" Cheryl asked.

"No. With my fiancé."

Ibrahim pulled away from the table gasping, "Fiancé?"

Cheryl and Wino slowly slid their disapproving expressions towards Ibrahim.

Cheryl disregarded him, "When did you get engaged?"

"Oh, about a month ago" Nedu replied taking a swig from his cup and turning towards the TV.

His gaze fell onto Ibrahim, kneeling on the floor. "What're you doing, Ibrahim?"

"I'm showing you how I broke the world record this morning for pushups." Rolling up his short sleeve, Ibrahim slapped his bicep, "Using all this ammunition here." Planting his palms on the ground, Ibrahim lowered his self and huffed *one* as he rose.

The trio watched him for a few moments. Wino eventually broke the concentration, "I don't think I ever met your fiancé."

"Oh, you haven't?" Nedu kept his blank focus on Ibrahim.

"I was thinking, maybe we should have a get-together. Just the four of us. Ibrahim can come along too if he likes."

"That would be nice," Cheryl supported him. "Except that last part."

The two smiled at Nedu but he steered away from them. For a second, Nedu glanced at the eager couple, acknowledging their interest.

He responded, "Yeah. That'd be nice. I'll let her know and maybe we can set something up." He remained distant and guarded.

Nedu twitched slightly. His focus re-centered on

what's before him. He reeled back his neck in shock.

Ibrahim maintained his rhythm, although he stacked one foot upon the other and balanced atop his pinky finger.

With a smirk upon his face, he counted, "Fifty-five, fifty-six, fifty-seven. You see this Nedu? This-is how professionals do-it."

Nedu's lower lip fell. Wino smiled nervously. Cheryl pursed her lips in disapproval.

Turning back Nedu inquired, "Ibrahim, y-you still have your?"

"Nope, this-is just-pure discipline." Ibrahim huffed as his wand shuffled down his shirt and onto the carpet.

"Busted," Cheryl hummed.

Ibrahim flopped onto the floor. He panted like an exhausted golden retriever. Nedu sat quietly. He retracted in his seat. The magician that stood before him on that fateful day still lived. Ibrahim still bore the magical artifact and wielded its powers to enhance his overall wellbeing. Judging from Wino's demeanor and Cheryl's untarnished body despite reports of what occurred a few days ago at Olu Park, Ibrahim surely dispensed his talent for the benefit of others. Wino asked about him earlier this month but it seemed he either backed down or never brought up the discussion with Ibrahim. In the end, a magician lived. The question is: should he?

***

Finally, the door to Nedu's apartment creaked open. The poorly lit room was empty. Rays stemmed beyond the curtains that lined the kitchen just around the corner. This space was more compact than Wino's. Nedu softly stepped into the room. A soft clack rang into the room.

He slung his gym bag over his neck, a voice chiming in from beyond the wall. "Is that you honey?"

"Yeah," he grumbled in a raspy voice. "It's me. How's your day?"

"Meh, I got another job offer."

"Oh?"

"But I turned this one down too. I don't like the way the office looks." Nedu paused. The rush of water gushed from the sink.

Her voice restarted the conversation, "Yours?"

"We got the whole city to come out."

"That's good. I would've come out too, but I was talking to that god-awful, boring coordinator all morning. Maybe next time, I'll join you and your friends."

The light flicked off. Nedu's fiancé strutted past him in the darkness. She made her way for the bedroom, a silhouette entered the doorframe.

"I'm headed to bed. Night."

Nedu tailed her until she's out of his sight. The bedroom door creaked but never shuts. A sliver of moonlight shined from the room onto the carpet. The bed crumpled and squeakd as she climbed onto it. Under the ambiance of her adjusting into bed, Nedu relieved a heart-quivering sigh. Within the darkness, his eyes glowed like the glint running along a stainless blade.

His final utterance for the day was a lackluster "Okay," as the room fell to silence.

The End.

EPISODE 8: WHAT A NIGHTMARE

Knuckles clonked against the front door.

"Ugh," a voice groaned reluctantly. Footsteps flopped over from within the room. "Coming," Wino said.

Crumpled papers crunched. Furniture shuffled along the carpet as he made for the door within the darkness. The front door to Wino's apartment creaked open. Before him twirled Cheryl, dressed in an all-black, glittery evening gown. She posed for him, her foot perked up along her shin, tails of her dress pinched up between her fingers and her head cocked against her shoulder.

She smirked in her supple pink lipstick. "Ta-da! How do I lo—whoa?"

Wino could barely muster the strength to gaze upon her. Bags hung from under his eyes and his lips parted subtly. "Hey Cherry," he muttered groggily.

"What happened to you?"

"Ugh."

Wino's eyes flapped out of sync like a lizard's. He slumped against the doorframe granting Cheryl visual access to the room. The two living room sofas were out of place: one balancing atop its sturdy frame, dividing the kitchen and the living area while the other stood on its side against the window panes. The center table had been relocated to the corner against the wall facing the hallway; the fridge, lying on its back with both doors open, replaced it. It opened to the ceiling with clothes bulging out. Ibrahim snuggled atop this colorful stack of fabrics, snoring as if he were a tranquilized hippopotamus. Shoes scattered across the room, with kitchen utensils and food staining them.

"Oh my," Cheryl gasped. "Did a tornado hit you? Or did it hit the whole U?"

"No," Wino wined. "It's Ibrahim."

"I'm guessing this means we're not having our date tonight, huh?"

Wino stared at her. She reluctantly scrunches her lips to one side of her cheek in response.

***

Cheryl tugged on her velvety pink pajamas decorated with images of strutting flamingoes.

"Thank goodness, I have a spare set of PJs here," she said climbing into Wino's bed.

She slid one knee atop the mattress, crawling over the sheets. Wino sat with the duvet folded along his lap. He flashed a melancholic smile.

"Thanks for cleaning up, Cherry."

Beyond his door, slightly creaked open, the room had been tidied. The fridge stood within the kitchen, the sofas had been realigned and all the food scraped into a seal-tight, white trash bag. Ibrahim lied unconscious, one leg stretched out along the sofa while the other dangled with his arm over the ledge. A puddle of saliva gargled from his open throat as he drifted deeper into cerebral twilight. Wino's room remained the only lit space within the apartment, replacing the front door as the oasis of illumination.

Cheryl tucked herself in, asking, "So, what did Ibrahim do this time?"

"He's been having nightmares this past week."

"He doesn't pee himself too, does he? Cus I touched him."

"No. He thinks it's real and starts, well it's like he's sleepwalking."

"Here we go. It's *like* he's sleepwalking?"

"Well, you'll see for yourself." Wino brows furrowed with worry.

She read into his anxiety, one arm cautiously pulling away for the lamp on his nightstand. She flickered off the lights responding, "O-kay?"

Later that evening, when the couple slept within each other's embrace, the wall bellowed with a boisterous clang. Cheryl's eyes flicked open. She paused, waiting for a follow up to confirm the noise. A few moments passed and she heard nothing. Suddenly, a secondary strike thundered from the living room. This noise provoked her to a seat. Her focus locked on the door. She siphoned a few glances darted out towards Wino. He lied undisturbed, unresponsive to all the stimuli generated by both his partner and the ominous ambiance. She contemplated if only she heard these noises. It could even have been caused by magic, like she's under a spell and didn't know it. She sat patiently. Another moment past before, finally, a third series of instruments drummed in cacophonous harmony. This concerto of discord preceded shattering glass solidifying Cheryl's suspicion.

She sprung out of bed, whisper-shouting, "Wino! Wino, did you hear that?"

"It's him," Wino nonchalantly responded. His body still unresponsive.

Cheryl tiptoed towards the door. "What's he doing? Is someone out there with him?"

"It's just him."

Cheryl pulled open the door, peeping into the entryway. The symphony of chaos flooded the room. It sounded as if a thunderstorm brew. A whirlwind whistled. Materials clanged against one another. She peered into the living room as Wino wobbled to a seat on the bed. Suddenly, Cheryl ducked out of the way with a squeal. In flew a white chair from the dining area. It banged against Wino's forehead, flinging his feet skyward and hurling the blanket off the bed. The chair tumbled onto the floor as Wino groaned in agony.

Thankfully, Wino leapt to his feet atop the bed. Down he marched towards the doorway, his palms wrapped tightly into fists. He stomped past Cheryl, fueled by frustration.

Wino growled, "I-bra-him!" exiting the room. "Would you wake u–!"

Another thud bellowed into the atmosphere as Wino flew back into the room with his hands thrown overhead. The second dining chair waddled past the doorframe having smacked him in the face. Immediately, the unconscious Wino mimicked Ibrahim with deep, erratic snoring. Startled, Cheryl popped away from him with a yelp.

She peeped around the doorframe to the swirling hailstorm of furniture. The fridge, the sofas, the television, and loose shimmering shards of glass gleamed in the moonlight as they twirled within the stream. Fearing the worst, another collision against the glass wall, Cheryl hastily dragged Wino by his arms into the bedroom.

Once Wino was out of the way, she bravely re-emerged to locate Ibrahim. It's possible that he was also in danger. For all she knew, it could be another magician. After all, they used to wage war against one another on a regular basis. What's more, the collateral damage these wars generated always overshadowed the dynamics of power that caused it. With Wino safe and snoring, she considered the option of rescuing or at least determining where Ibrahim was and if he was in danger.

By this time, the kitchen's glassware had pounded against the drywalls, jutting out more jagged blades into the typhoon. Carefully, Cheryl crept into the swarming chaos, crawling for fear of impact. She scanned the room. Her eyes dilated to distinguish any details resembling Ibrahim. Towards the corner of the adjacent wall, where the TV usually would sit, she observed the fridge crashing to a halt. Its front door creaked open as it's drawn back into the whirlwind. The torrent of wind hurled the sofa into the kitchen space, slamming it against the wooden-tile floor. Cheryl assumed the impact would have sparked Ibrahim to wakefulness or at least crushed him to deactivate the swirl of magic.

If not there, she wondered, glancing down the adjacent glass panels.

In this corner, between Wino's room and the living room, Ibrahim slumped against the wall, a string of drool dangling from his open lips. Upon detection, his howling of-a-snore roared into earshot.

Cheryl snatched Ibrahim, tugging him into the room. She slid the bedroom door closed behind her.

Upon shutting it, a heavy bang smashed along the door. Another second and she would've been crushed. She spun to Ibrahim, indignation in her heart and yanked him up by his white sleeping robe.

His beanie dropped onto the floor as she called, "Ibrahim!"

Prompting Ibrahim's eyes to flutter open. They revealed a haze of white light like the fluorescent bulbs. Wino's blanket slithered towards Cheryl as the lamp on the nightstand rocked and swayed.

He muttered, "Five more minutes," incoherently before drifting back into the dream realm.

Another object splattered against the wall, emboldening Cheryl to wind back her open palm.

She struck Ibrahim. Slapping him across the face, "Wake up!"

This slap deactivated the shine from his sclera as his black pupils rolled into view. The objects thudded against the floor outside. The whirlwind slowed to a stop. Silverware jingled, furniture slammed, and the fridge creaked. She panted anxiously, glancing between the door and Ibrahim.

Ibrahim rubbed his cheek, fully awake. "Di-did you just slap me?"

Cheryl unclenched Ibrahim's robes, dropping him onto the floor. She huffed a heavy sigh and examined Wino's door. She scanned it as if a monster was outside and it just finally surrendered to her will. She wondered how anyone could conjure such a horrific scene, and unintentionally for that matter. She knew magicians were strange and lethal, to say the least, but what should she make of this? More importantly, who's going to clean *this* one up?

***

That morning, Ibrahim sat at the dining table, fork and knife in hand, bags hanging beneath his lower eyelids, yet he eagerly licked his lips in anticipation. Wino strolled by, sliding a ceramic white plate stacked with buttermilk pancakes, cinnamon-and=chocolate icing drizzled over each one. Next, he passed a smaller plate with scrambled eggs and finally crispy, sizzling bacon. Ibrahim drooled at all the food before glancing at the bacon. Angrily, he glared towards Wino who stared back.

The two held eye contact until Wino growled, "What?"

"You know I can't eat this."

"It's *turkey* bacon."

"That's why I love you." Ibrahim grinned, tossing away his fork and diving into his breakfast.

Beside him, Cheryl rested her chin upon her palm. "You mean you really don't remember what happened?"

"Mmm," Ibrahim mumbled smacking his lips together.

Wino jutted his head out over the kitchen frame urging, "I-bra-him," in a stern voice.

Ibrahim replied, "No. I don't."

Cheryl scanned over his cheeks, puckered with food. She angled twowards Wino before descending back onto Ibrahim. "What going on? You're ignoring me?"

"It's because you got him to stop last night," Wino responded.

"It's because she slapped me!" Ibrahim barked.

"I saved your life!" Cheryl retorted. "That fridge nearly squashed the both of you. And the couches almost shattered the windows. Thank goodness it was just a cup. You guys should be thanking me."

"I never asked for your help," Ibrahim scowled at her.

"And what about Wino?"

Ibrahim waved his palm towards the kitchen responding, "Meh. Wino can handle himself. Next time, you just keep your hands to yourself or you're staying home."

"Oh no you don't," Wino interjected. "I'm not staying with just you until this nightmare stuff is resolved. Cheryl is staying here every night until your nightmares are gone, Ibrahim. That way she can slap you again."

Ibrahim twirled around in his chair, his face wrought with disgust at the very idea. Wino and him locked.

Cheryl interjected, "I am not staying here with you two! That whirlwind nearly killed me too. I'm sleeping at my own place."

She folded her arms and leaned back in the chair. Who were they to decide what role she would play? Wino's expression fell as he swept up scrambled eggs, decorated with ruby red tomato slices, lime green peppers, and toasty golden-brown onions from the sizzling frying pan.

"Good." Ibrahim faced his food. "It's better for you to stay out of it."

Wino whimpered from the kitchen, "But what about me?"

His shimmering, pouty eyes and dangling bottom lip met Cheryl's stern glare. He had a point. Wino did manage to *survive* Ibrahim's nightmares beforehand but there was no way someone could suppress that on a nightly basis.

"You'll be fine, Wino," Ibrahim mumbled as he

stuffed the bacon into his mouth.

Cheryl bounced her eyebrows, flashing a sarcastic *I told you so* expression at Wino.

This caught Ibrahim's attention as he whipped back at Wino. He flashed a disapproving stink-eye as Wino passed around Ibrahim. Wino towered overhead with two plates in hand. Wino slid one breakfast platter before Cheryl. Ibrahim tailed it, his gaze landing on Cheryl as she reflected his demeanor at him. Wino sat between the two, his own platter laid before him.

"So Ibrahim," he started. "What're you having nightmares about anyways?"

Ibrahim eagerly perked up within his seat. "I thought you'd never ask."

His eyes fell dim. The steam from Cheryl and Wino's plates wafted towards his nose, swirling onto him and fading into the atmosphere. The couple granted him their attention; Cheryl slowly chopping her omelets into chunks while Wino sat still. Ibrahim hands fell onto his lap.

Eventually, with a sunken expression on his face, Ibrahim started, "Once I fall asleep, I can see – well, there's this guy. Wino, you remember where I got my wand right?"

"Yeah, the diamond altar place, right? It was in the desert."

"Right. In my dream, I'm there again. Except this time, there's someone else. And they have my wand."

Cheryl took the first forkful into her mouth. What diamond altar place? Wino had never made mention of it despite countless tales of their journeys. And as always, Wino appeared caught up in Ibrahim's tale. His eyes were unwavering while his food cooled beneath his nose.

How could someone tolerate such behavior? Couldn't Wino see that Ibrahim's used their history as strings to puppeteer Wino and manipulate the situation to his favor? Their lives were in jeopardy from this guy – this magician – and yet no one wanted to acknowledge the walking hazard that Ibrahim was. This could not continue forever. Wino *would* have to make a choice one-day: either the wand went or Cheryl did.

"This guy," Ibrahim continued. "Pulls it out of the altar before I can even get up the stairs. He takes it for himself. Now, I know I can take him, I know I can but every time I try – you see I have a wand too, even though he takes his own from the stone, I still have mine. But for some reason, it's like his is the *right* one and I should have it. So, I always take mine out and challenge him. And then…"

His lips pursed to utter the next world but Ibrahim stared deeply into his plate. His lips hovered apart from one another. Cheryl took the next bite with intrigue.

Within the living room, the couch jittered. It rattled softly along with the carpet at first but then clanged as one leg lifted and dropped from a taller height. The fridge swayed back and forth as it marched from the wall. Cheryl noticed the shivering objects and wafting curtains. Wino centered his attention upon Ibrahim. The two appeared lost in time to the increased popping and sparking of the frying pan.

Cheryl mumbled, "Is the stove still on?" She urgently slides one foot out from underneath the table.

Immediately, Wino responded, "It's off."

His profile appeared chiseled out of stone. The TV flickered itself on. The channels accelerated. Cheryl nervously clutched the fork in her hand. She motioned towards Ibrahim. Suddenly, Ibrahim's focus snapped and he angled at her with a detestable look.

The two froze for a moment, breaking as Ibrahim faced Wino.

"I told you she shouldn't stay here."

Wino changed the subject, "Go ahead, what happened after you challenged him?"

Cheryl lowered her arm as the serene ambiance returned. The curtains draped over the carpet while the television shut off.

Ibrahim narrated, "Anyways, I take out my wand to challenge the guy. And when he turns to me, he's wearing my face with ruby red eyes. At first, I thought it was a mask, but eventually, I found out it's real – I mean he's real. He's me. The guy doesn't say anything, he just takes the wand and, and he's better than me with it."

Cheryl and Wino split their lips, jaws hanging slightly at Ibrahim's admission of weakness.

"So what're you going to do?" Cheryl inquired.

Wino supported her, "Do you think you can beat him? I mean he's you?" Ibrahim sat quiet. Upon his lap, he scanned his wand laid across his thighs. The violet scepter rested silently, its orb sleeping dormant beneath an undulating hue.

"Maybe it means something," Cheryl suggested. "Maybe you're scared of something and this is your way of dealing with it. It's showing itself through your nightmares."

"Are you scared, Ibrahim?"

Ibrahim snapped at Wino, "Are you mad? Me? Scared?" The couple retracted as Ibrahim continued, "Ibrahim fears no man, especially not some person that's not even real."

Cheryl grinned. "But do you fear yourself?"

"No one. No-bo-dy."

"What about the police or The General?" Wino added.

Sitting up, Ibrahim intensified his tone, "Listen, you may fear them, but I fear no-bo-dy." He corkscrewed his neck back and forth with every syllable, "No-bo-dy!"

"Another magician?" Cheryl smiled, egged him on.

"Ask this klutz." Ibrahim jerked his finger towards Wino, perking up higher in his chair. "We've fought tons of magicians and I beat them. I saved this world twice!"

"I wonder if Nedu would know anything about this," Wino suggested silencing the room.

Ibrahim reclined in his chair, still steaming from the absurdly insulting suggestions. Judging from their silent consensus, the trio believed Nedu to be the next best option. This would also grant Cheryl, who had little exposure to Nedu, to see him up close and personal. Who was this third member of their past? More importantly, was he as quirky and unpredictable as Ibrahim or timid and enabling like Wino?

***

Ibrahim stretched out upon the couch. His fingers interlocked atop his belly. His toes fluttered past one another, while a grin stretched across his face.

"That tickles," he giggled as a chocolate donut slid over his breast. Nedu towered over Ibrahim despite being seated on a dining chair beside the sofa. He dawned a white lab coat and uses a pair of white headphones plugged into the donut to measure Ibrahim's pulse.

"Hold still," Nedu commanded, a grin also sneaking onto his face.

Cheryl hunched over her crossed arms. She rested

her chin over her knees watching from the adjacent couch. Wino switched the faucet off from the kitchen as he stepped around the counter. He flung water off his fingers.

"Got anything yet Dr. Ned?"

"Let the man work, Wino," Ibrahim instructed.

Wino halted at the armrest of the chair, arching over and casting a shadow upon Ibrahim.

"Well," Nedu twirled around, slithering his hand into the pearl-white box seated on the table. He retrieved another donut, this one with polka dot chunks of milk cocoa and coffee brown chocolate icing. "I think he's okay."

Nedu sank his teeth into it. Ibrahim gulped the other donut. His mouth widened like a bear trap as he says *Aaah.*

"Sorry," Cheryl interjected, her face mushed into the couch. "I don't think this is how medicine works."

"Sure it is," Nedu replied, stealing another bite.

"Don't mind her." Ibrahim leaned over the cushion. "Did you go to med school?"

"I know you didn't," she retorted.

"Don't you know Nedu went to one of the best med schools in the country – in the whole world?"

"Which one is that?"

"Ibrahim School of Medicine," Wino calmly added with a smirk.

"Okay, so now I'm *sure* that's not how it works," Cheryl snapped back at Ibrahim.

Nedu tucked up his shorts and squatted down onto the white seat beside Ibrahim.

"Okay," he tossed the final fragment into his mouth like a black hole and asked Ibrahim, "So what's really going on? Are you scared? Anxious?"

Ibrahim's smile evaporated as he heaved impatiently, "Why does everyone keep asking me this? I'm not scared of anyone! You should know this. You were there."

"He says he sees himself," Wino answered.

Nedu read the seriousness of the room. "You see yourself, Ibrahim?" he asked.

Ibrahim relaxed his throat. His skull sank into the armrest like quicksand. He scanned the rooftop. "So what do you do with yourself then? Bake a cake? Make statues? Tell yourself bedtime stories? I know you love no one like yourself," asked Nedu.

"He fights himself," Cheryl responded.

"Oh, well then you can't lose, can you?" Nedu shrugged.

Ibrahim cleared his throat.

Wino commented, "This would be easier if we could just get inside his head."

"Good luck getting out," Cheryl snickered.

"That way, we could see the Nega-Ibrahim and figure out what's going on."

Nedu and Ibrahim glanced at Wino. They shared a thought and not long after sat Wino next to Ibrahim on the couch. Nedu angled Wino's head onto Ibrahim's shoulder. Ibrahim clenched his wand with a fist, cupping it within his other palm.

Wino worriedly protested, "I was just saying it would be a good idea."

"Yeah," Nedu responded. "That's why we're trying it."

Cheryl stood behind the table, knuckles against her hips and confusedly inspecting the setup.

Wino squirmed in discomfort. "But I didn't think

we could really do it."

"Welp, that sucks," Dr. Ned responded.

"Have you done this before or are you guys copying a movie or something?" Cheryl asks.

"We've done it before. Birdbrain just doesn't remember it." Ibrahim responded.

"He probably figured the dream was his own." Nedu grinned.

"How does it work?" Cheryl inquired. "Do they have to fall asleep?"

"With their heads touching," Nedu clarified. "Then someone acts as the host while the other *connects* into their dream through magic."

"What if Wino can't fall asleep?" She folded her arms.

Nedu buckled his knuckles with his thumb. Depressing each one, a pop crackled into the air. "I can fix that."

Nedu squatted down to the table behind him. He pinched a silver spoon, swirling it within a pool of steaming, creamy milk in a glass cup. He transferred half into another cup, clanging it along the glossy rim. Nedu offered them towards Ibrahim and Wino.

"Does it have magic in it?" Cheryl asked.

"Nope, it's my grandma's secret recipe. Puts you right to sleep."

Wino and Ibrahim retrieved the cups. Ibrahim stared at it with determination in while Wino panned towards Cheryl. He requested *mayday mayday* before he downed the shot in sync with Ibrahim. It's as if Cheryl should've dispatched of the two friends Wino had willingly brought back into his life. If he didn't want them to return, why did he insist on maintaining contact? At this point in his relationship, a former red flag had become the banner of his lifestyle. First, he invited them to his home. Now, he succumbed to peer pressure inadvertently projected by his friends for the sake of achieving their goals. Something, at the very least, seemed off about this connection. Could it have been that Wino was bullied the entire journey and really he was dragged along like a slave? It's clear that he's the minority of the trio. Two magicians and a powerless human made for nothing but a skewed relationship; a friendship founded on dependence. For all she knew, Wino's *relationship* with these two may have been nothing more than a fantasy – a misconstrued adherence to Stockholm syndrome.

Wino's vision blurred almost instantly. Waves rippled across his lines of sight, smudging Nedu and Cheryl into a bright pink blob. Ultimately, the light faded and the image fell black.

Upon the seat, Wino slumped over towards Ibrahim who'd also fallen unconscious. The light of his wand shimmered, prompting Nedu to couple their heads firmly against one another.

Soon after, he stood mumbling, "That should be it."

"What's in the milk?"

"Chamomile, Ramelteon, and loads of honey."

***

Within the recesses of Ibrahim's subconscious, a full moon came into focus. Its violet rays showered a sea of undulating dunes below. It blanketed them with its tinge. Individual grains sparkled like black diamonds, tumbling along the ridge down the slopes and swept up by howling gusts. The domed sky was polluted like ink dunked and diffused into a puddle of rainwater. Thick ribbons of particles danced as they stretched across the air. Perched at the apex of the greatest dune of the desert skyline, rested a shrine, an altar. It's a glass house, stair steps lead to a box table whose base flared out wider than its skyward face. Shimmering velvet curtains draped from the glass pagoda, too thick to be swayed by the wafting breeze.

Wino and Ibrahim emerged from the dunes before the altar. The falling grains stacked, drawing them up in columns. As their silhouettes formed, the grains merged to recreate their outermost shell. Once completed, they awoke and the pair scanned the landscape. Wino spun, gazing with Ibrahim at the altar.

Atop the highest step, shrouded in a murky haze, emerged an attendant. His eyes jutted out from his face, a pair of palm-sized stones as if the sands of a dune were compressed into chunks. His mannerism replicated Ibrahim as he started down the steps. Retracting one hand from his pocket, the creature reached for the altar, which had a stick plunged into its center.

Immediately, Ibrahim reached for his back pocket. "Watch out, Wino."

"Is this the guy?" Wino's voice shuttered.

"D'you see anyone else?"

Ibrahim withdrew his wand, synchronized with the silhouette. The dimness of Ibrahim's wand paled in comparison to the flare bursting from his opponent's. Out from the dunes erupted an enormous python slithering towards Ibrahim. It lunged at him, swiping its tail at Wino and propelling him down the steep slope of the dune. Wino tumbled, the black grains and royal purple sky flipped past with a rapid succession of inversions. He skidded some meters down its side, clutching at the dune with his every finger, feet and even his scalp trying to reclaim control of his momentum.

Eventually, he tamed his descent and reoriented himself. Wino scanned the landscape, drawn towards the screeching cry of the serpent. Ibrahim also propelled downhill by the extensive mass of the beast as it attempted to devour him. The serpent had captured his arm within its jaws and glared down at him with the intent to dismember him. Ibrahim, on the other hand, restrained his emotions, retaining his focus on the silhouette of Nega-Ibrahim atop the dune. Despite his initial performance, Ibrahim refused to be swayed into the gaping void of inferiority. He furrowed his brows, gripped at his wand, and unleashed an overwhelming torrent of magical energy, incinerating the serpent in a golden flash of glory.

***

In Wino's living room, Nedu and Cheryl watched as the pair snored peacefully upon the sofa. Cheryl tapped her foot upon the carpet, arms crossed, and a safe distance behind Nedu. She scowled over Ibrahim, he was just so certain that dragging Wino within the dream realm would solve the problem. The man had no magic in him. She'd probably experienced more magic control in her short time exposed to Ibrahim than Wino had in all his years of potential servitude.

Once again, Ibrahim had involved his reluctant roommate that followed him just because of some shared history. If for just once, Wino would simply tell him to take a hike, she'd support him and bring a certain end to Ibrahim's reckless charade. What if Wino never woke up? What if he was lost in the dream realm? What if only Ibrahim woke up? She was left in the waiting room with a false doctor for a hopefully decent outcome. Speaking of, his donut box had nearly slid off the rear corner of the table, closer to TV than to either of them. His arm reached blindly, pressing upon the table, but he never found it. One glance back and there it was. Now he reached for it, but how did it even get there? The box swerved away from Nedu's outstretched arm and made for the carpet — however, it wasn't. In fact, it levitated. That could only mean.

"The dream's becoming a nightmare," Cheryl gasped.

***

Within the dreamscape, Ibrahim and Wino stood back to back. Two sphinxes encircled them and the altar atop the grandiose dune. Nega-Ibrahim stood poised with his arms crossed behind his waist. He watched, amused, as the pair tracked their prey.

"I could really use Nedu right now," Ibrahim grumbled.

"I agree, how about I leave and send him in my place?"

Ibrahim poofed a Khopesh, a long Egyptian sickle sword, into Wino's arms. A raggedy stained cloth wrapped the handle in while the blade was studded with jewels along its curve.

"Sure, just skin yourself alive with that thing. Should be enough to wake you up."

"On second thought, never mind."

"Well, since you've already got it, why don't you use it on that guy? I'd do it myself but got my hands full here."

Ibrahim darted down the ridge of the dune, drawing the sphinxes towards him. As they gave chase, he leapt and skidded down the slope. His wand emanated magical ribbons that streaked energy as he descended. The sphinxes closed in on his anticipated position, leaping skyward as he approached. Before colliding, Ibrahim swerved down an adjacent dune, propelled by the wave of their impact. The beasts rose to resume pursuit, leaving Wino only a few meters from the altar. He turned around timidly hugging the Khopesh into his chest. He witnessed Nega-Ibrahim trailing Ibrahim's descent along the dunes before acknowledging Wino. Wino tugged his rattling foot forward, scattering sand from the ridge down its sides.

His voice cracked as he whimpered, "Um, ex-cuse me. Hi, um, is there any way you could l-let us, um, beat you?"

A snarling grin crept across the silhouette's charcoal face as it swayed *no* in response.

"Oh," Wino continued. "I understand. Sh-should uh, should I start running?" pointing down towards Ibrahim's trail.

Nega-Ibrahim's wand gleamed from behind his back and he revealed its brilliance to Wino. Ominously, it nodded *yes.*

***

Back in the living room, Nedu clutched his donut box as it dragged him across the living room, past the tables towards the front door. The curtains wafted, and Cheryl's hair fluttered in the developing whirlwind.

"Whoa, nelly! What's going on?" Nedu grunted, driving his heels into the oatmeal and raisin carpet.

Loose sheets of paper scattered into the brewing room from Wino's bedroom.

"This is what happens," Cheryl barked. "Ibrahim's

nightmare manifests itself in the real world."

"Okay, they did *not* teach me this in med school!"

"Oh brother." Cheryl scurried over to Ibrahim. She motioned towards his body, prompting Nedu to release one hand from the box and call her.

"Wait! What are you doing?"

"Waking him up!"

"No, we've come too far. Ibrahim has to finish the dream or else we'll have to start from scratch."

"This gets worse, y'know?" Cheryl pointed at the ceiling.

"Don't worry." Nedu yanked the box from the air, clutching it between his palms. "We can just hold things down until they wake up."

He confidently smiled at Cheryl, yanking a bite from the last donut with his jaws. Cheryl replied with uncertainty in her eyes; her brows furrowed and she nervously grinded her fingers atop one another. Once more, she turned towards the sleeping beauties that snored peacefully despite the ruckus.

***

Along the steep side of The Great Dune, Ibrahim propelled himself with the relatively low output of his wand generating thrust. He undulated his ribbon trail, outmaneuvering the tailing sphinxes and accelerating past their strikes. As he descended, Ibrahim engorged his wand with energy, jousting himself around their paws and coordinated assaults. Wino, on the other hand, backstepped his way down the dune ridge. Before him was an animated Egyptian Anubis engaging him with its magnificently brilliant staff. It twirled its weapon, striking at Wino who reflexively deflected it. With every *clang*, however, Wino lunged away, yelping in fear to the amusement of Nega-Ibrahim. The malevolent silhouette redirected its attention to the approaching Ibrahim. The sphinxes recovered from a head-on-collision, dazed and disoriented as the magician climbed altitude like a rocket-propelled grenade. Nega-Ibrahim witnessed this and with a flick of his wand erupted a pyramid of stones, not taller than a meter high, in Ibrahim's path. With his oncoming acceleration and the sporadic eruption of the pyramid surprising him, Ibrahim failed to evade. He swerved onto the side, splattering against its edge and flinging bricks skyward. He faceplanted into the gravel, tumbling to a stop midway up the slope. The sphinxes recovered and dashed up the hill to pounce upon him.

***

Within Wino's bedroom, a cyclone of ominous clouds swirled violently. It pelted Cheryl and Nedu with couch pillows, picture frames and shoes like ice blocks upon a moving car during a hailstorm. Ibrahim and Wino slouched upon the sofa as the whistling winds wound about them. Nedu and Cheryl shielded their faces, retracting from the concentrated eye of the storm. Its presence blacked out the light of the sun and casted an evening gloom upon the room. Dr. Nedu finally realized Cheryl's perspective.

"Can we wake them up now?" she screams.

Cheryl braced the doorway leading to the living room, between Wino's room and the bathroom. The dining table hovered until finally swept up into the engulfing storm. It hurled into Nedu's face although he managed to seize its legs. Tossing it aside, he met the sofa adjacent to Ibrahim and Wino. This furniture tumbled forward, rolling like a log at him. Nedu also caught this piece, although it shoved him against the wall. Hurling it away, Nedu met with the fridge as it slammed against him. His fingers slowly clutched onto it and tugged it away.

He surrendered. "Okay. Okay, yeah let's wake them up now."

Cheryl approached the torrent of furniture. She squatted down, crawling along the carpet, and avoiding any sharp objects. Clanging materials chimed from the kitchen. Out from the cabinets and drawers emerged silverware including knives and forks.

"Uh oh."

The gleaming silverware flung into the haze and swings towards Nedu.

"Oh no no no!"

***

Back in the desert, as the darkness faded, Ibrahim unveiled his face, shielded by his arms. The sand dunes quaked beneath the bouncing strides of the sphinxes. They leapt over him and proceeded up the dunes.

Flipping over like a pancake, the Anubis choked Wino. Wino kicked and squirmed in protest but failed to break free. The Anubis proceeded to offer him to the enclosing sphinxes.

Ibrahim watched in shock as Nega-Ibrahim casted a smirk down from on high. Marred with guilt, Ibrahim retrieved his wand, secured it within his palm, and casted a torch of energy. The brilliance captivated the Anubis and Nega-Ibrahim as they observed his last-ditch attempt.

Casting the wand skyward Ibrahim exclaimed, "You leave him alone."

The pair of sphinxes lunged at Wino who peddled his feet in desperation. Just as they descended upon him, a sarcophagus erupted from beneath the vast, crystal-black desert wasteland. The shimmering coffin depicted an Egyptian Pharaoh favoring Ibrahim's caricature. Its sheer distance coupled with its enormous stature culminated in a monumentally massive sculpture. As the eruption ceased, three strands of mummification bandages pierced through the case, shooting out towards the nightmares. The first of which pulverized the Anubis, releasing Wino; the second two strands impaled the predatorily-inclined sphinxes smothering them within the dune before launching them into the distance.

Nega-Ibrahim watched aghast as the trio swirled behind him, returning towards the sarcophagus in an arching motion. He ducked for cover as the bandages smashed the diamond altar, scattering its shards over the collapsing dune. The explosive disruptions destabilized the dune and tugged Wino across its slope with Nega-Ibrahim. The two watched in horror as the nightmares retracted into the gaping jaws of a mummy's head jousted out from within the sarcophagus.

The bandages were worn, bloodstained, and unraveled about the mummy's face revealing further resemblance to the caster. As the mummy casted its glare upon The Great Dune, its eyes consisted of rubies gleaming a fiery ember blaze towards Nega-Ibrahim. The mummy king growled, mirroring Ibrahim's passionate glare. Vibrations shuttered within Wino's body as he slid down the dune.

"The mummy king," he muttered with ominous familiarity.

***

The dream spurred on within the confines of Ibrahim's imagination, while in the apartment, the living room continued to shake.

"Are you okay?" Cheryl asked.

Nedu marched away from the front door, knives, and forks having stapled his white lab coat behind him.

Glancing back at the close call, Nedu asked, "O-kay, how do we wake them up?"

"I have to get close," Cheryl replied.

Turning towards the kitchen, the living room table swirled into view. It flipped and drew towards Cheryl. Nedu slid before her and palmed the table to a halt. Tossing it away, he allowed Cheryl to creep around his torso.

"Cover me!" she commanded.

Together, they proceeded step-by-step towards the sleeping duo. Nedu shielded her from oncoming cutlery and furniture. As they drew near, Cheryl outstretched her palm towards Ibrahim.

***

On the dune, Nega-Ibrahim outstretched his wand towards the mummy king, panic plastered upon his visage. The rays of his scepter dwindled as he drew nearer and was presented with the true mass of the fist winding back almost a mile away. Ibrahim reeled his wand back in sync with the mummy, both had fixated upon the sliding target.

***

At the same time, Cheryl clutched Ibrahim's collar, tugging him up towards her. The living room sofa twirled into her peripheral. She flinched, reflexing to cover her head. Nedu's muscular arm plunged into the sofa, restraining it despite the overwhelming pressure coming from the storm. The eye of the storm had drawn tighter about Ibrahim's body accelerating its centripetal winds.

It tugged at Wino's foot, sliding him away from Ibrahim. Nedu stood poised before Cheryl, one arm restraining the couch, the other bracing the fridge. Cheryl detected cutlery swerving beneath the couch and hurling towards her. A knife skidded along the carpet, hovering towards the nape of her neck.

Cheryl retracted her palm as Nedu fought the enclosing furniture.

"You're going to slap him?" he grunted.

"It's the only thing that works."

"I-bra-him is going-to-be pissed."

"Too bad."

She stiffened her palm midair, the hovering cutlery shot past her hand and redirected the knife at her neck. *Ouch,* she barked, releasing Ibrahim and inspecting her hand.

***

"Do it, Ibrahim!" Wino howled as he spun out towards the base of the dune, the sky inverting with the black grains of sand to occupy the upper region of his field of view.

Ibrahim indignantly slammed his wand upon the ground with a downward slice. The mummy king launched a right jab towards The Great Dune, displacing tons of air and overcoming the resistance dragging against his velocity. Nega-Ibrahim erupted stone pillars as ubiquitous as stones for the Pyramid of Giza from The Great Dune to combat the oncoming meteor. The pillars torpedo towards the impending punch yet crumpled and disintegrated against its blistering heat and immense kinetic energy. There was simply no force he could generate to compete with this blazing wrecking ball.

The mummy king's fist pulverized The Great Dune,

splattering waves of sand into the landscape with a tinge of violet streaking over the rippling surface. The waves poured over the horizon, washing away the dunes and carrying Wino off into the landscape.

"We did it!" Wino sang as the sea drifted him away.

The mummy king disintegrated into a waterfall of ruby red sand, mixing into the ripples of black grains. The hurricane approached Ibrahim as he retracted into an upright posture.

"You bet we did." The sea overwhelmed him and washed away his body into the landscape.

Wino's eyes flicked open. He sprung up into Nedu's bulging pectorals in excitement.

"We did – oh! What are you doi—"

A spank clapped into the atmosphere, snagging his attention.

"What the–!?" Ibrahim barked.

Cheryl jumped back into the room, releasing him onto the couch. The ominous violet clouds swirled away, revealing the tangy orange sunset beyond The U. The furniture pieces lost their pressure as the storm faded. The fridge and couch fell onto the floor. Nedu and the gang suspiciously watched Ibrahim as he rubbed his cheek grumpily.

"What just happened?" Cheryl inquired.

"We thought you guys were stuck inside," Nedu added.

A confident smirk emerged on Ibrahim's face as he replied, "We won!"

He threw up his arms in excitement, leaned back onto the couch, and rested his eyes.

Wino exclaimed, "Finally! I can get some sleep." Wino plopped onto the floor at Ibrahim's foot.

Nedu and Cheryl glanced at one another before returning towards the pair. Like tranquilized hippopotamuses, the two snored themselves into their own precious dreams. Nedu turned back to Cheryl smiling.

"I swear these guys never change." He pounced above the pair, planking midair and plopping on the pile.

Cheryl watched the trio fake-sleep like old friends in a restful pile. Ibrahim and Wino wore smiles in his dreams while Nedu smiled at the immersion of himself atop his friends.

A blanket draped over them, unwittingly covering Wino and Nedu's head but leaving Ibrahim's exposed. Cheryl spun towards Wino's room, closed his door, made for his bed.

"Nope," she mumbled to herself. Climbing into bed and tucking herself in. "I'm not even gonna bother anymore."

The End.

EPISODE 9: JUST A FRIEND

The afternoon sun baked Wino's room, generating a toasty atmosphere. Bourbon-toned wood panes lined the kitchen floor beneath a sweeping gust stirred by the air conditioner. Its wind rushed over the stainless steel sink, over the granite countertop, and around the furniture. As it crossed the entrance, the front door swung wide open. In stepped Wino, polo, khaki and briefcase as uniform dictated.

"I'm back."

Wino scanned the room. He stood alone within the space and paused to detect Ibrahim. An ominous serenity blanketed the room. Since Ibrahim's arrival, quiet like this stirred his mind to contemplate the innumerably horrendous possibilities this invited. Passersby strolled along the corridor, prompting him to enter. Inside, Wino wandered towards his bedroom.

The sliding door rolled open as he called out, "I swear if you're wearing my robe, I'm–"

Inside his bedroom, navy blue walls framed the space and calmed the mind. Coupled with his neatly laid king's bed, the decor and architecture culminated into an inviting sleeping space. It's the kind of room anyone would hate to have to leave. The opposing wall mirrored the living room, panes running across it with a deep blue curtain embroidered with baby blue crystals. The drapery flowed under the rustling of the air conditioning unit. This draft permitted a dancing haze of light upon the cosmic carpet, like that of an arcade studio.

The bathroom door swung open, "Are you clogging my toilet again?"

Wino's porcelain throne lied in wait. The seat was down with an empty shower stall standing further inside. Checkerboard tiles ran along the floor, stainless steel and crystalline porcelain alternating in the room.

Wino's cell chimed as he strutted back into the living room. Kicking off his shoes he answered, "Hey."

"Hey, love."

"Have you seen Ibrahim?"

A moment of silence fell upon the conversation. Cheryl audibly retracted her phone with a displeasing groan.

"No don't hang up," Wino protested. "Hey, babe!"

"What are you doing?"

Opening the fridge to inspect it, Wino replied, "I just got back and–"

"And Ibrahim's not there. Y'know he has to get out of the apartment sometime?"

Checking underneath the sofa, he responded, "I know, it's just weird that's all." Wino peered out the window towards The U's courtyard. "So how was your–"

A sudden herd of eager stomping raced down the hallway. It drew Wino's attention, growing louder as it approached. The stomping trampled up to his doorway before pausing for a brief moment. In flew the door, Ibrahim charging inside, his black thawb-robe fluttering in his exhilarated panic. Ibrahim slammed into Wino, propelling him like a bowling pin against the shove of a speeding bowling ball. Behind him, two girls both armed with colorful rifles gave chase. One jumped atop the living room couch to Wino's bewilderment.

He barked, "Hey!" as his phone glided beneath the sofa.

One woman was slim and dawned dust-stained white socks, striped lime-green shorts, and had waist-tall flowing jet-black hair. It's smooth with a clean shimmer but flopped violently as she hosed Ibrahim down in a jet stream of water. A bright smile blossomed between the two as he squirmed in protest. Her roommate, a slightly larger woman also in her PJs, rammed her shoulder into the doorframe, bringing herself to stop.

She froze at the entrance, spotted Wino rising from behind kitchen counter hand-on-head and whispered to her roommate, "Psst! Get down."

The playful laughter of Ibrahim and her roommate overwhelmed her voice. The girl glanced woefully between Wino and their roommates. Ibrahim flooded the thin girl's hair with his own water. He retracted to retrieve Wino and proceeded to use him as a human meat shield.

"Bring it on!" he merrily shouted, prompting the girl to take aim.

Wino and her brunette roommate protest respectively. "No, not my shirt!"

"No, don't shoot him!"

Wino was drenched. Ibrahim shot from behind Wino, propelling the girl off the couch. Gaining ground,

Ibrahim took charge. He tossed Wino from his front, forcing her regression back into the hallway. The two stormed the hallway while her roommate remained within the doorframe.

She whispered, "Sorry," and shut the door.

Wino analyzed his soaked uniform, pouting at the aftermath. His chairs and carpet were also watered in the crossfire. He rose, turned into the kitchen, and slipped on a puddle of spouted water. Luckily, Wino's head plopped onto the crunchy carpet while his feet slammed onto the polished hardwood.

"Ouch," he groaned.

"Hello?" He marginally detected a voice through a phone speaker. "Wino? Hello?"

Wino scrambled to his feet, rushing to the living room to retrieve his phone.

***

On the bus from work, Cheryl braces a standing pole.

She gradually raised her voice asking, "Who were those laughing voices? Wino?" The turquoise bus line entered a steep incline, shuffling the occupants and their luggage towards the rear. Cheryl relinquished her handrail, attempting to control her volume, "Answer me, Wino."

"Ladies and gentlemen," the bus driver chimed through the intercom. "Please take hold of a handrail if you're standing as we're going up a hill."

Cheryl stood erect, unmoved by the swaying force everyone is subject to. A nearby passenger even lost grip and braced her shoulder for stability. Cheryl stood quietly, her eyes clenching in response to the silence on her line. She wasn't worried at the grip of the stranger who shined his eyes upon her like a child in distress. She understood his distress and couldn't care less about him.

Next thing, Wino's voice broke through the phone, "Hey. I'm back."

"Good. Now, who were those voices?"

***

Wino climbed onto the couch from his kneeling position. "Ibrahim and some girls he brought with him."

"Oh."

"Oh? That's all you have to say?"

"Well, what happened?"

"They were playing with water guns and drenched my freaking uniform." He sighed, slouching in his seat. "Now, I have to do laundry again."

"That's strange," Cheryl nonchalantly responded. "I didn't even know he had friends."

"You seem awfully calm about the whole thing."

"Well, look at it this way, now you'll have a fresh batch of clothes for the weekend. You could lighten up too."

Wino sighed a gut-wrenching groan as he slouched even further in his seat.

***

Later that afternoon, Cheryl and Wino stood before the windowpanes casting their gazes of displeasure upon Ibrahim. Ibrahim sank into the couch, his sight had set on the soccer match on the TV. Cheryl folded her arms in a golden yellow shirt and jeans, a thin leather watch on her wrist.

She lectured, "You ruined his uniform for work tomorrow, Ibrahim."

"It's just water, tomboy," he calmly responded. "Calm yourself."

Wino chimed in, "Its not just that. You soaked the

couch and the kitchen floor. I slipped and could have broken my head."

"I'd put you back together, it's not a big deal." Ibrahim turned into Wino. "By the way, how come you wait for her to be here before you mention anything? We were here a while before she came. What do you need her here for?"

"That's not the point," Cheryl retorted. "You could have hurt him."

"Shut it. You're not part of this."

Cheryl palmed the ridge of the couch, insisting, "I am a part of this."

"No, you're not. You're just jealous you don't live here."

This response left her speechless with imbued rage. Her cheeks flushed with a rosy blush.

"That's still not the point, Ibrahim," Wino calmly added. "You can't just bring your playmates in here anytime you feel like."

Ibrahim remained silent.

The couple exchanged glances as Wino asked, "Did you hear me?" Still no response. "Answer, Ibrahim, or I'm kicking you out."

"What am I supposed to answer to that?" Ibrahim erupted. "Playmates? What am I twelve?"

"Could've fooled me," Cheryl mumbled.

"Well, what are they to you?" Wino inquired.

"I prefer the term *pari pari*," Ibrahim responded.

Pari pari – magician's slang for friends.

"*This* guy," Wino huffed. "Whatever they are, you still can't bring them over."

"But you bring *this one* here almost every day. She even sleeps over."

"Too bad, my house."

Wino's resolve drew Cheryl's surprised admiration.

"Whatever," Ibrahim dismissed.

A moment passed before the TV shut off and Ibrahim strutted out of the room. He disappeared behind the closing doorway.

As it closed, Cheryl spat her tongue out, adding," Good riddance."

She made for the bathroom as Wino entered the kitchen. Suddenly, she yelped from the restroom, prompting a rapid response.

Wino slid into the doorway. "What? What is it?"

Cheryl cringed over the bathroom sink. Following her gesture, Wino spotted fine strands of jet-black hair littered all about the sink.

"This. Is just nasty," Cheryl started. "I hate it when my roommate does it and I just can't stand it." Her fingers clawed at the air, stiffening like a Halloween creature clutching at a victim's skull.

"Isn't that your hair?" Wino casually inquired.

Cheryl scrunched her face in displeasure, casting a gaze like a purring predator. Wino could hear the metaphorical growling lion.

"This is him again, y'know? Him and his – his *pari pari*'s." Cheryl plucked the individual strands, releasing them over the trashcan.

"Well, at least, we have a treat for later," Wino cheerfully advertised.

"I hope you don't mean the hair."

"No. I went to the Pie Factory yesterday and bought your favorite: Mocha Volcano Cake with cookie crumbs."

"Where'd you keep it?" Cheryl asked unfettered by his statement.

"It's in the freezer," he replied, making his way towards the kitchen.

"I bet you it's not there."

"No way, I put it in the back so – what!"

Cheryl curiously jutted her head beyond the doorframe. She stepped out, dabbing her hands within a paper towel.

"Told you."

"It's completely gone, and it's covered in hair."

"Yup." She tossed the towel into the kitchen trash, a fur ball emerging as it descended. Turning to Wino, she added, "Cus you won't kick him out."

"He's on the streets for this."

"Come on, we both know you won't do it."

"I paid forty dollars for this!"

"Hmm, not bad."

"I swear this guy is gone." Wino reluctantly squashed the container within the trash. Cheryl flicked off the bathroom light and made for the front door.

"Let's go," she commanded. "I'm getting my dessert one way or another."

"Aren't you going to use the bathroom?"

"Come on, Wino."

***

That late afternoon, Wino and Cheryl returned from their insulin frenzy to Wino's apartment. The couple strolled down the corridor, an extra cake in Wino's hand and smiles on their faces.

"Ibrahim's gonna love this," Wino cheerfully exclaimed.

"He ate your whole cake, Wino. Why are you bringing him another one?"

"I know, but he's never tasted this flavor."

"I swear." Cheryl motioned for the door.

"He's going to freak."

As it swung open, Ibrahim howled in laughter, clacking his ankles over the sofa. His head rested upon the ground while his arms were outstretched towards the center table that'd been shifted closer to the TV. Across from him was his *pari pari* playmate, a bucket over her head as she stumbled around in confusion. The more polite, brunette roommate sat adjacent Ibrahim, her palms folded atop one another and a cup sat within her grasp. She chuckled, retrieving the 20-sided die from the table. The playmates froze at the sight of Wino and Cheryl, the bucket-headed roommate still chattering inaudibly. She seemed to be Ibrahim's favorite and brought a smile to his face. She plucked the bucket and tossed it onto the carpet. The room went quiet as Wino and Cheryl entered. Cheryl made for Wino's room, ignoring the gaming trio.

"Hello," the seated brunette sang.

"You're playing the board game?" Wino asked.

"Yeah," the standing roommate responded. "Wanna join? We have plenty of cards."

"No, thank you," Cheryl coldly responded as she turned the couch corner.

"Why?" the seated woman asked.

"Because they're squares," Ibrahim grumbled. "Come on, Senny! Let's keep going." He grinned like a child eager to play.

Gently, Senny's roommate placed her fingertips upon Ibrahim's robe, drawing his attention.

She whispered, "Should we leave?"

"No!" he selfishly responded. "Don't mind them. Let's keep going."

This prompted a stern glare from Wino that Ibrahim ignored. After a moment, Cheryl motioned for Wino to come. Wino entered the bedroom, and she shut the door. Their debate started the moment the couple faced one another.

Their attempts at a hushed discussion penetrated Wino's door into the living room. The trio of playmates all angled towards the door, drawn by the increasingly tenacious argument. Senny's roommate anxiously cleared her throat. She attempted to catch Senny's eyes, but Senny pretended to ignore her, only exchanging glances with Ibrahim.

***

Inside Wino's bedroom, Cheryl strutted away from Wino, her hands combing through her hair. Her face flushed as she approached his bed.

"Just listen, okay?" Wino pleaded. "Those girls, his friends."

"His *pari pari*."

"Yeah. They're making him happier than we could."

"What?"

"Think about it. Have you seen Ibrahim this happy – ever?"

"Cool, great. Why can't he be happy in their room? Do you even know who these girls are? Do they even live at The U?"

"I think so. They look like..."

"I mean, do you hear yourself? He's happy, but you and I are going insane. Magicians don't rule us."

Wino paused. He scanned the room until the sound

of the front door climbed into earshot. He opened to the living room. The board game sat neatly arranged atop the table and the furniture had been realigned; most likely the work of Senny's roommate.

"They left." Cheryl huffed from inside Wino's room. "They heard us talking and left."

She plopped herself onto Wino's bed, hands on her head and groaning from her abdomen. Wino quietly emerged from the room. He opened the freezer door. Cheryl glanced towards the wall. She rose from the bed and exited.

Within the living room, she approached Wino. The cake he had bought for Ibrahim was in his hand. Fortunately, it was still intact.

"Is it *hairless*?"

"Yeah."

"What now, you going to go give it to him? Beg him to behave around his *pari paris?*" Cheryl sat at the white dining table. Wino inspected the desert. He drew a blank face, stitching together a scenario within his mind.

"What?" she inquired.

"I'm...thinking. Maybe we're looking at this all wrong."

Quietly, Cheryl folded her arms. Her legs crossed. A curious gaze, aimed at Wino, suggested she reconsidered their relationship or his sanity. A crooked smile crept along the crevice of Wino's cheeks. He faced her, an awkward silence growing within the space.

"I have an idea."

***

Down the hall, the floor elevator dinged. It's stainless steel doors softly glided apart. The wheels made no more than a slight squeak as they separated. Once divided,

Ibrahim peered into the hallway. Cautiously, he scanned the L-shaped intersection, one corridor lead towards Wino's room and the other connected the two wings. A common room within the connecting corridor hosted a congregation of movie-watchers. Although masked by the darkness of the room and struck by the electric flashes from the screen, Ibrahim discerned a handful of occupants curiously looking back at him. One stood to close the door, disconnecting him from their space. Ibrahim redirected his focus towards the hallways. He initially tiptoed but proceeded to towards Wino's room. His head was on a swivel, scanning his rear while maintaining awareness of his surroundings. This hypersensitivity had him leaping back from opening doors. He locked onto those that emerged before they simply ignored him. Passersby shuttled along in a herd, marginalizing him against the wall. Nonetheless, Ibrahim stared into the crowd, checking for any potential threats. He's like a foreigner, fresh off the boat and into the big city. He was startled at all the sight and sounds that greeted him from all angles.

Making his way to his room, a stampede rushed towards him from down the hall. He spun to see Senny and her roommate, once again armed with decorated elliptical rifles charging him. He took off. His cloak rattled in the rushing winds. Their giggles echoed over him as he threw open the door.

Inside, Ibrahim slammed the door shut, holding it closed for dear life. The girls sieged the entrance. Their combined efforts yanked it open by a sliver. The tug of war raged on, Ibrahim bracing his feet upon the doorframe while Senny wedged her nozzle within the gap.

Ibrahim howled in defiance, "You'll never take me

alive!"

"Fine!" Senny barked. "Then I'll take you dead!"

The women laughed in giddy exhilaration. She and her roommate pried open the gap. Ibrahim rearranged his foot placement, trying to establish a tighter grip but failed to overpower them. His heart raced while an excited smile worked its way onto his face. The thrill of the chase beat across the doorframe, as the pair inched closer. They'd soon breach the doorway and he'd be exposed to their weaponry. He flicked glances into the room, searching for shelter. And as he scanned the living room, the kitchen, and the dining area, he discovered something. Ibrahim almost relinquished his grasp on the doorknob upon discovering what awaited him.

Stationed at the dining table, Wino and Cheryl stood in all matching clothing: black socks, black shorts, black V-neck, and for Cheryl, a black headscarf. A wooden crate labeled 'La Munchies Farmer's Market!" mounted the table between them. It's brim overflowed with fresh fruit including Cantaloupe, Tomatoes, and Guavas all spliced into halves and sprinkled in chili powder. Wino and Cheryl glared incisively at him; Wino rife with pent up frustration and Cheryl glowing with a grin coupled with a voracious thirst for revenge. The couple delved their claws into the crate. Ibrahim's grip on the door sluggishly relaxed. He's wobbled upon the doorframe as Senny's villainous laughter howls louder and louder.

To his dismay, Cheryl sang, "I-bra-him."

His gaze fell to her retrieving a red-hot pepper-stained tomato, her smile bursting across her face.

Turning to Wino, he head, "Out."

Softly, Ibrahim asked, "Wha?"

"I said out!" Wino exclaimed, hurling his own tomato in sync with Cheryl.

The food splattered on Ibrahim's face and robes. He flopped to the floor, swiping some of the pepper and inspecting it. Another flurry descended upon him, prompting him to shield his face, flailing his arms. The door flew open and Senny sprung inside. She hosed down Ibrahim, giggling and hopping around him. He fled the scene. Outside the room, Ibrahim darted around the door and down the hall, shouting in protest. Senny's roommate detected the red splotches on his robes only to be pummeled by unstained guava. Out from the room, Senny retracted squirting her gun back at the armed couple.

"Returning fire!" she shouted. "We're taking too many casualties, let's get out of here!" She yanked her roommate from the floor and sped the opposite way down the hall. Her jet-black hair had been struck with fruits still dangling from within. Her socks and her thighs were also pummeled.

Inside the room, Cheryl leapt with joy before Wino. "That-was-so-much-fun!" she squealed. "We're so gonna get in so trouble for this though."

Wino maintains his focus outside the doorway, where Senny's roommate had fallen. He lowered his arm, loaded with shaven pineapple to ask, "Do you think we should have left her roommate alone?"

"No, she hangs out with them."

"Yeah, but she always cleans up and she's a lot nicer."

"So? If she hangs out with Ibrahim and I see her, she's getting another tomato to the face." Giddily, she asked, "But wasn't that fun?"

Smiling, Wino confirmed, "Yeah, that was a ton of fun."

"I know, we should have done this earlier. But I didn't know you'd even come up with something like this."

"It just came to me, plus I wanted to get back at Ibrahim for being such a jerk."

Wino's eyes climbed from Cheryl to the doorway as footsteps crossed along the hallway. He yanked his arm up with a gritty look on his face. Cheryl responded, retrieving a chili-stained orange and aiming with him. The two stared down a mid-thirties blond woman, cautiously tiptoeing in heels across the battlefield. Her wandering eyes met their hostile ones, prompting her to clutch her purse. The couple relaxed, allowing her to proceed into her room directly across from them.

Cheryl leaned in, mumbling, "We should probably clean this up."

"Yeah, that's a good idea," Wino replied.

***

Wino and Cheryl cuddled on the couch. Their legs scrubbed against one another, entwined over the table. They fluttered their feet together wrapped in cozy black stockings. Within Cheryl's grasp sat a ceramic bowl decorated with swirling baby blue bands. Inside were diced fruit showered in the ruby red chili pepper. She plunged her fingers inside, lifting them to Wino's face. Her lips were stained as if she wore lipstick and Wino soon joined her. She grinned up at him, watching him work his way through it.

"What is it?" She grinned.

"I think it's guava," he responded. "What was it?"

"I don't know," she giggled. "I can't tell what anything is anymore." Cheryl fished for another fruit slice. "I'm pretty sure this is pineapple." Making her way towards it, Cheryl watched Wino dart his jaws before her.

Chewing it, he confirmed, "Yup, pineapple."

Cheryl made her way to the dining table, searching through the crate for other sugary fruits. Her chili-smothered fingers disappeared in the sunset haze of mixed sweets.

"What're we going to do with the rest of these? I don't think The U wants anymore chili on their carpets."

"Well, I was thinking we could give it to the shelter."

Cheryl pointed. "Like this?"

"I guess you're right. I'll ask Nedu if he wants some."

The front doorknob twisted. Cheryl and Wino glanced over at the white flag jousted into the half-inch gap. It waved in surrender before the door slid further open. Senny carefully popped her head inside, laced with ember-streaked hair.

"We surrender," she said apologetically.

Cheryl and Wino exchanged glances.

Turning back to her, Wino responded, "What about Ibrahim?"

To this, Ibrahim tugged the door open wider. His robe hung drenched by a cascade of varying watercolors, chili, and pungent fruit. Against the charcoal backdrop, the flowing colors almost resembled a painting. A sunset, punctuated by the large tomato clump stuck to his breast, marked the horizon as a bubbling river wavered about his knees. His brows were slightly furrowed and bags tugged beneath his eyes. Cheryl and Wino focused on his dress, attempting to discern the intended portrait as Ibrahim marched inside.

"What happened to your other friend?" Wino inquired.

"She went back to our room," Senny responded.

"Wait," Cheryl inquired. "You live here?"

Pointing towards the TV, Senny responded, "I'm down the hall from you guys." She stood with her silky hair fraying at the ends. Her legs were painted similar to Ibrahim's clothes. Her shirt was mostly unfettered; however, fruit smothered her back.

Ibrahim flopped onto the living room sofa adjacent to the couple.

This action prompted Wino to shout, "No! Ibrahim, you're dirty!" in protest.

Wino flailed his arms over Ibrahim but the magician simply gestured his palm towards Wino.

With his eyes on the TV, Ibrahim lifted his palm to Wino. "That was pretty good."

Starstruck, Wino cautiously high fived him before continuing his protest. By this time, an exhausted Ibrahim stretched his feet over the table.

Rolling his head back onto the sofa, he started, "Was that idea yours, tomboy?"

"It was Wino's," Cheryl responded.

"*You* came up with that?" Ibrahim snapped.

"Get off my couch."

"How'd you come up with something like that, huh?"

The two debated on the couch. Wino nudging Ibrahim off while Ibrahim stubbornly resisted him. The magician clutched the chair in defiance. Cheryl made her way across the room towards Senny.

She started, "So, do you have your *own* room?"

"Nah, I moved in with my roomy last fall. She won the lotto and I came with. You stay with?"

Senny nudged towards the boys. Ibrahim propelled Wino onto the adjacent sofa using his feet like a kangaroo. Alone, he sprawled out over the couch, attempting to relax. Wino jumped and retrieved a tomato from the crate. With an outstretched wagging finger, Ibrahim attempted to dissuade Wino but was pelted nonetheless. Outraged, Ibrahim hopped to his feet, conglomerated the splatted remains into his fist and proceeded to pursue Wino across the room.

The girls shifted closer to the kitchen wall while Cheryl responded, "Oh no. We don't live together. Not- not yet. We were planning to but, um."

"I gotcha. Things changed."

"Yeah. Change of plans. I guess."

"You know, he really appreciates you," Senny said in a breath of authenticity.

There was stillness in her eyes and a touch of deep-seated wisdom in her tone like she understood the overarching situation.

Cheryl responded, "I know, I just wish he'd stop putting it off. I mean we were supposed to–"

"No," Senny corrected Cheryl. "The other one."

Cheryl paused. Her mind clearly struggled to locate this *other one* from the available option.

Wino squirmed through the corridor, exiting his bedroom with haste. He scurried over the couch with Ibrahim in hot pursuit. Tumbling over its ridge, Wino dodged the torpedoing tomato paste, allowing it to slap Senny in the cheek. The trio gasped. The paste flopped from her face into her anticipating palm. Her eyes remained shut while she processed the impact.

Cheryl tentatively turned and yelld, "Ibrahim! You hit her in the face, you dolt!"

"Shut it, tomboy!" Ibrahim retorted. Turning to Senny, he gently asked, "Are you okay?"

Senny chomped into the tomato, responding, "I'm taking this with me."

She made for the door. As she planted her foot beyond the doorframe, Wino chimed in. He knelt atop the carpet. "So, does this mean we'll be seeing more of you, Senna?"

"It's Senny," Cheryl corrected.

Senny smilesd from the doorway responding, "Actually, my name is Seneca and you'll see more of me. Ciao."

The door closed. Ibrahim immediately huffed a sigh of relief.

He mumbled, "Fun times over," as he hopped off the couch.

"Ibrahim, go and take a shower!" Wino commanded.

"Yeah, yeah, I'm going."

Ibrahim jammed his arm under the couch cushion, retrieving his wand from it. As he slung it over his shoulder, the gleaming orb morphed into a fluffy violet sponge, his robes swirled into a bath towel with sunset art drawn across it and a transparent shower cap atomized on his head. The stains from the room slithered into a rubber duck dangling from his wand-sponge.

Cheryl and Wino came alive with surprise.

"You mean your wand was here the whole time?" Wino asked.

"What'd you expect? I can't take it with me. What if it falls out when we're playing?"

"So, then she – Senny doesn't know?" Cheryl asked.

Ibrahim paused. Then he started towards the bathroom. "No."

"Why don't you tell her?" Wino inquired. "Don't you two spend a lot of time together?"

"Yeah, but she's just a friend."

The door to the bathroom closed and, immediately, a blaring karaoke strung by a live jazz band roared from within.

Inside the living room, Wino turned to Cheryl who inquired, "How did we not notice? We could have turned in his wand and given him the money."

"But, why d'you think he didn't tell her?"

"I don't know, probably because he doesn't trust her or something. She might work for the police – but we could have turned it in. I'm so mad."

Cheryl pouted towards the crate, crushing the remaining fruit in her fury. Wino glanced between the doors of his room, the bathroom, and the entrance door. He reflected on the label Ibrahim selected to rebrand his former *pari pari*. She was just a friend? After all that, Ibrahim was still so selective of who he let in? Moreover, someone who would think they'd forged a bond with him was just cast aside as nothing more than an acquaintance? Granted, he did only just meet her or at least introduce her to Wino and Cheryl. There was still no way he could have not felt some connection to someone he favored so much. Maybe Wino read too much into a few words. But it made him wonder. It made him conjure a whole list of questions stemming from that one phrase – *just a friend.*

The End

EPISODE 10: NOSTALGIA

Faded like a coffee-stained film, my mental album flickered through a memory reel. It splintered open with the crackle of a vinyl record player being scratched by the needle. This contact conjured a stream of hazy scenes filtered vinaigrette and down poured upon the retina of my subconscious. Now, I can't say for certain that this all happened as recanted, but a voice deep within me swore the content to be true. Every night, the dream unfolded like this:

    The starry night twinkled up above with the galactic backdrop arching as a dome overhead. The hovering moon highlighted the path for us. Ibrahim and I scaled a swirling mountain by horseback. Our two-headed stead trekked up the winding path as it narrowed. We're so high up that smaller hills and valleys flickered their lamplights down below. A reversing trail of light shrank to the size of ants while the mountain breeze washed over us. Glimmering villages, castles, and campsites littered across the vast nightscape. They were lands ruled by magicians in a time of persistent unrest. Most had failed to expand out to the size of the city we occupied now, a hallmark of the time. Of course, there were some exceptions, but they were few and far between. The sites contained non-magicians, but these peasants always lived under one magical powerhouse or the other. Security was fragile as the toppling of one dictator lead to the scramble for another. There certainly was no U and there was no Cheryl.

As we scaled this fuzzy hill, blanketed with invasive and persistent horsetails and wheat, a trickling stream of magicians descended with haste. Some bore precious metals, artifacts and treasures looted from up above while others still carried armor and fine cloths down the hillside. They scrambled on foot, riding tamed beasts such as ours and others still flew, taking off into the skies beneath curtains of raining starlight. They fled in bands, punctuated by brief periods of relative quiet. In these moments, I questioned our objective. Flocks of rescue teams were already dispatched to contain the site yet even they retreated as we made our ascension. What then were we to do?

My eyes fell to Ibrahim, his costume reflecting the moonlight into my face. He wore a beige cape that fluttered atop his deep ember silk robes. A heavily embroidered, Hausa-styled, cylindrical cap rested over his head. It was studded and suited him, like a traditional ruler that rode into town. Ibrahim was calm and a glance at his face almost revealed grateful servitude coupled with a sense of duty. We came about the final sway of the mountain's spiral. As we rose, our beast's marching eased to a stop. I noted our pause and Ibrahim took to hurdling his self into the tall grass.

"Come on," he commanded. "It won't go any further."

I followed his lead and disembarked. Retracting from it, I watched our vehicle scurry away with a fleeing bandit. He was adorned with ill-gotten goods and having seen that we didn't need it, he hopped right on. Ibrahim now marched up the knee-high wheat blades towards the tip. I tailed him, lunging across the grassy fields until coming upon the sight.

It was a searing inferno; a torrent of fire that burrowed a gaping hole into the heavens. It soared under the crackle of crumpled and charring wood. This was an estate or possibly a temple that erupted under the scorching indignation of a wicked magician. It was much larger up close than I had imagined it to be. One extended family had lived here for generations and made very little contact with the world beyond their bubble. Their lives were shrouded in conspiracy. Living so high in the clouds, their existence towered over everyone else. And so the people made the most of it. They generated folk tales with the minute factual information they could elicit from passing couriers and supplemented it with copious amounts of creative absurdity. But from the evidence presented, it seems magicians got involved, possibly by bloodline, and now this happens. Perhaps someone lost at a game of cards and was a bad sport about it.

Ibrahim tucked his palms within his cloak, strutting off towards the melting estate. His robes swayed past bent blades of wheat. My cusped hands anxiously tucked into my chest; my heart throbbed into my ears and my vision wobbled under the sweltering heat. I could feel the blood in my arteries beginning to boil or at least simmer. Blistering heat swathed my forehead as beaded water bubbled out. I was at my baking point, it all came to this. The various cooling measures built into my anatomy collapsed when suddenly the warmth was swept away. It felt cool under my nose and my shoulders shuttered in response to a passing breeze.

Like matted sheets of soot, our feet kicked up coiling black dust as we proceeded into a clearing. The walls of the estate enclosed us, forming a boundary with the starry backdrop. The estate mirrored an ancient city, brick roads linked bungalows sweeping into a central road. There were small ponds and little arched bridges. The houses hung wind chimes with household names decorated on wooden planks. The extended eaves shaded the encircling porches, casting a shadow upon those hidden beyond the toweled entryways. Unfortunately, many of the buildings were constructed using locally sourced wood and so the flames consumed them in a blaze of fury. The ponds dried up, koi fish splashing in the dwindling puddles. A mystical field repulsed the flames like a magnet and sheltered us within a cool bubble.

Ibrahim proceeded into the clearing, me trailing close behind him for my own protection. We marched before the porch of a disintegrating home. The red-hot ember shone like the sun heralding the descent of dawn. Ibrahim, without a second thought, headed inside, leaving me behind to scour for survivors. Soon after, he emerged with women and children adorned in silk robes scorched at the hems. They clung to him just as I had until their flame-repellent field merged with mine. As a group, we then proceeded along the main road, the rescued families highlighting some homes of their friends and spotting survivors. In his flamboyant fashion, Ibrahim confidently commanded the flames to bow and clear a path from which the victims could approach our herd.

Our crowd swelled as we made our way across the estate, reaching the cliffside-gated exit. At first, I assumed we'd return the way we came, but Ibrahim had other plans. With a fling of his wand, the estate walls crumbled, the bricks restacked themselves leaving open a central path. There was no road beyond the cliff, but Ibrahim proceeded, and the families followed him without hesitation. I stayed behind, counting the heads of those that had joined us and made sure the weak were escorted out.

After completing the headcount, I took one last glance at the blazing homes as they succumbed to their faulty support beams and pillars. There were some unfortunate members of this clan that fell. Judging from their injuries, it was the initial flare that scorched them and not the engulfing trails the later ensued. It was the handiwork of a magician, as clear as day.

Ibrahim once told me, in a moment of honest weakness, "Nothing good ever comes from the magicians."

His words always echoed in times like this. We had spent most of our lives by this time cleaning up their messes. We made things right where we could and even put our lives on the line, facing magicians head-on when necessary. We made a great team, even more so when Nedu later joined our gang. It was what we lived for, and we loved it. It's how we ended up facing the threat of our time on two separate occasions. We saved not just ourselves but also the whole world – twice.

I turned to follow Ibrahim out of the estate walls when I discovered the entourage had disappeared, leaving me within the brewing flames. The tangerine blades swarmed the exit towering over the walls like a raging furnace. The repelling field had abandoned me for the torrent to consume me. The fog of charred wood bellowed into the sky veiling the moon behind its shrouding curtain. I was alone encircled by the unleashed fury. My throat sored, like grated cheese the air scuffed against the spongy walls of my insides. It stung and choked me. Like men on horseback, the flames approached, weapons drawn to eliminate the intruder. I was captured and to be eliminated on sight. I fell and my vision blurred, a swirl of red-hot soot and charcoal skies washed away paths of escape.

***

Next thing I knew, my eyes flicked open to the darkness of my room. The only discernable image was that of dancing moonlight shimmering on the carpet adjacent to the fluttering curtains to my left. It was supposed to be a nightmare, but I wasn't not scared. A little anxious – yes, but only because I couldn't breathe. It was a nightmare kind of choke, I clearly could still breathe, but the perception that I can't disturbed me. Either way, I still had time to go back to sleep, but why bother when it'd just restart itself again? I didn't get if I was supposed to make something out of it or what, but it kept replaying inside my head. Usually, I just laid there and reminisce some of our travels together, quiet to make sure I didn't wake Ibrahim. Sometimes, I'd giggle out loud at the funny moments or shrug my shoulders and cringe when I remembered the embarrassing times. Overall, I was very nostalgic about the whole thing. And I'd be lying if I said that sometimes, I wish I didn't have to go to work. Instead, I'd love for Ibrahim to burst in here in his usual flamboyance and command us to go somewhere for the day. With time, I learned that he'd make up most of the adventure as we went along. It'd be stressful, but it'd be fun.

I strapped on a jacket and made for The U's middle courtyard. It was the first frost of the season and Mrs. Miyamoto always sold green tea in coffee cups for about an hour for early morning commuters. I helped her set up on her first day and ever since then, I made it a habit to see her on the morning of the first frost.

I made my way out the sliding double doors when a voice called, "Hola mijo."

Turning around, I saw Fabiola, a hefty front desk worker in her dress suit and signature gold air hostess's tie. She fluttered her fingers towards me, attending to the line of guests waiting for her.

"Hola," I hollered back to her.

Outside, I stepped up towards Mrs. Miyamoto's stand. She was a thin-framed lady with straight black hair similar to Ibrahim's sporadic friend – Senny. Her age hid, masked behind a charming smile, her face rife with soft cheeks and pink lips like a baby. Mrs. Miyamoto's shop lined the wall of The U on the same wing as my room. It blended into the vibrant community, a Mediterranean shop and miniature indoor ice rink on either side of her.

"Ohayo Wino-san!" she bowed.

"O-ha-yo," I butchered in response. I insisted in sharing my friends cultures and this included their language.

"Ocha wa ikaga desu ka? Would you like some green tea?"

"Yes please," I dug my frosted palms into my coat pockets. I retrieved a wad of straggling ones. "How much are they?"

"It's free!"

Leaning back, I pointed to the vertical black banner with white stylish kanji script deciphering, "But it says four dollars for the–"

"No it's free!" she insisted.

I froze, puzzled by the missing price tag that was clearly lost in translation. Mrs. Miyamoto spoke crystal clear English so the issue wasn't an accent or anything. More concerning was the fact that the client before me clearly had a cup of the same green tea and paid for it.

"You helped me when I first moved here – so it's free."

"No, no, I can't do that."

"It's alright,"

"No, cus' I'm buying two cups. One for my roommate," I displayed the peace sign while unfolding crumpled bills.

Not to be outdone, she poured the cups, slid brown cup sleeves onto them and jousted them towards me before I had enough money assembled. Looking up, her head was bowed so she couldn't receive the money, I presented. Culturally outsmarted, I stuffed the money back into my pocket and humbly accepted her gifts.

Mrs. Miyamoto rose, smiling in victory and asked, "So Wino, are you going to pick pumpkins today?"

I sniffed the steam from my cup repeating, "Pumpkins? Today?"

"Oh yeah, my friend and I will be over by the Highlands later tonight. It's a small festival for the city. You get to pick pumpkins and they hang beautiful lights everywhere and you can hang out with your friends. It's a lot of fun. You should come so you get to drink more tea!"

"You're selling your tea there?"

"Yeah, they asked me if I could sell tea to the families while they pick the pumpkins. So I'll be there, yeah. You should come."

Her eyes hinted at a person behind me, glancing between the two. I started away from the conversation, sipping my tea and nodding to her. I thanked her for the tea. She gestured goodbye, turning to her next customer and I made my way up.

***

Back in my room, Ibrahim sat at the dining table.

I slid into the doorway singing, "Hey, I got us some green tea from downstairs."

He was quiet. He scanned over the courtyard. It was his first winter with me since stasis. One silky and stainless white robe draped down his body. One leg rested on the chair with his elbow on his knee. Ibrahim turned into me and received the cup.

"Is it any good?" he cautiously asked, taking a sip.

He waited a moment before accepting its flavor and tilting the cup over his face. We spent a few moments drinking in silence together, me standing beside the table and him seated. Eventually, I broke the quiet.

"So, what's the adventure for today?" I asked.

It was a throwback from our traveling days. In response, he'd usually point us in some direction – any direction and we'd head out. We had no idea what awaited us for the rest of the day but we took it as it came. It was almost our unofficial routine. Instead, Ibrahim tore from his drink and gazed at me with subtle shock in his eyes. I smiled back at him but he was speechless. Awkwardly, he turned back into his cup, like a solemn memory stirred in his mind. Ibrahim wasn't one to really reveal his emotions, but this one clearly caught him by surprise.

His voice was raspy when he said, "There is no adventure."

"But there's always an adventure," I protested.

He turned towards the window. "Not anymore."

"Then I'll make one," I responded. "How about we pick pumpkins?"

Again he snapped to me, this time brewing with tamed confusion. "How 'bout we pick pumpkins?" he recited.

"Yup. Mrs. Miyamoto, the lady I got the tea from," he turned to the queue snaking along the courtyard, "She said they're having a pumpkin picking party tonight."

"Where?"

"The Highlands, it's across town."

He pondered it for a moment. "And you want to do this?"

"Yup."

Ibrahim planted the cup on the table. He scanned it from base to lid, scrubbing his thumb along the cardboard sleeve. He looked out the corner of his eye with suspicion asking, "And you want me to go with you?"

"Is there an echo?"

He turned away. Gazing out the window he replied, "Fine, I'll go with you. If you want me to."

"Cool, then that's our adventure for the day."

I chugged my tea retreating to my room. Escaping the cold silence of the living room masked by the whistling, frosty, fall breeze outside, I hid inside all day.

I wanted to do something for Ibrahim – with Ibrahim since he'd been alone all this time. Cheryl and I would spend most of the day outside, only to return when the daylight fell and that was if we didn't have something planned for that evening also. Since he'd appeared, I felt bad leaving him in this apartment by his lonesome. When I brought him out, it turned into trouble because of his attachment to his wand. It conflicted with my life with Cheryl, and juggling the two hadn't been easy. I knew his pause was to consider what this meant for Cheryl and me, but I was glad he left it alone. I hoped that by going out tonight, just us two, the nostalgic candle that burned during our adventures would rejuvenate him – would wake him up. Maybe it'd bring out the old Ibrahim; one that wasn't always clutching for power, but instead the one who made sacrifices for random strangers. And who knew, maybe this was how I could get him to give up his wand.

***

It was only when the sun began to set that I reemerged from my room. Only now, I had on boots, oak brown slacks, and a flannel shirt. My jacket dangled, strung by two fingers. I slid the beddoor open and there stood Ibrahim in the entryway. He wore a sweater, with denim jeans and a beanie.

"Lemme borrow your brush," he commanded. He walked past me into my room. "Where is it?"

I shifted from his path. "On uh – over the counter," I fumbled. "Where's your jacket?"

"Don't have one." Ibrahim snatched the brush. Removing his beanie, he stroked it over his head. "How far's The Highlands from here?"

"About a thirty-minute walk. People are already heading over there."

"We're walking?" Ibrahim exclaimed.

"Yeah," my voice dwindled. "I thought we'd walk it."

He sighed. "Alright." Plopping the brush onto the counter. He shuffled his beanie onto his scalp and made for the door. "Let's go."

Again, I motioned from his path and we headed out the door. As I locked the apartment I noticed Ibrahim shoving his hands into his pockets, within one of them was a violet glowing orb. A frosty chill swept along my spine. It split and frayed into my limbs like an electric jolt. By now, I expected him to carry it, but the sight still struck me as a red flag. I paused, took a breath and made my way out.

***

Along the sidewalk, we strolled amongst the trickling trail of attendees. The people around us chatted freely. Groups of teenagers jogged across the street to merge with their friends. The streetlights flooded the road and the moon hovered high above. Clouds scantily occupied the sky and apartment lights climbed the concrete towers. Despite the enchanting environment, Ibrahim and I were unusually silent. The harmony of our shoes scuffing the chalk-adorned sidewalk was more productive than our communication.

"So," he eventually started. "What happened with you and Cheryl?" His gazed reached across the street.

"Hmm?" I replied. "What does that mean?"

"You two aren't fighting?"

"Nope." The teenagers squealed before us, giggling as they made for the festival lights in the distance.

"She out of town?"

"Uh no. Why?"

He paused. "So nothing's wrong?" looking at me.

"I hope not."

We shared another moment of quiet. Ibrahim returned his focus towards the footpath. We crossed underneath a shattered streetlamp casting darkness over a segment of the road. It provoked the teenagers to a howl, but our passage was undisturbed. His voice broke out, "Then why did you –– so why didn't you invite her like you normally would?" as we reemerged.

"I don't know," I shrugged. "I just thought that maybe you'd like to go. She and I can find another day."

"And that's it?" he asked.

"That's it." I turned to him, "So, you thought we had a fight?"

"Well, I figured *something* must've happened. You two are," He searched for the word.

"Pari pari's?" I mocked.

"Inseparable," he fought against the encroaching smirk.

We came on to the dancing tangerine lights in the distance. The city blocks receded behind us as crunchy fall leaves gathered along the alleyways. The Highlands was mostly a residential district meaning the houses were a lot closer to the ground. Abundant landscaped vegetation decayed or at least jettisoned their leaves for the upcoming season. The brick homes were tucked away and we happened upon a small park for the local community. It bordered a small forest, lightly decorated with trees like a painter that applied a few strokes for the scenery. The concrete and asphalt transitioned to grass and wood panes beneath the hazy gradient of fall-colored leaves.

The park was almost half a football field and a fraction of Olu Park's space. Half the field was covered with pumpkins, laid out in rows encroaching upon the nearby woody forest. The opposite half stationed a few stands, benches and an outdoor wood patio. Select attendees came and went through a gated alleyway leading to an adjacent neighborhood. It lay just beyond an eco-friendly fence with a screen of climbing vines. Dazzling orange pearls strung from patio posts to the trees across the field. Its display brightened the area and made the place livelier than it admittedly was.

"So that's it huh?" Ibrahim mumbled.

"What?"

My name was called from a distance. It looked out and spotted Mrs. Miyamoto, flailing her arms at me. I made my way over and heard a second voice as I drew near.

"Wino. I didn't know you were coming, mijo." Fabiola stated, a cup of steaming tea in her hand.

"It's beautiful isn't it?" Mrs. Miyamoto fluttered her palms.

"Mijo where's Cheryl, your hermosa chica?

I attempted an explanation while Ibrahim made for the benches beneath the pergola. He sat by himself and planted his chin upon the table. He sat with his eyes He closed his eyes. His hands jostled awkwardly in his pockets.

***

Families took photos of their children grappling pumpkins almost as large as the kids. Guests inspected the pumpkins and some took to carving them with the tools left out at the benches.

Out amongst the patches where the elderly strolled with arms crossed behind their waists and couples kissed beneath the shower of fallen leaves, stood a man. He was wrapped in an all-black sweater, with a shawl veiling his lips, black slim jeans, and midnight black boots. He was slender and his hair draped over one eye. His back turned to Ibrahim and wavered calmly just like every other guest. He even bought a cup of Mrs. Miyamoto's green tea, placing it on the ground to retrieve a pumpkin.

As the evening went on, I regrouped with Ibrahim having snuck away from the two ladies. At her behest, I appeared with two complimentary green teas from the stand. My presence made no difference to Ibrahim who glared out at the pumpkin patch.

"You want to go out there?" I offered.

Ibrahim glanced at me with conviction in his eyes.

"No," he swiped the cup and took a sip. "There's something about that guy."

We watched as a blond woman in a cream jacket and fluffy brown boots made her way over to him. Ibrahim's wand glowed in his jacket pocket. A textbook technique, it echoed their conversation closer to us like a wiretap.

She stepped up to him asking, "D'you like that one?"

He turned to her, softly replying, "Yes, I do. It feels," he pondered, "full."

"If you like, you can take it," she offered. "We also have tools if you want to carve it up.

"Oh no," he replied. "I've never carved a pumpkin before."

"It's no problem." she cheerfully responded. "I used to carve pumpkins all the time as a kid. I can help you if you want?"

"How generous," he responded with his cold steel eyes falling to the pumpkin, "It's just that. What I meant by that was: I'm much more skilled at carving people up."

The woman froze, startled by his statement. The man stood with his eyes calmly locked with hers. At this moment, the woman must have deciphered his statement and timidly retracted from him. Her shuffling feet knocked over his tea, spilling it onto the adjacent bundle of leaves. Their voices were so quiet, that no one in the vicinity was drawn by their ominous conversation. In fact, the presence of a male and female must have lead people to assume they were a couple. It wasn't until the tattered wing of a crow spurted out from the shoulder blade of the man that people noticed he was on his own. The blond woman shivered in fear as her legs shuffled baby steps from him. She then fell over a pumpkin, squealing in terror. Her voice drew the crowd towards the situation and out rang screams and barks of a magician.

Ibrahim instinctually bounced over the bench. He yanked me behind Mrs. Miyamoto's stand. She hastily followed suit in a panic.

As a trio, we peeked around the corner as the man continued, "I apologize. I don't mean to frighten you." He appeared sad while snow-white bands streaked down his hair, dying it in the process. "It's just so hard living as a magician nowadays."

With this, the man drew his other arm across his chest, unleashing a second wing. The crowd dispersed, crying of a magician gone mad. The stampede flooded the streets and hid within the woods. People tugged at their children, their loved ones and their smartphones. Pumpkins splattered all over the floor, smearing thick tangerine globules over the scenic sunset orange fields. It was like an ink splotch on a painting; the kind that ruffled the skin as one passed their fingers over an artwork.

The magician towered over the terrorized volunteer. Her breath quivered in the sprinkling downfall of fall leaves, swept from their branches by the passing evening breeze. Like a jagged hook, the first wing anchored the magician as he rose. It suspended him above the tree line. With his crossed arm, his fingers clenched the other wing that refused to grow.ABodragging it slowly, erratic thorns snapped off and flung out into the crowd. They punctured the ground and devastated anything in their path. Then, in one swift motion, the magician ripped it out. In his hand, he bore a scythe. Its arched blade drifted across his torso. It reflected the moonlight upon his pale face, revealing eyes as red as a ruby gem.

"Guys," Mrs. Miyamoto squealed. "We have to get out of here."

Her voice trembled behind me. I turned to inspect the gated exit. The panic had flung it open, providing a direct path into the adjacent neighborhood where we could take refuge. The only problem was our number. Just the two of us would be a lot, but with Mrs. Miyamoto here, Ibrahim and I would certainly be spotted by the magician and targeted. Even worse, we might have escaped, but she might not have been fast enough. We were stuck behind her stand, obscured by the latticed pergola roof, or whatever remained of it.

I hated being in these situations. My mind raced. *Do we run? Can we make it? Can she make it? And what of the volunteer? Do I just take off and run?* The wheels kept turning until a stern voice shook me from my thoughts.

"Wino," Ibrahim called. His back faced me.

"Yeah?"

"You think he's noticed us?" His voice was still. Like a veteran, Ibrahim's heart and mind may have churned, but he strove to distill focus.

"No," I responded. "Not yet. But–"

"I think we can take 'em."

"Are you crazy?" I hunched over him. "We're not fighting this guy. We have to call the police."

"You do that and little miss pumpkin's a goner. Long before they get here."

I turned and witnessed Mrs. Miyamoto's panicked expression. Her eyes bounced between mine. At a glance, I spotted attendees huddling behind a mound of pumpkins in the distance. Guiding them was Fabiola, a silver Glock 9 millimeter in hand. She used her finger and hushed the members under her care as they witnessed their loved ones stranded amongst the fields. There was no clear path of escape for them. They clearly were to be prey of the magician following his descent upon the volunteer. Fabiola glanced over and we made eye contact. It hurt to see a friend like this, and it hurt even more to be powerless.

"Come on Wino," Ibrahim urged with distilled resolve. "We can take this guy."

In the distance, the crooked limb crackled as it undulated in the breeze. A cold stare descended from the magician as he ushered soft words to console the woman.

"This life," he said. "Is just not fit for us magicians."

"Oh my god," the girl uttered in hysteria. "I'm going to die."

"Yup," Ibrahim grumbled. "Unless *someone* decides to make-a-move."

I turned to him. His profile glowed in the moonlight. An unwavering conviction shone through his eye, glaring at the magician. In all my attempts at revitalizing our nostalgic past, none struck a chord so piercingly as the determination in Ibrahim's eye. A violet hue gleamed from his pocket. I watched as its light rose and fell in this nightmarish twilight.

Ibrahim retracted from the corner stating, "We could wait for the police if that's what you want to do."

"No," I instinctively responded, gesturing closer to him. "Let's fight him."

This provoked a smirk in the corner of Ibrahim's mouth. He stuffed his hand into his pocket and withdrew his wand. Mrs. Miyamoto watched with mouth opening shock as we made our way around the patio.

"Get to safety when you can," I commanded her and headed out.

"Although, I admire The General's effort," the magician spoke as he arched nearer to the girl. His arm rose towards the moon behind him. "We were not meant to live as captives, as it were."

The razor-sharp blade of his scythe gleamed along its crescent. A crooked smile rippled across his face. The maniacal magician swung his scythe over the girl carving a "C" with his strike.

The woman flinched. Next, she'd probably expect to feel the blade splitting her. It's blade driving into her flesh and tearing her asunder.

His blade delved into the material, puncturing it but failing to splice it into two. The magician struck a pumpkin. His eyes flapped, trying to correct the false image. This was supposed to be her head right, but the woman lay beside the pumpkin. Her arms were thrown over her face in reflex. They withdrew to behold the failed strike with as much bewilderment as the magician.

"You sure bout all that?" Ibrahim called. The magician glanced towards him. "Cus some of you aught to be rounded up and caged." Ibrahim strolled towards the man, leaves crunching beneath his every step. The magician analyzed Ibrahim, retracting from the girl as Ibrahim came to a halt. "Bring a bad name to the rest of us."

His eyes wander towards Ibrahim's wand. Calmness swept over him.

I watched from the man's rear as he retracted into an upright position. The woman glanced over towards me, a similar panic to Mrs. Miyamoto's. I hushed her and motioned her to come towards me. All eyes on were on me: Mrs. Miyamoto's, Fabiola's and the onlookers – all except for the magician.

"An artifact," the man responded.

"Yeah, so what? Don't start thinking I'm one of you." Ibrahim responded.

The woman shuffled towards me, creeping as gently as she possibly could.

"Oh? But you are." The magician responded with a smirk. "The General would have your head if only she knew that which you held."

The woman made it to me and I drew her up. She clung to my flannel shirt. We panicked as to which way we should go.

"Too bad she's never gonna find out."

The man smiled, "Spoken like a true magician."

The woman and I made for Fabiola's group that motioned for us to approach behind the stack of pumpkins. Outstretched, the magician's scythe jousted towards us. We froze. His back faced us. The sharpened edge glowed in the moonlight.

"And just who are these two to you?"

"I've no idea who the girl is." Ibrahim shrugged.

"And the other?"

Ibrahim maintained his silence. Out stepped Fabiola from behind the stack, gun drawn and blasting a few rounds at the magician. I grabbed the volunteer and escorted her. We pounced over pumpkins in a frantic charge. Fabiola's gang waved hurriedly for us to rush. The magician swung his weapon, twirling it to splinter the barrage of bullets. I shouldered the girl from the deflected shrapnel. Ibrahim seized the opportunity to withdraw his wand, the orb gleaming with the Witch's violet aura. I glanced out the corner of my eye to see the magicians standing off.

Their weapons clashed in a brilliant white-hot explosion scattering crystalline shards as debris. The screech of their strikes was that of two samurai katanas followed by the deafening explosion of cannon fire. It was a concerto of magical warfare.

The volunteer eventually made it to Fabiola's gang. I spun around and spotted more onlookers too afraid to make the journey. Instinctively, I ran to gather them. One by one, they trickled along the piles of leaves, between barren tree branches and across the pumpkin patch.

Ibrahim danced with the magician, exchanging earth-shattering blows; the shockwaves of whom tumbled over the pumpkin heads, flung gusts of leaves skyward and threw escapees into a stumble. Despite the immense danger presented, I started to feel at home with the scene. It was as if, watching Ibrahim duel a magician was almost comforting – nostalgic.

The magician flung Ibrahim back towards the pavilion. In a crouch, Ibrahim skid along the moist grass, shuffling to a halt.

"Nothing worse than a tamed magician," the man

spat.

Ibrahim furrowed his brows, as violet light filled his eyes.

He growled, "I already told you that I'm not one of you."

With this, Ibrahim's wand glowed. He jousted it towards the magician and out gushed a golden glimmering stream. It struck the blade of the man and the impact generated an earthquake that propelled me into the trees. The forest flew past me until I plopped onto the ground. The impact rattled me. I fell unconscious. Time slowed. Like an energetic child tugged to a seat sternly by their guardian, I was wrestled to silence. The evening breeze swept over my face and the darkness of my eyelids brought me to a sudden halt.

***

During this down period, I could see the finale to my nightmare. The encroaching flames receded from me. They parted and Ibrahim emerged in his royal regalia. Arm outstretched and confidence in his eyes, he yanked me out past the searing flames and into a free fall over the cliff. Despite the impending danger below, the dazzling city lights took me in across the twilight cityscape. The wind rushed past my ears and my pounding heart raced. All worries left me. For as long as I lived in Ibrahim's care, I just knew everything would be all right. I embraced the torrent of roaring winds, the adrenaline rush and the potential life-ending consequences such a decision I made. I knew little of the intricacies of magic usage, but I did know that I trusted Ibrahim with my life. We fell for a few seconds longer before the dreamscape faded to black. Black oceans overflowed from the horizon. They swallowed the dreamscape and the world collapsed.

***

After an unspecified amount of time, I heard sirens singing in the air. The fall leaves not yet jettisoned reflected a red and blue tinge at their tips. Groggily, my vision came to and I hazily recalled the preceding events. People were in danger, Ibrahim fought the magician and I did my part of escorting them out. But then, it looked as if I was left in the fire alone.

I climbed to a seat against a nearby tree and discovered the battle site. Pumpkins were launched nearly as far as me, their skulls punctured or even worse melted from the blistering energy of the impact. There were no attendees left, only military personal strutting about the taped off park.

Upon the ground crept a spiny creature, whose limbs jutted out in all directions. It was like a conglomeration of all the fallen branches into an anthropomorphic monstrosity. It was the maniac. They had seized the magician. This meant the others made it out. To my right, scoured officers with flashlights, flooding the forest as they searched for survivors or accomplices.

I attempted to make it up to my feet but my head spun. I wobbled on my arms until plummeting back onto the tree. It was too difficult and I couldn't muster the strength.

Suddenly, a hand shook me.

It was violent and an accompanying voice called out, "Wino, Wino!"

A shadowy silhouette skidded in front of me. Its eyes shone like a cat, the moonlight hiding behind its face. "Come on," it said. "Let's get the heck out of here."

"I can't," I groggily protested.

It didn't listen. The violet-eyed creature yanked

me up to my feet, energy engorging my body from toe to hair tip. It dragged me through the forest, around the floodlights, and onto the street.

We made it beyond the taped-off perimeter of the search area and onto the asphalt of the road. I still struggled to keep up but was tugged by the arm at all times as we escaped the eyes of the police. Suddenly, we crossed the street, under the flickering light of the broken streetlamp. Its struggling bulb grew alight and I spotted the beanie Ibrahim had worn earlier that evening.

He glanced back at the scene with his shining eyes and huffed, "They're not following us. Let's keep going." He released my arms and we jogged down the road back to The U. As we made it towards the courtyard, he giggled, eventually howling, "Not gonna lie. That was fun. Just like old times!"

It went nothing like I had planned, but at least I could say that I lead the adventure today. It really was just like old times.

The End.

EPISODE 11: BIONICA

Soft-soled boots stepped over the crunchy carpet of the office. A uniformed man, bearing his beret pressed against his breast stepped up to wooden door with a one-way glazed screen. He flew his arms, submitting his self for inspection. Another officer twirled in his chair. He climbed from his cubicle and patted the man down.

"Oh boy", the inspector huffed. "Here comes the bearer of bad news." He retracted from his comrade. Using his thumb, he gestured the man to enter.

"Hey, I'm just doing my job," the soldier responded.

"No but seriously, we appreciate you guys. She's going to love to hear this."

"Much obliged." He pulled his beret on snug, tipping it as he nodded to the cubicle guards. He palmed the door open and marched into a dim boardroom full of high-ranking officers in military regalia. The air was stuffy, like they'd been there all morning. His intrusion broke their conversation and demanded the stern attention of these grumpy officers.

"Officer Gale, reporting sir."

The men turned towards the head of the table. Here, The General masked her chin behind her interlocking fingers.

"This had better be good," she responded.

"Yes ma'am! At exactly 0600 hours, delta squad apprehended the rogue magician formally known as The Blue Bandit ma'am!" The General paused. Her stoicism scrutinized by the men for any slip of expression. "As we speak, he is being taken into custody."

"That's the best news I've heard all morning," The General responded. "I think this calls for a celebration don't you gentlemen?" The roundtable broke into smirks and scoffs as The General rose to her feet. "Let's prepare for his arrival then."

"Yes ma'am!" they respond.

***

The sun-kissed sands of the outlands surfed along the horizon. The grains hurdled over the jagged terrain. A caravan lied scattered like an off-road jeep, shattered and battered upon the dusty ground. The area was predominantly inhabited by scarce and scattered vegetation. These blooming bouquets consisted of deep-sea blue shrubs, turquoise berries, variegated zebra-stripe cacti, and skyscraping palms that lied marred by a sea of golden brown clay and ember laterite soil. Glittering wisps of topsoil wafted over the jagged crevices and creaking wheels of the demolished vehicle. Planks and splintered wood jutted out from the blood-stained blanket.

The hooves of a huffing beast trampled over splattered wreckage, weaving a trail of carnage over the terrain. Gusts of grains washed the transient footprints away. Atop its back rode an ecstatic Neanderthal. The beast, like an expired Spinosaurus, drifted to a halt revealing the hazel-eyed, Mohawk wearing, bandit. He sat with his torso clad in armor plates, fox-fur boots, a bear-hide skirt wrapped about his lower body and finally an extensively engraved medallion dangling from his neck. Centered within the necklace glints a turquoise opal. The horizon descended behind him as his medallion gleamed like the underside of a churning furnace. It's a blinding solar flare. This light rose and fell in tune with the hue of his passionate eyes. In conjunction, the beast beneath him huffed from its snout. It encircled the wreckage in a creeping motion.

Out stepped a soldier before the snarling animal. She marched into the center of its swirling encroachment. The beast rider crackled his tribal-tatted knuckles, gripped his bronze trident spear, tugged upon the leather harness and fixated his gaze upon the officer. She stood fearless before him. Clad in a uniform constructed of derived metallic textile alloys, her chest puffed out and boots skidded apart. The faceless officer hid behind a biker's helmet accented with ominous strings of twirling LED lights upon the faceplate. From head to toe, her suit enclosed her person. The only exception was her occipital lobe, exposing two coiled, hot-pink puffballs of hair.

Amongst the wreckage, a squad of soldiers and hunters lied groaning in agony. They tossed and tumbled, gripping at their battered and bloodied headscarves, khussa shoes, and drenched ember robes as if for dear life.

The beast rider approached cautiously, observing the officer, as still as a leaf upon a tranquil lake. Her head tracked him silently. With increasing tension, the bandit thwacked his companion barking, *"Hiya"*, and prompting it to charge her. The four-legged animal, like an expired dinosaur, howls. It bounded over the dusty wasteland, accelerating towards her. Atop its back, the rider waved his spear like a roman chariot with his flag.

She sprinted towards him in response. Her fists clenched together, as the charge dawned upon her. She hopped –– arms first, as if diving onto the rider. He jousted at her helmet scuffing her face. The officer knotted a wire about the bandit's throat. Her legs rolled overhead as it drew tight. The string pressed into his pharynx. She flipped onto the ground, the cord drawn by the stampeding beast. Snagged, the rider whisked from his seat with a hydraulics-reinforced tug, throwing him across the wasteland. He flopped upon the red-baked sea opposite his unruly companion.

The beast scurried off into the distance, encircling its trail as if reconsidering its retreat. The soldier tracked the animal before dismissing its potential as a threat. She faced the squirming miscreant.

He scratched at his throat in a futile attempt to grip the nearly invisible spider-thread. It threatened to decapitate him. The soldier drew her index finger upon her forearm presenting a message: *Calling Base.* The bandit glared at the silent officer standing before him, her face veiled behind the accent lights that darted not only across her screen but extended all over her suit.

Eventually, a voice projected into the atmosphere, "I'm guessing that's a catch. We're sending backup and medics. You sit tight."

The encased officer strutted beside the miscreant. He scanned her callous demeanor unfettered. She towered over him, amused by his discomfort. She made for the downed officers. Pressing into their wrists, she confirmed the kill count and sorted them into two piles.

Shortly after, the sirens of The General's Police Force rang into earshot. The conflict took less than a minute once the woman arrived. Whoever this machine was, she threatened the whole realm of magicians.

***

Cheryl paddled her fair-skinned feet, submerged ankle-high within a pond of crystal clear water. Her toes flicked past one another as she grazed her legs past one another. Her denim jeans rolled up to her knees. The sleeves of her magenta and black flannel shirt reached her elbows.

She reclined over the forest floor huffing a sigh of relief. "This feels a-ma-zing."

"You could say that again." Wino responded.

Wino cheerily parked his hiking gear adjacent Cheryl's. He strolled over, matching her shirt but wearing cargo shorts to join her.

"This feels a-ma-zing!" Cheryl sang, giggling in her response. "We should do this more often."

"It certainly is nice to get out of the city every once in a while," he added, untying his hiker's boots.

Sinking his feet into the pond, Wino mimicked Cheryl's sigh, uplifting an abdominal groan from his belly.

"I know right?" she confirmed. "It's like an oasis in the forest."

"The General keeps such a tight lid on things, you'd think more people would come out here."

The couple lied on the crunchy forest floor surrounded by towering pine trees. These trees littered the sky and jettisoned clusters of dark chocolate seeds upon the ground. There's no trail behind the couple, suggesting that they wandered off the path. It rewarded them handsomely, as the two shared a moment of meditative quiet.

Cheryl lifted her gaze skyward. Wino locked his elbows inward, dropping his upper body weight upon the tripod of his arms and his hips. Birds tweeted a harmonious melody as critters scampered along the shaded halls of the wilderness.

"I could stay here forever," Wino said.

"We definitely found a great spot."

"Yeah, I—— wait, do you see that?"

Cheryl lazily cocked her head towards her significant other, scanning her surroundings with a smirk on her face.

"It looks like…"

Wino squinted towards the center of the wall of trees, climbing meters from the ground. Suddenly, yodeling chimed in accompanied by the screech of a hawk.

Cheryl jolted her fingertip skyward. "Is that what you're talking about?"

A charcoal silhouette stood midway along a branch. Behind it, a hawk encircled the forest floor from on high. Upon the branch, Ibrahim stood bare-chested, inked tribal marks stroked across his cheeks. He dawned cargo shorts, a halo of twigs and associated berries, and a mossy vine in hand. He regressed, as he gripped tighter upon the hanging vine.

"Look out below!" he sang, charging towards the ledge.

"Oh no." Wino grumbled hysterically. "Oh no no no."

Wino retracted his feet from the pond. Cheryl scrambled to rise from the water, clawing at the carpet grass with her gaze fixed on the descending Ibrahim. He plummeted like a cannon ball, accelerating rapidly, as he dove towards the ground.

"There's not enough water," Wino said.

Ibrahim withdrew his wand, He conjured a concave pan, larger than his body and sat on it. He plunged into the pool. Up climbed a hurricane of water, hurling Wino towards his hiking materials and blanketing Cheryl within a sheet of liquid diamond.

In its aftermath, hanging leaves channeled excess water along their tips. Beading drops dripped off like a running faucet. The forest floor soaked with mud accumulating into brown water puddles. Stacks of leaves assembled, masking sunken pits in broad daylight. Cheryl and Wino were washed ashore. Their clothes hung drenched over their clammy skin as they shivered in the frosty mist.

Cheryl peeled herself from a woody log hollowed by beavers. She clung to it in the wave like a boat-wreck survivor washed into sweeping currents. As she rose, she detected Wino, also recovering from his collision with their hiking equipment. The two met eyes before glaring at the pond. Within this crater sat Ibrahim. He smiled from inside the pit and eagerly waved at Wino.

"Now *that* was fun."

***

At The U, a crowd of city residents swarmed the courtyard. It's a second for the apartment complex, the first being its grand opening. Since then, occupants never exceeded that record. The city's blue bus pulled up along the curb. Out climbed the trio, arriving home from their hiking trip.

Wino and Cheryl emerged first –– visibly grumpy and littered with deep green foliage, twigs, and mud stains. They stomped onto the pavement, ruffling with their luggage slung over their backs. Behind them came Ibrahim. Stepping into the doorway of the bus, he's starstruck. Ibrahim's eyes peeled wide open at the human herd. Without any luggage, he slowly strolled down the steps of the bus. The trio weaved about the maze; Cheryl carved a path, as the men tail her. Ibrahim peered between a heart-shaped conjoining of two couples as their chins closed together for a kiss. He detected a podium stationed just before the entrance of The U. As they moved closer, Wino approached Cheryl, closing the distance between them.

"Do you know what's going on?" he asked.

"Not a clue."

The double doors opened to The U. Ibrahim turned to see Cheryl and Wino already inside. As Ibrahim made his way into the corridor, a delegation of officers marched past. Like a procession, two armed soldiers led a small ensemble beyond the doorway. Caught off guard, Ibrahim glared at them. His breathing halted. His expression froze. Visibly unfettered, he continued past the business execs accompanying the procession.

Centered within this flock, marched The General herself. She snagged Ibrahim's attention. Like a bubble or a magnetic field projected about her person, she struck him electrically. A chill quivered down his body, causing a misstep. The General casually guided this parade into the waiting courtyard crowd. Her beret stood meticulously puffed, a freshly pressed uniform fit snugly atop her sturdy frame, polished boots swayed sequentially, and she wore an air of confidence. On either side, she commanded the attention of the businessmen and women. She generated a lethal aura reverberating within the atmosphere. What was truly three seconds translated into a minute for the magician caught so close. Considering the lingering aftereffects of her impression, the realization lasted about a minute total. Enough time for Ibrahim to miss his elevator, catch another one, and recap what just happened.

He's alone.

The meter counted up the floors as he muttered. "That's The General. But did she just see me?"

As Ibrahim crossed paths with The General, he did manage to capture her presence rooted within the proceeding crowd. But despite all the focus directed towards her, The General glanced out the corner of her eye detecting him as well. Her detection skills were likely more mature than Ibrahim's; however, it's also plausible that he projected some of his spirit upon her. As Ibrahim entered the doorway to The U just then, he harmlessly scanned the exiting group until electrified. Her inspection, however, was directed precisely towards him. The General watched Ibrahim as he turned the corner, returning her focus onto the congregation stationed within The U's courtyard as she emerged.

***

The elevator dinged and Wino's door slid open. Cheryl flopped her pack upon the carpet, unzipping it as Wino entered from the bathroom. Ibrahim drew their attention. Quietly, he paced towards the paneled windows. He yanked the curtains closed, exposing only one eye between them. The couple exchanged glances before returning to Ibrahim. Wino drew near, tapping Ibrahim's shoulder.

"Um, Ibrahim? What's going o–?"

"Shut up, Wino!" Ibrahim hissed.

"Isn't The General out there?" Cheryl asked defiantly.

Unresponsive, Ibrahim continued to monitor the situation. Wino slipped beneath the curtain, draping it over his neck to accompany his roommate.

Along Ménage Boulevard, a fleet of armored, turret-fitted, jet-black vans screeched to a halt. They parked across the street, triangulated about a central vehicle. Out poured squads of dutifully armed soldiers. They encircled the armored van. A latch released, compressed air squeals into the atmosphere, and a caged trunk rattled open.

Barefoot and scantily dressed in tattered animal skin, soldiers dragged the bandit from the wasteland onto the concrete. They restrained him -- one cuff encircling his torso with three connecting chains drawn by squad members. They also cuffed his wrists and his Mohawk descended into wavy, slumped strands. The General's soldiers guided him through the courtyard. Guests hollered chants, cheers, and boos at him. He slumped into every step, heaving with his head hanging over his knees. The crowd divided, encircling him as he proceeded towards the podium.

"Who is that?" Wino asked.

"A magician," Ibrahim solemnly responded.

The General climbed up to the podium, the bandit knelt at the foot of the block.

"Ladies and gentlemen," she started. "It is with honor that I stand before you today to announce that we have finally apprehended the Blue Bandit."

The crowd jubilated, arms thrown skyward, and a round of applause gestured for the General.

"For months, this man has terrorized innocent travelers, caravans, and even my own soldiers as they traveled from one city to another. But his reign of terror has come to an end and the law has caught up with him. This man, like many others, was enticed. A rare relic tempted him."

The General raised his studded medallion to the amusement of the crowd.

"This. This medallion is another rare artifact, one that granted him immense, unbridled power. Unfortunately, he, like many others, was unable to tame it and so it tamed him. There are two things that we should take away from this experience. One is that magic and those that practice its arts face severe consequences for any mishappenings anywhere. And rest assured," she turns towards the criminal growling, "you will be dealt with."

This display of aggression prompted chanting and cheers from the crowd, and another round of applause swept over the congregation. Wino glanced out the corner of his eye towards Ibrahim, who watched silently. After all this time, Ibrahim's true emotions still eluded Wino. It's just as Ibrahim watched the news the night of the Witch. *What does he think of this? What does he feel?* Cheryl shifted towards the pair from the center of the living room.

***

A soldier stepped up beside the podium. She stood at Parade Rest –– with arms crossed behind her back and feet shoulder with apart. Her desert cream vest matched her jacket above military cargo pants and boots. The brim of her hat nearly veiled her eyes. Two hot-pink puffballs hung beneath her hat like pigtails.

"And two," the General resumed, prompting the soldier to unlink her arms and trigger her suit.

The very stitches of her uniform refabricated into

polymer chains, forming a skin-tight bodysuit culminating in a turtleneck just below her jaw. It resembled a biker's suit with elliptical pads bracing her knees, ankles, hips and other joints, accentuating creases detailed with ambient light strips and a glossy carbon fiber finish. The overall design was sleek, black, and strung together as one piece, like a luxury sports car. Crowd members jumped to climb over one another. They snapped selfies, took videos, and attempted to graze the augmented super-soldier. Her subordinates stablished a human shield, fencing the onlookers behind them and containing the bewildered viewers.

"I present you with ADEX, the first fully functional human-augmenting super-suit. It's self-repairing, absorbs nearly all forms of magic energy, it's lightweight, sturdy, and it's eco-friendly. Once again, my team has demonstrated our resolve to overcome unruly magicians and protect those that would otherwise have been left to their own means of self-defense. We have displayed our willingness to strive for justice everywhere and our dedication towards a free and fair world; a world where everyone has the opportunity to achieve greatness and not one where someone can take greatness and brandish it to compensate for their insecurities."

Cheryl, Wino, and Ibrahim towered meters over the congregations. Not a word uttered between them. The rustling of Cheryl's bag as it slumps onto the ground prompted no response.

"Lastly, let this be a warning to anyone who would threaten the sanctity of our way of life. We will stop at nothing to protect what we have from those that would see to it that we are left begging for our basic human rights. We're not scared, and we dare you to come at us."

The soldier's hat refabricated into her helmet, completing the transformation. This, along with the conclusion of The General's speech, yielded a resounding round of applause. Suited executives of The U watched from the doorway, clapping in support as chants climbed over the audience. Camera crews broadcasted the overall enthusiasm before signing off.

***

Upstairs, Ibrahim peeled away from the windowpane. Wino tailed him.

Cheryl gasped, "Wow. She's amazing."

Before Wino emerged from the curtains, Cheryl clutched at his wrist. With a glimmer in her eye, she inquired, "Did you see that? Her suit just popped out of nowhere."

"It looks like they've been working on it for a while now," Wino responded.

Turning back to the courtyard, Cheryl added, "I bet that cost a fortune to build. Magicians better watch out."

Wino slipped beyond the curtains into the living room. He spotted the front door sliding to a near close as Ibrahim's silhouette disappeared behind it.

***

Downtown, atop a skyscraping glass office building, cubicle workers typed away at their documents. The elevator door dinged open. In walked Ibrahim, twigs, figs, and leaves dangling from his person as he strutted along the center aisle. Within the conference room before him, danced shadows of board directors discussing the future of their company. An ongoing presentation stirred discussion as the room lights dimmed and the shades drew along the windowpanes. Ibrahim tugged open the door, slipping inside as it closed behind him.

Within the room, the light penetrated as it would any other day. There was no presenter, no executives or discussion. The gray office chairs were neatly tucked along the barren polished oak table – all except for one.

Ibrahim made for the conference table. "Did you see that?"

"Could you miss it?" her voice responded as she twirled around in her seat. The Witch casually crosses one leg over the other as she gazed out the windows. "She called us out."

"You think she meant all of us, or?"

"Or what? Who else is there?" The Witch rocked from her seat, crossing her arms. "Us. You and me and the big guy."

"But what if she meant every magician, not just us three?" Ibrahim asked.

"I'm sure there were others on her list, but she was definitely thinking about us."

"So what are we doing?"

"How many options remain?" The brutish Whitesmith emerged from behind Ibrahim. The man plopped onto a seat. "We provide that which she seeks most."

"A war," the Witch responded.

Facing table, the Witch retrieved and unraveled a large map bearing a satellite snapshot of the city. The trio gathered around the plan.

"You ready to get back in the game?" she asked Ibrahim.

Following his nod, the Whitesmith grumbled, "I certainly hope so."

"Stop," the Witch rebuked. "He's the reason you got out alive."

"False. See, I had prepared a thorough exit plan from which—"

"Yeah right." The Witch grinned with the Whitesmith. Turning to Ibrahim, she continued. "So, you up for another break out?"

"We're getting more magicians?" Ibrahim asked.

"Yup. I found you out something."

Above her map of the city, the Witch undulates her fingers, raising her wrist towards the ceiling. Her motion elevated a violet wireframe overlay. The vibrating electrical projection revealed a network of subsurface roads with routes culminating into clusters beneath parks, offices, and city service buildings. The ensemble decentralized like levitating calligraphy disconnected at the hinges.

"What is this?" Ibrahim inquired.

"This," the Witch responded. "Is where your friends are locked up; it's where *this* guy was headed to until we saved him, and it's where we're going to recruit backup."

"They're containment units," the Whitesmith elaborated. "Individually constructed to nullify a magician's techniques."

Ibrahim's lips pursed at the sight of the hologram, brows slightly furrowed, and eyes glared deep into the projection. His fingers clenched his wand tightly, tucking in close to his hips.

"And look at this." The Witch drew her index towards a gap between two corridors. "There's no way to go from one cell to another."

"So we must coordinate," the Whitesmith concluded.

"But why are we saving these scrubs?" Ibrahim inquired. "They already got caught."

His companions paused momentarily.

"Do you want to fight that thing yourself?" The Witch asked.

Ibrahim jousted his wand towards her. "Try me."

"Cybernetic monstrosity will shred you to tattered bits, sprout," the Whitesmith warned.

"Call me that again and I'll dunk you six feet under."

"Take your best shot."

The Witch interceded, "It's not just about that cyborg. This is about The General. I mean, aren't you sick of this place?"

Ibrahim's fury dwindled as his focus descended to the hologram. His fingers ruffled his wand as his lips relaxed.

"I know I am." She answered.

The Whitesmith added, "We live with clipped wings, branded bodies, and shackled ankles. No life for a magician."

"Exactly. I've had it with The General and her city. That's why when we break those *scrubs* out, it's every magician for herself." The witch displays her signature crooked grin.

Ibrahim glanced at her. "I thought you wanted to run this place."

"I did, but this city's her core. We break her here–"

"Then it's only a matter of time before the others fall the same," the Whitesmith concluded.

Within the boardroom, the Witch's ethereal wireframe image disintegrated into a dispersing swarm of butterflies with crystal trails. They fluttered into the plaster walls, disappearing behind them. The Witch and the Whitesmith gazed at Ibrahim with varying degrees of interest.

"So, you in?"

"I think he's grown far too attached," The Whitesmith audibly whispered. "This life's tamed him" prompting a stern glare from Ibrahim.

Ibrahim's resolve shined through his eyes. He replied, "When are we doing this?"

***

Later that evening, Ibrahim spread over the living room couch. One leg dangled onto the floor while he stared blankly into a news report on TV. Bags hung under his eyes while the ambient glow from his wand highlighted them from underneath. Wino's bedroom slid open to him chatting on his phone while heading towards the kitchen.

As he reached Ibrahim, he paused. "Alright, I'll see you tomorrow. Love you. That's all they've shown since this afternoon." He continued towards the kitchen.

"It's on all the channels. Some of them don't even show news on a regular day but they're talking about it."

"Yeah, because the whole city's talking about it. How many times have you see-"

Ibrahim whipped over the couch. "But if she hates magic so much, how come she's using it? It's not just tech running that cyborg y'know?"

"Oh. Well, I don't think she hates magic."

"Yeah, just magicians." Ibrahim slid down the sofa.

Wino approached the living room, taking a seat with a plate of deviled eggs.

"Come on, Ibrahim. Without it, no one can handle yo– the magicians. You have to fight fire with fire."

"That's stupid, you'll just set the whole city on

fire."

"It's a metaphor."

"It's a stupid metaphor."

Ibrahim stretched his arm, swiping a deviled egg from Wino's plate. The news reporter interviewed a soldier from the force on TV.

She started, "So officer, what can you tell us about this new, uh, super suit? Cyborg? I don't even know what to call it. What do you call it?"

A uniformed soldier seated within his office responded, "Yes, well, you can call it whatever you like. We've heard cyborg, robot, augmented human, and the like. I personally like to call her *Bionica*. That's a little inside joke between us."

His lips curled into a smile beneath his combed mustache as he wheezed in laughter.

The news reporter asks, "And what does this mean for the force? I mean is this something that eventually every soldier will have?"

"I hope not," Ibrahim grumbled.

The reporter continued. "Should we expect to see, cyborgs running the city in the near future and what does this mean for magicians?"

"Well, I hope so," the soldier responded. "I'd love to get me one of them too. But, in all seriousness, that particular uniform, just that one, cost the department a pretty penny. So, it'll be a while before people can expect to see more of them. As for the magicians, as for *all* criminals really, this should be a warning. If any of you watching this, have yet to turn in your artifacts or magical equipment, you still have time. There's a number you can call or a box in front of every office where you can just drop your equipment. Often times, you can get a reward to encourage others. So it's never too late. We've had many people show up and turn in their artifacts and they left with cash in hand."

Wino glanced towards Ibrahim.

The man continued, "So don't be afraid. And as for those of you that seek to endanger everyone else's personal safety for your individual gain or for fun, you've seen what The General has in her arsenal. The moment you decide to fight her or her police force, she's gon use it."

Ibrahim frowned at the reporter and soldier image as they playfully discussed the cyborg. Wino glanced between the screen and Ibrahim. He hovered his egg before his lips.

Eventually, he inquired, "So what do you think?"

Ibrahim retained his focus on the TV. "I think it's stupid."

"You think a lot of things are stupid."

"'Cus they are."

"But what about your wand?"

"What of it, Wino?"

"He said you could make a lot of money for it."

"I'm not handing it over to that war maniac."

"So are you going to join the police force then?

"You try'na say something, Wino?"

"Didn't you see the Bionica?"

"So? Let them build a hundred of them. I'm not scared."

"You're not invincible, Ibrahim."

Ibrahim sprung up from his seat, glaring at Wino. He was speechless, but passionately gripping his wand.

"Even you have your limits." Wino persisted.

"What does that mean?"

"It means." Wino flicked a glance towards the TV. The headline read *Cash Reward for Artifacts. Call number.* His voice dwindled. "Maybe you should consider turning it in. You'll get money for it and–"

"Did you forget that I took care of you when we were traveling?"

"I know but–"

Ibrahim leaned towards Wino. He rasied his voice, "That I gave you *everything* you needed and never complained *once*?"

"But that was then and now–"

"Or that I helped every single person that we ever met with my own magic? All because you asked me to."

"But now The General's doing that. And she's got a whole army."

"So what? Where was she and *her army* when we were saving the world, two times?"

"I don't know. But she's here now. And I don't think you can stand up to her," Wino defiantly responded, his gaze grazed the carpet.

Ibrahim stood erect, pausing for a moment over Wino's claim. "Really?" Ibrahim angled towards the TV. With a cold stare, his pupils dilated with a deep purple hue polluting his iris. The TV buzzed as the image flickered. He raised his wand. The screen imploded. LCD chips splattered within the thin black frame.

Wino leapt to his feet squealing Ibrahim's name. His plate flopped onto the sofa, staining it with smeared Hors d'oeuvre.

He clawed at the TV screen, crying, "What're you doing?"

Calmly, Ibrahim lunged up to Wino.

The latter being slightly taller, Ibrahim looked up

to him and in a gentle yet stern tone, growled, "We'll see about that."

He then spun and strutted out the doorway. Wino stood in the chaotic aftermath of the detonation. Ibrahim disappeared into the hallway, as neighboring residents reeled open their doors to the sound of the explosion. The found Wino standing flushed, tomato-red, arms layered atop his head and visibly flustered.

The End

EPISODE 12: BREAKING SILENCE

Wino's front door opened to a casually dressed Cheryl, dawning a crimson dress with three-quarter sleeves, leather wristwatch, and a pearly pawprint necklace. She slipped into the living room knocking on the door behind her as it closed.

"Knock knock," she sang.

The early morning sun broke into streams of glittering dust particles beyond the fluttering curtains as the rustling of the AC rumbled into the air.

Cheryl motioned further inside to the call of Wino's melancholic voice, "Almost ready."

"Okay," she answered, scanning the room.

Cheryl attempted to have a seat until she discerned the current state of the TV. She hopped back to her feet, exclaiming, "Whoa!"

Wino calmly emerged from his bedroom buttoning his flannel shirt.

"What happened to the TV?"

Wino mumbled an inaudible response, as he attempted to find his words.

"Did it explode?" Cheryl asked.

"I think it imploded," he responded. "Since all the pieces are still inside. Oh, and I spilled food on the couch. I tried to clean it up but…"

"How? What happened? Was it Ibrahim?"

Wino lowered his head, capturing and buttoning the final notch. He glances at the TV, speechless.

"Were you hurt?"

"No."

"You missed a button," she added, prompting Wino to toss the tail of his shirt, allowing it to hang. He sighed, frustrated.

Cheryl approached him as he whined, "Can we just stay inside today? I really don't feel like going out."

Cheryl corrected his mis-buttoned shirt as she softly inquired, "After yesterday, you asked him about his wand again, didn't you?"

"Yeah, and he got angry and blew up my freakin' TV."

"And after?"

"He walked out the door."

"Has he come back since?"

"No." Having adjusted his shirt, Wino reeled away from Cheryl into his room. "And he's not staying here anymore unless he gets rid of it. I'm tired of him pushing me around."

"What if he says no?" Cheryl asked. "What if he threatens you?" This prompted a questionable gaze from Wino. "I'm just saying," she added. "He may not want to give up his wand. And what if he says he's staying here?"

"I'll make him," Wino responded. "Either he turns his wand in or he's getting out."

"So you'd call the police then?"

Wino paused. His hand slid off his dresser.

"Because that's the only way I can see you getting him to leave. Besides Nedu, you are the only one he knows in this city. But if he doesn't listen to you, then you have to cut him off, or else he'll drag you down with him."

"I know." Wino sighed.

"So you'll do it?"

Following a pause, Wino responded, "If he forces me to, then yes."

Wino centered on Cheryl. Fear gripped at his expression, as worry adorned her own. The two shared the silent moment.

"I just want you to be safe. He is a magician after all."

Hearing the squeaking of the city bus from the roadside before The U, Wino answered, "I know." He swiped his room key off the counter and made for the door. He commanded, "Come on, let's go."

***

A scalding sunrise burned over the horizon. A towering office building bisected its gleaming light. At its base stationed an underground car park. The entrance saw little traffic, but on this particular day, it didn't expecting any visitors. The gate opened for a bulletproof armored van to descend into the darkness beneath the building. It was a remote corner of town with no outlet for cars and no paths for pedestrians, only a cul-de-sac for tall office blocks. As such, the space was barren with little to no activity at the ground level.

Despite this, one onlooker approached the desolate area, marching along the center of the asphalt gray street. From his hand, dangled a silver mallet, its studded head swinging in tune with his arm.

***

In a separate portion of the city, The General's officers rounded up their work. Half the office spaces stationed soldiers dismantling their equipment, returning their weapons and artifacts while others suited up for the evening shift.

They undressed before their lockers, chatted about their days and any plans for the evening. Beyond the wall of their lockers were the desk workers, restocking supplies, dispatching units, and monitoring city cameras. Both their private and public security services funded the force while granting them access to nearly every system within the city.

This was truly The General's stronghold. Despite the volume of employees, this particular unit was not police HQ. As such, The General herself was not present. Instead, she appeared periodically to monitor progress, tally artifact quantities, and boost unit morale.

From the dressing room, emerged a bronze-skinned black woman with hot-pink puffy ponytail balls at the back of her head. She strutted out in pink sneakers and snug, black shorts. She stuffed her head into her shirt, drawing a long-sleeved black compression shirt, with tessellated gray diamonds across her torso. A fellow officer emerged from his office, stepping into her path.

"Bianca's off to the gym?" he sang, his combed mustache wiggling over his lips.

"Yup."

"You really ought to take a day off, y'know?"

"I can handle it." She cheerfully responded, "I'm not complaining yet."

"I know you can. I'm just looking out for your safety. I mean, doesn't that thing make you tired?"

"No. If it did, I wouldn't be going to the gym." She giggled. "I saw your interview today."

"Oh you did? How did I look?"

"Like you should've retired with your mustache." She started past him.

"What are you crazy?" He subconsciously stroked his mustache. "Ladies love the 'stache."

Bianca shook her head, "Nobody loves the stache," skipping past him.

"Bianca, you're breaking my heart." He faced an on-looking typist. "You like the 'stache right?"

His coworker immediately focused on her screen, replying, "No. Wrong time period."

***

Along one barren sidewalk, Bianca jogged with her ears plugged. Music screeched from the LED trim of her earbuds as she chanted along with the lyrics. The sun had set for the evening and stars twinkled across the skyline. The roads emptied with few people meandering about the maze of intersecting avenues. The evening buses began their route, but none intersected with this street. The street was narrower than Ménage Boulevard.

Bianca merrily made her way along this corridor. Her eyes peeled to a light projecting from an open storage garage directly adjacent to a small restaurant. From down the street, a person stood within its light. They stared blankly into it, dressed in a slender, maroon thawb with an embroidered neckline. He noticed her, turning to watch her approach from the darkness. The streetlights had yet to ignite and this back road was otherwise poorly lit. She continued, intent to cross his line of sight until she spotted a violet glint from atop an apartment building behind him.

Up above, the Witch planted her foot along the building frame with her arms folded. Her signature energy emanated so brightly that Bianca slowed to a stroll. Bianca unplugged her ears and paced into the street.

She mumbled, "Is that someone? Are they going to jump?" aloud as she maneuvered behind the man.

He trailed her, casually inspecting her hair and carefree personality.

Bianca audibly informed herself, "Oh no, I think they're going to jump."

Quickly, she swiped her palm across her shin, activating her *Bionica* transformation. Carbon fiber polymers crept up her thighs like compression pants.

She shook her legs like an athlete warming up as she barked, "No, no no. Don't jump! You have so much to live for!"

Behind her, Ibrahim curiously watched her flail her arms at the Witch. The polymerization of her uniform snagged his attention. Atop the building, the Witch spotted the panicking woman.

Confusedly, she asked, "Who's this?"

Below, Ibrahim turned into Bianca, visibly astonished at her veiled legs.

Bianca skipped over to him excitedly commanding, "Sir, sir. I think this person is trying to jump okay? I'm going to need you to move…"

She flicked a glance at Ibrahim before doing a double-take at his wand. Turning to his face, she read his sinister interest while realizing the similarity between his eyes, his wand, and the glint of light from the Witch above. Finally, Bianca met with Ibrahim.

"Look who I found." He sang.

Ibrahim raised his wand, expelling a surge of magenta energy that burned across the asphalt like an electrical fire.

Bianca whispered, "Oh no," to herself before taking off.

She sprinted down the street as fast as she could. Her ADEX propelled her around the building corner at blistering speeds but failed to escape the pursuing lion's head that tailed her. It chomped her torso within its jaws, retracting along its magenta band towards Ibrahim. She kicked and squirmed as it lifted her. Sparks jolted from her torso under the piercing grip like an exposed live wire. She struggled to break free. As it rewound, the translucent lion's head flung Bianca into the storage garage, splattering a hail of merchandise, brown boxes, dust, and rubble street side.

"Who is that?" the Witch asked.

"Bionica," Ibrahim answered waiting for the smoke to clear.

"Oh, perfect!"

Within a few seconds, the smoke cleared and a gaping hole remained in the concrete wall of the facility.

Ibrahim smirked. "She's running."

A few streets adjacent to the encounter, Bianca skidded to a stop. She started down an alleyway until she detected an approaching silhouette. The moon appeared within the sky. Its light veiled this person's appearance. Twin violet gems matched glittering purple nails.

"I got her," The Witch answered

Bianca twirled to flee from her. As she lunged away,

Ibrahim crept into the street outlet dissuading her. Sandwiched between the predatory magicians, they drew nearer. Bianca angled towards the walls of the two buildings facing her. She glanced between them until drawing her attention skyward. Bianca charged one building, scaling it with ease and bounding from wall to wall. She maintained her momentum. Jumping over its rim, she sprinted across the rooftop.

The soldier hurdled from one building to another. Bianca screamed into her forearm, "Command, come in command! Hello?" A satellite tower displayed upon her arm, beside a *Looking for Signal* message. She nervously clenched her fist, "What? But I'm in the city?" She angrily rattled her fingers, ravaging the screen in a frenzy, "Why aren't you working? Urgh!"

An upcoming gap between buildings prompted her to dive forward like an Olympic swimmer. Parallel to the floor, she spotted a fast approaching projectile. Bianca rolled to a premature stop as Ibrahim rose over the gap. He enwrapped her within a magenta python bearing venomous teeth drenched within a corrosive acid. Quickly, Bianca shrouded her torso with polymerized pads and fabric. Her helmet appeared just as the Witch swooned up to her, palm outstretched and electrified with magical energy.

The eruption propelled Bianca like a bullet, soaring past buildings tall and stout until she landed beside Ménage Boulevard. Her descent collided with the courtyard fountain, hurling shattered stone fragments into the glass entryway. The ensuing stampede burrowed past her and into the shops.

Residents peered from their windows at the disruption emerging from the streets. Bianca groaned amongst the rubble. She cupped her blood-tinged forehead within her palm. The impact weakened the integrity of her incomplete suit, which wasn't fully functional. It exposed a quarter of her face and the scratches therein. The spaghetti fibers of her uniform dangled from the gashed opening upon her eye.

A voice cracked from her suit, "HQ, how may I direct your call? Bionica? Hello? Hellooo?"

The pair of magicians arrived atop the buildings across the boulevard. Their eyes and tools gleamed with the signature violet-magenta glimmer.

The Witch, the taller of the two, started, "I couldn't have asked for anything better."

"It's almost too easy. You think they caught the Whitesmith?" Ibrahim inquired.

Police sirens chimed. Red and blue lights sped away from their position, beeping against adjacent buildings as it receded along a perpendicular boulevard further into the city's downtown core.

"I think he's doing just fine," the Witch scoffed.

The first responders descended upon an office block cul-de-sac to witness the emergence of two magicians armed with a silver mallet and bronze trident spear. The two marched up the street, dead set for the oncoming traffic. Having left a menacing trail of disaster for the jail-keepers, they're eager to deliver a bewildering baptism of fire upon the unfortunate soldiers and medics hurriedly arriving on scene to aid their comrades.

Their eyes surged with silver and turquoise luminescent fury. The squad cars swerved dramatically, cutting off the ambulance. Out swung officers with pistols drawn and oversized puffy jackets with the word *POLICE* written across their backs.

"Freeze!" they commanded as the men strutted unfettered by the demand.

The spear-bearing combatant swirled his weapon overhead, spiraling the clouds and even the stars in a cosmic whirlpool of galactic dust and heavenly bodies. A central eye formed within the heart of this elemental concoction, discharging a bolt of static electricity upon his weapon. Over his chest, the opal medallion shined like an eye gazing upon the sun. It bathed the barbaric magician behind a curtain of its engulfing brilliance, swathing his spear within a film of electrostatic sparks. The brutish Neanderthal parked his glamorous weapon adjacent to his torso.

The Whitesmith brandished his mallet commanding in his deep base-full voice, "Together now."

"Fine," the magician chuckled. "You're the boss."

The pair impaled the asphalt in unison, upheaving a cataclysmic hurricane of galvanic gravel directed at the first responders. The clash bellowed a cacophonous roar that howled across the night sky. It rippled throughout the city, reverberating as it soars.

***

Within Wino's room, the couple leaned in close to one another. They're seated opposite the all-white dining table. Moonlight shined from beyond the windowpanes glittering along the rim of slender glass vase bearing a single rose. Hot air, steaming from their shared meal, whisked past their nostrils. They stared deeply into one another's eyes, Cheryl visibly smiling at Wino with her arms crossed over the table edge.

She sighed in relief. "Y'know, I could get used to this."

The rim was dimly lit, the living room lights faded

with candles lit across the space. They burned of sweet cherry blossom over roasted cinnamon, adding the floral accent to the ambiance of the couple's dinner date. Wino spun his fork over the ceramic plate. He wound it over the Alfred sauce, enwrapping the fork with spiced noodles topped with cilantro. Lifting it, he smiled cheekily at Cheryl who assumed her role, parting her lips.

She hummed sharply, noting, "It's spicy. But it's so good."

"Hey," Wino called her attention while she munched. "So, I've been thinking lately." He prodded the food as he scoured for the appropriate phrasing. "I wanted us to try moving in together."

Cheryl muffles her lips, cautiously asking, "But, what about Ibrahim?"

Facing the rising moon, he answered, "I doubt Ibrahim's going to turn in his wand. So, he'll just have to find somewhere else to stay." Wino pressed his torso into the table. "But I want you to stay with me. Here."

Cheryl tried desperately to conceal her murky tears. Her face lowered to the table before she could meet with Wino's eyes.

"I was starting to think you'd never ask."

"Is that a yes?"

"Of course." She eagerly popped from her seat with arms outstretched. Wino rose to embrace her. The couple squeezed tightly, enjoying a moment of silence.

Cheryl whispered to Wino, "My roommate is so going to kill me," to which they chuckled lightly.

"Mine too," Wino responded, laughing louder.

Suddenly, the U quaked in the aftermath of the magicians' conflict with the ambulance and police. The violent gyration tumbled Cheryl onto the couch, Wino clutched at her for safety. The startled pair flicked beyond the windows in confusion.

"What was that?" Cheryl exclaimed.

Wino motioned towards the table, hopping over the toppled meal. He set his focus upon The U's courtyard. Marginally, he discerned the downfallen Bionica amongst the scattered rubble. Disturbed, he shoved the chair from his path, pressing up against the window.

"Oh no."

**

Within The U's courtyard, Bianca uprooted herself from her stone-bound coffin. Her weight fell onto the concrete slabs of the public area. Her arm displayed a *Signal Found* message followed by *Connecting to HQ*.

A voice chimed in, "Bianca, we're picking up multiple distress signals from your suit. Are you alright?"

"No," she whined hysterically. "I need help." Bianca glared between the loose strands of hair fallen upon her face. She noted, "There's two of them. Powerful. Magicians. My suit's not working."

"Sit tight, we're dispatching a squad to you now. Are you able to get to safety? Hello?"

A few meters towards the street, Ibrahim hovered like a descending angel until his toes kissed the ground. He strutted towards Bianca.

"Calling your friends? Call them, I'm not scared."

"She's their VIP," the Witch added.

"You're the only cyborg they've got," Ibrahim watched Bianca crawl away from him.

The lobby doors automatically slid open as she stumbled to her feet, limping indoors.

Ibrahim calmly maintained his pursuit, walking onward until addressed by the Witch, "Wait! I've got a better idea."

The Witch extended her palm, swathed in a swarm of particulate matter reflecting the moonlight in striking brilliance. Like painting her hand across the sandy beach, the grains encircled her fingers. A gradient of magenta to deep purple enshrouded her palm. It formed an aura blanket. Ibrahim watched with rising concern for where her hand was pointed. He traced her anticipated point of contact and witnessed Wino slide apart the curtains to his apartment. The Witch's eyes gleamed as a sinister smile crept along her face.

"Let's bring the whole building down on her," she growled.

A glare reminiscent of her first appearance over The U resurged upon the Witch's face. Like a child, she squealed in anticipation. Her fingerprints glowed with a violet ambiance like an electric stove. Steam seeped from beneath her nails and a searing sizzle rippled out from them.

Ibrahim gawked at her. His lips parted while his heart throbbed with unsettling intensity. Originally an adrenaline-fueled throb, his pulse quaked with the earthshattering bellow of a thunderclap.

First, a glint, and second, a blast torpedoed into The U, smashing into a room and flickering the electricity off for the rest of the building. The electrical shuttering resolves into a blackened building. Piles of concrete, plaster, and wood flung out from the scalding blast. The beam sears along the walls as the Witch carved a trail of destruction across its center. The walls caved in around the tunneling torrent of magical energy. The building gushed a cocktail of structural support beams, pipes, and what appear to be civilians like a fresh wound.

The descending flood crashed upon the floor as the backup generator relights the central lobby.

Suddenly, a flash of light shined upon the Witch's face and she's evaded an oncoming streak of energy. It burrowed through the roof in a baby-blue haze, scalding the shingles around her foot and burning a few strands of her braids. In shock, the Witch peered down at the courtyard. Ibrahim aimed with wand outstretched and brows furrowed.

He barked, "What're you doing?"

She failed to respond, bewildered by his authoritative attitude. Her mind raced at the realization that Ibrahim just fired upon her. In any case, he spun towards the trail of wreckage and flew into the shattered glass frame of one apartment room. The Witch silently observed him. He disappeared into the shadows.

Sirens came into earshot. Ménage Boulevard teemed with officers, weapons drawn and turrets angled towards the Witch. Snipers mounted their rifles along alternating rooftops, the glared from their reticles glinted across the horizon. She swept over the landscape, returning towards the carved entrance of The U.

***

Inside Wino's room, Ibrahim popped over the dining table onto the hazy snow-white carpet. The moonlight casted a rectangular stain encircled by shadows. Ibrahim carefully strolled into the living room, scanning over the discernable furniture in search of his roommate.

Glass fragments crackled beneath his footsteps. He paused along the frame of the sofa, running his finger along the ember-glazed ridge engraved by the beam. Soft steam smelling of pungent scorched fabric mixed with the floral accent of the candle burning at his feet. Ibrahim kicked his foot out to extinguish the flame as he proceeded around the sofa. He discerns a number of tattered fragments scattered about the room, yet he calmly panned for his friend.

Alternating red and blue lights climbed from Ménage Boulevard. These rays highlighted the edge of his cardboard game, the rim of a fallen glass vase and the silhouette of a boulder. Ibrahim analyzed this last object, detecting subtle fluctuations in its position. It swayed like a pendant, as muffled words emanated.

"We're going to be okay. Shh, don't worry. The General's out there. She'll protect us."

Ibrahim gently called, "Wino?"

Prompting the uppermost corner of the figure to reveal a piercing stare directed at him. The gaze projected fierce hostility, like a bear protecting its cub. Careful inspection revealed stains upon the couple. They sat drenched in a strangle liquid like a pipe burst open and splashed on them.

A moment passed and not a word was spoken. Ibrahim glanced out the shattered window to observe the ongoing struggle between the Witch and The General's forces. He heard the clashes and explosions in the distance, snapping along the skyline as the other magicians rampaged downtown.

He associated with this chaos. Ibrahim was a magician, and he supported this rebellious movement from its onset. But at this point, he reconsidered its value and whether it merited the downfall of this peaceful city.

Ibrahim twirled and started out the front door; Cheryl scrubbed her head upon Wino's chest to witness his exit with Wino.

***

Below, in the lobby, Bianca laid out along a navy blue lounge chair. A handful of workers accompanied her. They fanned her, retrieve glasses of water, and a phone for medical treatment. Carbon fiber shrouded Bianca's legs while fragmented strands dangled along her torso. Her materialized helmet partially masked her face. Bianca's chest undulated signaling that she was at least alive.

Ibrahim strolled into the lobby, marching past the coffee shop and directly towards Bianca. His wand hung from his loosely enwrapped fingers, snagging the attention of the bellhops and receptionists who glared at him with anxious uncertainty.

At the entrance, the Witch regressed behind the front doors. Using her powers, she slammed the automatic screens shut, reinforcing them with a jail-cell wireframe and heavy bolt. She spun to identify Ibrahim walking past.

"There you are!" she called. "Feel like helping anytime soon? I'm not the same ever since that sniper shot me, y'know!"

Ibrahim continued his unfettered approach towards Bianca. He was the center of attention for the workers, onlookers, and the Witch. A hail of bullets, beams, and blasts pelted at the electrified double doors. The Witch tailed Ibrahim.

Standing over Bianca, Ibrahim hovered his wand above her torso. Out radiated a pulsing aura of energy, similar to the Witch's.

Her eyes peeled as she barked, "Now what are you doing?"

Bullets permeated the magical membrane, whistling past her braided hair and snatching her focus on her defense. Ibrahim centered his wand over Bianca's chest. Tentacles from his orb seeped beneath the epidermis of Bianca's skin, revitalizing it and mending any sustained injuries. Bianca's body recalibrated with a deep diaphragmatic sigh, relaxing her subsequent breaths as she rested soundly. The Witch's gaze lashed out from her peripheral. She witnessed a traitor, Ibrahim perform a miracle against his better judgment. The solemn magician casted his gaze upon the onlookers. They'd seen him and thus needed their memories wiped by the end of all this. But for now, Ibrahim performed his duty.

He raised his wand, culminating its power within the orb that shined with a brilliant glimmer. The crystalline fragment, generated from colliding sparks shattered into a concussive wave, warping reality with its combustion. Rippling bands climbed the walls of the complex, washing over anything in their path and reassembling it as a consequence. The streaking lights flowed along the hallways, crossing between boundaries with no resistance.

Wino tucked Cheryl into his arms, as they rested on the carpet before the couch. Her arm stroked the bloodstained scorch marks on Wino's torso – his leaking wound. Waves rolled over the couple, calling their attention to their surroundings. The rolling ripples realigned any mismatched fabric, restructured all the obliterated furniture and revitalized any sustained injuries. The living room light bulbs snapped alight.

Wino and Cheryl watched as the room reconfigures itself. Cheryl inspected her hand. The bloodstains faded as if she never felt them. Wino's torso appeared untouched.

"What's happening?" She asked.

"I think," Wino responded. "Ibrahim's doing this."

Downstairs, the Witch's wall wavered under the onslaught of The General's onslaught. They'd only multiplied as reinforcements arrived on scene and volleyed bullets, lasers, and mystical attacks onto the force field. Despite this intense barrage, the Witch's cold glare settled with Ibrahim. A sinister distaste plastered her venomous countenance.

Ibrahim exchanged a glance with her. His gray wand dangled, drained of its energy. The lobby onlookers slept alongside Bianca. Their bodies dangled over the lobby furniture as Ibrahim stood central to them all. His expression revealed inner guilt, but resolve in his decision. It may not have covered for all his misdoings, but it was a great start. Moreover, it put an end to the magicians' raid on the city. What's done is done.

***

The General arrived on scene in a black SUV. She and a dozen other high-ranking officers emerged and quickly called off the siege of The U. With a raised palm, the roars of gunfire quieted. The ceasefire swept across the field. The attention of the soldiers rose to the engorging bands of energy stemming from The U and pouring into the city.

Droves of fire responders littered the streets, soaked in pools of their own curdling blood and their life force draining from their cores. Fortunately, the haze of magenta gradient light rejuvenated their bones, body, and brains. Their eyes flashed awake to the asphalt bed. As they drew themselves up, they're struck by the agony of whatever damage remained. The magic only served to keep them alive it seemed. Its efficacy dwindled as it radiated outward. They huddled together; those capable of walking tended to the most injured first. They utilized their own tools and techniques, motivated by camaraderie to endure the pain and persevere.

At this time, The General, adorned by her draping black jacket strung over her shoulders, sought counsel with her specialists.

"Can we enter?" she inquired.

"It appears fortified," the official answered.

Murmurs crept about the various units of mystical bands reinforcing the Witch's barrier. They considered the implications of a magician stronghold on their tactics. They're prepared to hunt and overwhelm individuals, but not a castle, at least not within the city limits. The use of deadly force within limits was more or less illegal but definitely frowned upon by city dwellers. If the General wanted to play military, she should've taken it outside.

"Retrieve the rail gun," she calmly commanded to her officials.

They turned to pass down the message when the restructuring of the plaza fountain snagged their collective attention.

The clunky chunks slithered atop one another bound by violet fibers.

The rising sun climbed into the horizon, projecting its pinnacle ray against a towering apartment complex. Its light flashed into Wino's apartment, highlighting the gaping hole funneled into the concrete and glass wall. The shattered fragments glittered in the sunlight as they realigned into the windowpanes. Concrete secured them in place.

"Belay that order," The General called.

***

Within the lobby, the Witch's boots clomped as she strolled towards the rear exit. The space was quiet besides her footsteps. Ibrahim panned over the glossy tiles as she drew near. Once upon him, the Witch casually passed by without uttering a word. She marginally scuffed his shoulder. She exited from his peripheral. With a full turn, Ibrahim found the Witch had disappeared.

***

By now, the pursuit for the accomplice magicians had stemmed beyond city bounds as reported by a news crew. Video footage captured The General's force tactically maneuvering into The U's central lobby. Guns drawn, they stormed the area in two columns. The courtyard teemed with the police force as noted by Wino and Cheryl. The two occupied one couch, although Wino inspected the panels with curiosity.

The morning sun relentlessly showered everyone beneath its magnificent warmth. Wino shut the curtains. The slits of light were plenty to illuminate the room and, besides, no one was eager for its presence.

Cheryl and Wino sat in silence as news reports streamed in. Social media feeds flooded. On one hand, a gaping hole was rammed into Wino's home, but, on the other hand, it's as if no lasting damage was inflicted. The only remnants of what happened were injured first responders and the news report. The couple exchanged curious looks, almost lost to the chain of events.

A knock sounded at the door. It drew their attention. The courtyard commotion coupled with prolonged wakefulness convinced them of illusions.

"Did you hear that?" Cheryl whispered to Wino.

"I think so," he responded.

It sounded again, knocks clonking against the doorframe. This time it prompted Wino to a stand. He opened to a downcast Ibrahim, standing in his draping robes and dangling wand.

Next thing, Ibrahim's seated upon the couch, adjacent Cheryl's chair while Wino stood within the odd gap between the two. Ibrahim watched the TV. Bags tugged beneath his eyes. The volume had been reduced to a whisper but it revealed Bianca. Her comrades escorted her on a stretcher to an ambulance. The couple followed his eyes as he glanced out towards the ruffling curtains. He was silent.

"Y'know you did this?" Cheryl sternly condemned him.

Ibrahim refused to reply. He gently unveiled his wand from his robe. Laying it upon the table, the couple observed its barren condition. The orb was gray like a lifeless heart. Its pulsing gradient had ceased, leaving only a stick in its wake.

Wino's lips fell apart at the sight, as Cheryl continues berating, "You could have done a lot more good if you'd just turned it in like Wino asked you to. Now, look at what you've caused."

"Wino," Ibrahim muttered. The rasp of his voice tugged at their focus. "What do you think?"

Cheryl turned her attention to Wino. It was time to inform Ibrahim of his condemnation, that he rebuked the actions of the magicians; as well as the time for him to formally expel Ibrahim from his home. Cheryl's fingers curled into fists upon her lap as her demeanor soured. Wino, unfettered by her reaction, extended his arm. He cusped Ibrahim's shoulder.

Leaning over, he gently responded, "I think you

just saved the world again."

To this, Ibrahim huffed a sigh of relief. His shoulders plummeted, as a smirk crawled along his face distraught with guilt. Cheryl unraveled her fingers as her bangs veiled her. She fell silent.

"She'll be back, y'know?" Ibrahim asked with rising confidence.

"Who, the Witch?" Wino asked in shock.

"Yeah, and she'll be coming right for me."

"Well, she knows where to find you." Wino smiled down at him, adding, "And we'll be ready."

The men shared a smile. It's a familiar sight, explored throughout their extensive history. It endured trial and tribulation and revealed itself in the flickering curtain of energy pouring down from the sun. The two were here to stay.

The End.

ABOUT THE AUTHOR

Kevin Kalu

An oral storyteller, Kevin has delved into the realm of literature as a means to share his stories beyond his immediate landscape and expand his horizons. "Ibrahim" is inspired by close friends and former classmates of his. He employs a snapshot of their school days in order to create colorful caricatures and embeds a human touch woven into the fabric of his characters. We follow the magician, Ibrahim and his human best friend, Wino, as they navigate the bumps and winding roads of their friendship in a world where magic has been banned. The tides have turned and humans now dominate the magicians but what does this mean for Wino and Ibrahim? To what lengths will they go in order to preserve their friendship or will they pursue ulterior motives?

Made in the USA
Las Vegas, NV
18 December 2021